TITLE I
HOLMES JR HIGH
2001-02

SOMETHING'S WRONG

The dining hall in the center of the kibbutz was all lit up for supper, and people should have been drifting in to eat, but something was wrong. There were groups standing on the big veranda outside the main doors. The young kids, who were usually out playing ball, were just standing silently. Nimrod saw something else. There was a square of white paper on one of the double glass doors. Suddenly it all added together and spelled something worse than some high school kid in trouble . . .

Something really bad had happened.

LYNNE REID BANKS

BROKEN BRIDGE

AN AVON · FLARE BOOK

Epigraph on page xv from *An Evil Cradling: The Five-Year Ordeal of a Hostage* by Brian Keenan. Copyright © 1993 by Brian Keenan. Used by permission of Viking Penguin, a division of Penguin Books USA Inc.

AVON BOOKS
A division of
The Hearst Corporation
1350 Avenue of the Americas
New York, New York 10019

Copyright © 1994 by Lynne Reid Banks
Published by arrangement with the author
Library of Congress Catalog Card Number: 94-26636
ISBN: 0-380-72384-0

Published in hardcover by William Morrow and Company, Inc.; for information address Permissions Department, William Morrow and Company, Inc., 1350 Avenue of the Americas, New York, New York 10019.

First Avon Flare Printing: April 1996

AVON FLARE TRADEMARK REG. U.S. PAT. OFF. AND IN OTHER COUNTRIES, MARCA REGISTRADA, HECHO EN U.S.A.

Printed in the U.S.A.

RA   10   9   8   7   6   5

For Tamar Sachs,
For all the years.

Contents

ONE   The Last Morning 1

TWO   At the Airport 14

THREE   Nimrod 27

FOUR   On the Edge 42

FIVE   The Notice on the Door 48

SIX   Nili's Nightmare 60

SEVEN   Questions 71

EIGHT   Dale's New Name 86

NINE   Flowers on the Sidewalk 98

TEN   On the Tel 105

ELEVEN   News of a Capture 114

TWELVE   Mustapha in Prison 125

THIRTEEN   The Lineup 137

FOURTEEN   Noah's Spending Spree 150

FIFTEEN   Conscience 161

SIXTEEN   The Trick 174

SEVENTEEN   Ways to Help 184

EIGHTEEN   A Dilemma 194

NINETEEN   Nimrod Has a Headache 204

TWENTY   Yoni Tells a Story 213

TWENTY-ONE	The Man on the Roof	221
TWENTY-TWO	Shoot and Cry	230
TWENTY-THREE	Lev at Work	242
TWENTY-FOUR	The Informer	250
TWENTY-FIVE	Bruises	258
TWENTY-SIX	The Shoplifter	265
TWENTY-SEVEN	The Big Bang	277
TWENTY-EIGHT	The River—The Border	291
	Epilogue on Two Hills	302
	Glossary	312

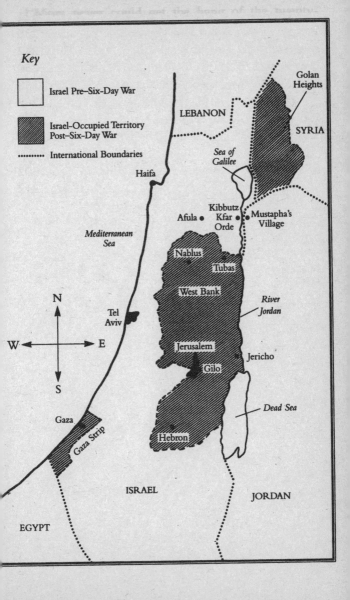

Key

☐ Israel Pre–Six-Day War

▨ Israel-Occupied Territory
Post–Six-Day War

⋯⋯ International Boundaries

LEBANON

Golan
Heights

SYRIA

*Sea of
Galilee*

Haifa

Kibbutz
Kfar
Orde

Afula

Mustapha's
Village

*Mediterranean
Sea*

Nablus

Tubas

West Bank

*River
Jordan*

N

Tel
Aviv

W — E

Jerusalem

Jericho

S

Gilo

Gaza

Dead Sea

Gaza Strip

Hebron

ISRAEL

JORDAN

EGYPT

Shelby Family Tree

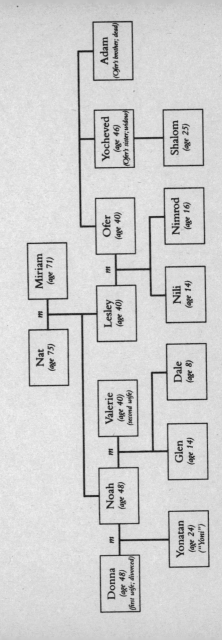

Donna (age 48) (first wife, divorced) — m — **Noah** (age 48) — m — **Valerie** (age 40) (second wife)

Nat (age 75) — m — **Miriam** (age 71)

Lesley (age 40) — m — **Ofer** (age 40)

Yocheved (age 46) (Ofer's sister, widow)

Adam (Ofer's brother, dead)

Yonatan (age 24) ("Yoni")

Glen (age 14)

Dale (age 8)

Nili (age 14)

Nimrod (age 16)

Shalom (age 25)

AUTHOR'S NOTE

Kibbutz Kfar Orde is a fictional place, and none of the characters in the story are based on real people.

I would like to thank Jane Nissen, my British publisher, for suggesting that I write this sequel to *One More River,* telling what happened to the characters in that book twenty-five years later. A number of people in Israel helped me with background material for this story. They know who they are, and that I am grateful.

There are those who "cross the Jordan" and seek out truth through a different experience from the one they are born to, and theirs is the greatest struggle. . . . For here is the real conflict by which we move into manhood and maturity.

. . . Unless we know how to embrace "the other," we are not men, and our nationhood is willful and adolescent. Those who struggle through the turbulent Jordan waters have gone beyond the glib definitions of politics or religion.

The rest remain standing on either bank, firing guns at one another.

—Brian Keenan (Beirut hostage),
from An Evil Cradling

ONE

The Last
Morning

Nili yawned and stretched her feet deep into the enormous hotel bed. The cool percale sheets, the down-soft pillow under her cheek, the general feeling of luxury, were delicious. Before opening her eyes, she did a sort of double roll from one side of the king-size bed to the other and back and then dived under the covers and burrowed like a mad mole in all directions through the warm, silky darkness.

Perhaps because of the contrast—her bed at home, and her other one at school, were small and narrow, the sheets not nearly so smooth— her first real thought of the day was: *By tonight I'll be home!* It was a thought full of joy. But that didn't mean she wasn't going to get the last ounce of enjoyment out of being *here*.

She emerged from her tunneling with her long dark hair all over her face and sat up in the wreckage of the bedclothes. She took a good-bye look around the room where she had passed the last seven nights in solitary splendor. She thought of her room at her kibbutz boarding school, shared with two others—companionable but small, cramped, and chaotic. Yow! This one was ten times as big. It had elegant peach-colored walls adorned with beautiful paintings, her very own luxury bathroom, thick floor-to-ceiling curtains patterned with bronze leaves, and a view, when they were drawn back, over Hyde Park.

Hyde Park, London!

Nili jumped off the bed and ran to check that it was all still there, that it was real. Even though she'd been here for a whole week, it still felt like a dream. But it had all really happened to her.

A trip to London by air, seven wonderful days of fun and newness and luxury. The shopping, the bus rides, the waxworks, the Tower of London, the London Dungeon (scary! She hadn't liked it at all, but her Canadian cousin Glen had!), the best seats at *Starlight Express,* the fabulous restaurant meals—nobody could take it away from her. Her uncle Noah was the best uncle in the entire world, no matter what anybody said.

Standing in front of the wide window, looking over the sunny park, its greensward patterned with huge lakes of yellow daffodils, she vowed that nobody at home in the kibbutz would say one single word against her uncle, ever again, in her hearing, because she just wouldn't let them.

Nothing. Not even hints.

Well, she thought, they wouldn't be able to for a while. Because her cousin Glen was coming back with her. No one would say anything mean about Glen's father while Glen was around.

Nili turned and ran, the squudgy carpet bulging between her bare toes, to the door that led through into Glen's room. She opened it with a rush, and it banged back against the wall, but that didn't wake Glen. He lay humped, motionless, under the covers of *his* king-size bed. Nili flung herself onto the bed full length.

"Come on, you lazy, wake up!" she said happily, tickling his neck.

He stirred and stretched the way she had. She bounced about on the acres of spare bed surface.

"Last morning in London," he murmured glumly.

"Last morning!" she agreed, but her voice was full of excitement. "Today we back home in kibbutz!"

"You mean you back home in kibbutz," mumbled Glen. "Me not back home, me in weirdo farm village in crazy country full of barbarians."

She stopped dead, staring at him. Something rough and unpleasant was happening inside her.

"You don't say that," she said thickly.

Her cousin opened his eyes and looked at her. He had a round, freckled face, a bit puffy from sleep. But his blue eyes were sharp.

"I just did say it," he said. "Israelis kill people, so they must be barbarians."

Suddenly, without knowing she was going to, she picked up a pillow and banged him in the face with it. He flung it off with an angry shout. She jumped on him and started pummeling him with the pillow. The next minute they were grappling.

3

They rolled over and over until they fell on the floor. Glen was on top. He grabbed a handful of her thick hair and pulled. She screamed and pushed his face back, with both hands under his jaw, until he had to let go. She rolled away fast and jumped to her feet.

"Are you nuts?" he panted from the floor.

"You don't say bad things about Israel!" she said fiercely. She felt very upset. She had never fought like that before. Never wanted to hurt anyone the way she had wanted, just for a second, to hurt Glen.

"Only joking, you idiot!" Glen shouted, his eye watering where she had caught it with the pillow. He got to his feet more slowly. The first button of his pajama top was off. He examined the tear.

"That's not a joke to say 'barbarians'!" she said. "And you shouldn't tease about my English! When we get to Israel, we see how good you speak our language!"

"Who wants to even go?" said Glen, turning away.

Nili lost part of her anger in astonishment.

"You *don't want to go*?" she asked incredulously. "Why not?"

Glen said nothing and went into the bathroom, banging the door. She could hear him running some water to hide the sound of peeing. She sat down on the bed. To stop her hands from shaking she stroked them down the sides of her disordered hair, tossing it back over her shoulders with a flick of her thumbs. She felt ashamed but still angry.

In the kibbutz, kids didn't fight. Not kids of fourteen. They just didn't. But then no one in kibbutz

4

would say that Israelis were barbarians. Even the new kids from Russia wouldn't. What kind of joke?

She turned her head as Glen came out of the bathroom, looking mulish.

"You should apologize," he said. "Girls shouldn't start fights; it's not fair."

"You too," she said shortly. "You was very rude."

They faced each other. His face was still flushed, his fair hair damply on end. His eye was red, and she felt sorry for that, enough to be the first to say, "Sorry I hit your eye."

He grunted.

"Now you," she prompted.

He shifted his jaw and his mouth worked. He didn't want to say it. But he could see, reluctantly, that she had a point. If she'd started bad-mouthing Canada—! No, he shouldn't have said that, even as a joke.

But it had come out of him because he wasn't easy about this trip to Israel. It had sounded exciting at first. A foreign country, so often in the news, so often talked about by his dad. A sort of storybook place. Kids at school were envious. . . . But as it got closer, he started to feel differently.

The news from Israel, which his dad had involved him in since he was small, was always about fighting, bombs, terrorist raids and counterraids, and full-scale wars. Glen was keen on guns, planes, warships, armies. When he was younger, games about soldiers and all the paraphernalia that went with them had been his delight, and now all his Nintendo games were about war and battles. But . . .

5

Well. The truth was, he had a sort of idea that he was being sent to Israel, to the kibbutz, where his father had once lived, because his dad couldn't go himself, or didn't want to. Glen felt resentful deep down about this. His dad had planned the trip without a word to him, as a surprise, and it had been, but, he now thought, not such a wonderful one. Glen was his own man; he didn't like people rushing him into things without asking, and certainly not a trip to a basically pretty scary place. Not that wild horses would drag his scared feelings out of him.

What he actually liked best was being home with his friends and his family, where everything was safe, comfortable, and familiar, where *he* was in control. In Israel everything would be strange; other people would know the score and he wouldn't.

One of these people would be Nili.

He looked now at his cousin. He secretly thought her very pretty. She'd given him a good bop in the eye for attacking her country. He admired her for that. Anyway, he liked her well enough for a girl; she was fun and a good sport. He was going to have to depend on her a lot when they got to Israel. So he muttered, "Yeah, well. Sorry."

She started back toward her own room. Just as she reached the door, he couldn't resist.

"I guess I'll meet a few who aren't. *If* I get real lucky."

She turned, her eyes narrowed. "Who aren't what?"

"Barb—"

"*Shtock!*" she shouted.

6

He grinned. Surely she could see he was fooling. "What's that mean?"

She stood with clenched fists, controlling her urge to fling herself at him. "It means, shut up your big fat face!" she said between her teeth, and then turned and walked out, banging the door in her turn.

Noah Shelby, who was Glen's father and Nili's uncle, stood before the mirror in his hotel bathroom and stretched his top lip carefully over his teeth to shave around his mustache. His electric razor buzzed and rasped, dragging his skin. He winced. He'd have liked to grow a beard, but his bosses would not have approved. Execs of Bulwark Engineering (Canada) Inc. were expected to conform to the dress code, which didn't include beards.

Noah was forty-eight. He was successful and he was rich. He had most of what men are supposed to want, including a wife and children, a very comfortable home, and two cars, one a Jaguar. His firm sent him all over the world. . . . In short, he'd made it. It seemed to him unfair that he had to remind himself of these happy facts daily, to make the face in the mirror come up with a faint good-morning smile.

He put on his shirt and tie and brushed back his graying hair. Then he put on his glasses. He looked ready, and felt almost ready, to telephone his mother long-distance to Israel. Now he did smile—ruefully. He always did this, made himself look smart before phoning her, as if she could see him. He knew it was ridiculous.

He made the call without looking up the number to Israel. He knew it by heart, though he seldom used it. He was not in very close touch anymore with what he thought of as his first family. Or even with his second. Noah was on his third family now.

After five rings he was about to hang up. In her tiny kibbutz apartment it couldn't take his mother long to answer if she were there. But then he heard her voice.

"Hi, Mom." He spoke loudly. At seventy-one she was getting a little deaf.

A brief pause. There was always that brief, chilling pause.

"Oh! It's you, Noah. Is everything all right? How's my darling?"

She meant Nili, of course, not him.

"She's just great. We've had one terrific week. I think they've had a really great time."

"That's good. And when . . ."

The line went crackly, but Noah guessed the rest and shouted: "That's why I'm phoning! El Al has changed the flight time. They'll be arriving at Ben Gurion Airport at thirteen-fifteen your time!"

"When did you say?" he heard through the static.

He repeated it. "Have you got that, Mom?"

"I've got it."

"Write it down."

"I don't need to. Do you think I'm getting senile?"

"No, I don't. How's Les?"

"Your sister's fine. She'll meet the children at the airport with Ofer. He's in Tel Aviv; he gave a concert last night. We heard it on the radio. Nimrod's fine too. Tell Nili her big brother sends his love."

There was another brief pause. Noah's hair

crawled on his neck. He swallowed and said, "How's Yonatan?"

His mother answered with a stiffness that easily traveled three thousand miles. "Your son is well. Why don't you try writing him a letter?"

"I gave him a computer for his birthday, Mom. State-of-the-art."

"A letter would have been nicer."

"Well, I will, Mom. I promise." He felt like a told-off child, stubborn, shamed, defiant.

"Don't promise me," said his mother. "Promise yourself. I notice you don't ask about Donna. Or your father, come to that."

"I was just going to—"

"I think we should hang up now; this isn't the cheap-rate time. Good-bye, Noah."

"It's my nickel, Mom, don't—"

But the line was dead. He closed his eyes with the pain of that deadness as he hung up.

After a while he opened his eyes and stood up. *You'd think Mom'd give me a mark for neatness.* He'd done his best to give her beloved granddaughter the time of her life. Maybe when Nili got back and told them all her traveler's tales . . . And she would, with relish. Lovely kid. She really was. It had been a pleasure to give her treats. So full of enthusiasm, so excited about everything. Just like her mother when she was young, and not just in looks.

Noah remembered his sister, Lesley, when she was that age. At fourteen she had left Canada and gone to live in the kibbutz. She hadn't wanted to—and how she hadn't! Emigration to Israel had been their father's idea—well, his obsession. Lesley'd fought the whole scheme tooth and nail. Gone on strike, the lot. Noah knew he had managed to help her then. He, who had been the family black sheep, an outcast. Then, as now . . . Well, not quite. At least they spoke to him now.

He closed his eyes and gave his head a little sharp shake. He hated thinking about his relations with his parents, his first wife, Donna, his first son, Yonatan. . . . This time it wasn't his father's fault, his pigheaded father, who'd once, long ago, kicked him out of the family for marrying outside their faith. Marrying a Catholic instead of a Jew.

Nope. This time, Noah thought, he'd really brought it on himself.

The word for what he was, the word he hated, forced itself into his mind. He couldn't keep it out.

Yored. Emigrant. Only in Israel was emigration somehow the same as desertion.

And in the nineteen years since he'd left Israel and gone home to Canada? The frenzied hard work, the new, *Jewish* wife, the new family, all his career successes, his money, his jet-setting? They counted for nothing with the people who mattered most. *The people who mattered most . . .* At forty-eight, in this year of grace 1992, could these people who mattered most still be his parents, his sister, his first wife, and his first son? The people who counted *most* should be his third family, his now-family—his wife, Valerie, his little daughter, Dale, and Glen. He knew that. But he couldn't feel it. The burden of his first family's disapproval went on weighing him down.

Yet they'd let Nili come, when he'd got up nerve to invite her. Their precious Nili. They'd lent her to him for a week, to keep Glen company, to have a trip abroad.

Surely that meant that at least they trusted him. Sort of.

He pushed the hard thoughts away and put on the new jacket he'd bought at Aquascutum in Regent Street. Very much within the dress code, he thought wryly, glancing at himself in the long mirror. Then he went into the silent, carpeted passage and knocked on Glen's door.

"Morning, son! Breakfast time! Are you ready?"

He heard Glen's answer, then moved to the next door along and knocked again. Before he could make his announcement, it was flung open. Nili stood there, her face all alight between the curtains of hair.

"Boker tov, dodi!" she said, and kissed him. He knew this was an honor. Israeli kids are usually not very demonstrative. But she did love him. Not just for what he could give her either. He hugged her back, feeling warmed by her sweetness.

"Are you all packed?" he said. "We have to leave for the airport right after breakfast."

"Yes! Just—I make my hair. Wait, Uncle."

She left the door open, and he stood in it, watching her brush the long hair, dark and a little curly, like her mother's. You'd think they'd wear it differently after a quarter of a century, but no. Nili had the same thick bangs, the same loose, over-the-shoulder style as Lesley had worn at the same age. She looked so like Lesley he might have been looking at his little sister brought back, as if nothing had changed since 1967. He watched his niece with a strange smile, as

11

if watching the past when the choices could still have been different.

He remembered how he'd left Donna in Saskatoon (pregnant with Yonatan, though they didn't know it then) and rushed to the rescue of his family in May 1967, when it had seemed Israel was about to be overwhelmed by its enemies. How his parents and his sister had welcomed him, how the traumas and hurts of the past had been swept aside ... He hadn't done much rescuing, as it turned out—the Israeli Army hadn't exactly needed his assistance—but he had thought his worst troubles with his family were over. That was all he knew!

Nili stuffed the brush into the top of her duffel bag, which was packed and ready, and almost skipped toward him. Glen was waiting in the corridor behind him. Noah smiled from one to the other: the Israeli niece and the Canadian son.

"Well, kids, a quick bite and then we must be off."

"Aw, Dad! I want a seriously big breakfast!"

They walked down the corridor to the elevators. Nili held his arm. "Are you sure that *Aba* and *Ima* know when to meet us?"

"Sure. I've just spoken to your *savta*."

Nili's voice rose excitedly. "You spoke to her? Did you speak to Ima? Did you talk to Nimrod?"

"Hey, take it easy. You'll see them all tonight."

"What if the plane's late?" asked Glen.

"They'll wait, don't worry."

"And then they'll take us home to Kfar Orde!" crowed Nili.

12

"What a name!" muttered Glen. "Sounds like 'Cuff fraud.' "

"Kfar Orde," repeated Nili. "It was named after a very brave English soldier who trained our soldiers to do night raids, back in the nineteen thirties. His name was Orde Wingate."

"Big deal," said Glen, though he was impressed.

"It *is* a big deal," she said. "You'll love it."

"What's to love?" Glen knew he was being surly. Night raids . . . the words made him feel excited, but somehow his stubborn reluctance was still there.

"Oh, come on, Glen," said his father, putting his arm around his son's shoulders.

"Do I have to go, Dad?" he asked, just to assert himself.

"Yes," said Noah shortly. But he squeezed him affectionately. He was thinking, *You know you have to go; it's all fixed. And I want you to. I want you to see it, to love it, and maybe—one day—you might succeed where I failed.*

The elevator came and they stepped in. Glen twitched his shoulders, and Noah took his arm away.

It was only a thoughtless movement because the elevator was hot and Glen was feeling grumpy. But it hurt Noah, then and later, as if Glen had rejected him, withdrawn his love, because he was making him go to Israel.

TWO

At the Airport

Lesley sat beside Dov, the driver, and watched the Israeli countryside bounce by. It was an old car, and Dov was an old driver. Come to that, it was a pretty old road, with more than its quota of potholes. But Lesley didn't even notice. Her mind was rushing ahead to the airport.

"Nili coming home today, then," grunted the old man. He spoke Hebrew with a thick Polish accent.

"Yes!" Lesley said happily. "And she's bringing her cousin with her."

The word "cousin" in Hebrew tells not only whether it's a boy cousin or a girl, but the exact relationship. In this case Lesley called Glen Nili's *ben-dod,* "son of her uncle." So the old man at once asked, "That makes him Yonatan's half brother, right?"

Lesley said, "Right," more subduedly. A

14

kibbutz is a gossipy place, and Dov was living proof that old men love gossip no less than old women. But of course there'd be talk when Glen came. There'd always been talk about Noah ever since he'd gone back to Canada years ago with a new partner, and Donna, his Christian wife, had come to live in the kibbutz with Yonatan.

She glanced at her watch. It was lunch break at school. "Could we just stop by the high school for a minute?" she asked. "I told Nimrod to watch out for us." She had a treat in mind for her son. A surprise.

"We're cutting it fine for the plane," grumbled Dov. But it was only a routine objection. The old car screeched protestingly and leaned against its worn tires as they turned into the long school drive.

Nimrod was waiting at the school bus stop, lounging with one unlaced sneaker on a seat. He straightened up as the car drew near. Lesley found herself looking at him through the windshield, as she might if he were someone else's sixteen-year-old son. Medium tall, slender, not bulked out yet, his face still beardless. That hair! Straight, dark, and a good foot long, pulled back and tied like a pirate—no other boys were wearing it like that now. Trust Nimrod to be different.

Lesley thought of her mother's Yiddish saying *"Klaine kinder, klaine tsoros; graiser kinder, graiser tsoros."* It might have been coined for Nimrod, who had been making *tsoros*—problems—most of his life, little ones when he was little, and recently, as he grew, getting bigger. Still. There hadn't been any for a long time now.

Two weeks at least.

She got out as the car drew up and hugged him. He didn't respond. Instantly she knew that the trouble-free patch had ended.

She held his shoulders and looked into his eyes, which were just level with hers. "Now what?" she asked.

He gave a brief shrug and looked away, beyond the high school campus with its white buildings and green lawns, over the flat Bet She'an Valley fields to the hills of Jordan.

"Come on, Nimrod!" she said, more sharply than she'd intended. Her heart had already sunk.

"They're going to write you a letter," he said.

A letter! She gave his shoulders a shake. "*Nu!* Tell me!"

"Oh, nothing. Some *shtuyot.* Can I come to the airport with you?"

She shut her eyes and her teeth. This was to have been the surprise. But what now? Whatever he'd done, it was not nothing, obviously. The school didn't write letters to the parents about nothing.

"First, tell me what you did."

He dredged up a heavy *mothers*! sort of sigh, and finally said, "Micki kicked me out of History."

"What for?"

"Nothing. Kidding around."

"So what else is new?"

A slow grin tugged at his mouth. "I got bored of sitting outside, so I went back into the classroom." He paused for effect. "On my bike."

"Oh, for God's sake," said Lesley wearily, in English.

She let go of him and turned away so he couldn't

16

see her face. What made him do these pointless, infuriating things? He never, ever admitted he'd done anything wrong. He really thought it was funny to disturb the class, to defy his teachers' authority. And the other kids didn't help. *I'll bet that just broke them up, seeing him ride into the lesson on his blasted bicycle!* she thought furiously. Last time he'd slid a small dog in through a tear in the window netting. That had been the end of that lesson too. No wonder his marks were so lousy.

"I suppose you've been suspended this time," she said. She hoped they darn well had done it at last instead of endlessly saying they would.

But he shook his head. "No. Just the letter. If they ever get around to it."

Stupid school! thought Lesley. *Discipline! Never heard of it.*

"So you've got another lesson now."

"Ima, it's Friday. End of week. End of story."

"You've got one more lesson."

"It's only English. Who needs it?"

She ground her teeth. It was too bad of him! She'd love to have had his company on the long drive to the airport; it would have been great to have had him there to meet Nili and Glen. And he'd have enjoyed it. But if the school wouldn't punish him and bring him to order, she had to. It made her mad! She couldn't even take his side!

"No, Nimrod, you can't come."

Now the cocky who-cares look fell off his face. A sour satisfaction twisted in her; at least she'd got to him. But his obvious disappointment got to *her* far more. *It's not fair!* she thought childishly. *I wanted him to come!* She felt as if she were the one being done out of a treat.

"Oh, come on, Ima, give me a break!"

"No. You don't deserve it. Go to your English lesson and behave yourself."

"Mom, I know English!" he almost shouted, in English.

"You can understand it and you can speak it. You can't read it and you write it like a drunken monkey."

"Who needs to write English, *l'khol harookhot*? Anyway, I can when I want to! Mom, let me come, be nice, do me a favor!"

Lesley drew back and stiffened her jaw. "Stop it. Go back to school. I'll see you when we get home tonight."

Before he could say more, she had got back in the car and slammed the door. Dov, who had been leaning out of the window openly listening, grinned maddeningly at her. She felt her face flush with embarrassment.

"Let's go," she said shortly.

The old man let in the clutch with a chuckle, and the car performed a U-turn. Lesley longed to look back, but she wouldn't let herself. She felt suddenly close to tears. At the last minute, just before the car turned onto the road at the end of the drive, she allowed herself a glance in the rearview mirror.

He wasn't heading back toward the school; he was walking after them!

She knew what that meant. There was no bus at this time. Not content with cutting his last class of the day, he was about to break another of the school

18

rules; he was going to stand on the road and catch a *tramp* back to the kibbutz. This was one rule the school did try hard to enforce, because getting casual lifts might be dangerous.

Lesley almost asked Dov to turn around and go back for him. But she just couldn't make herself do it.

She sat seething all the way to Afula.

Nimrod slouched along the main road to the public bus stop. In the school drive he had deliberately walked in the dust cloud behind the car that was taking his mother to meet his sister, the car he so badly wanted to be in, and now he could taste that dust between his teeth. *Dust and ashes,* he thought. *Dust and stinking ashes.*

Why had he gone and told her? He'd thought she might see the joke of it; she had a great sense of humor about some things. It'd been a major coup when he'd sailed back into class ringing his bike bell and the whole class fell on the floor laughing. . . . If he'd just kept his trap shut, he could have been on his way to Tel Aviv. . . . He kicked a large loose stone hard and felt the twang of pain in his toes as it flew into the ditch.

He wasn't looking ahead, so he didn't notice till he reached the bus stop that someone was there ahead of him. It was one of the Russian kids. What was his name? Who cared what his stupid name was?

Still, you couldn't stand there and not say anything. Nimrod gave him a grunt.

"*Shalom,*" said the boy politely. Shalom, *indeed!* thought Nimrod. *Who says* shalom *nowadays?* Made you sound like some old-timer. Everyone said *aha-lan,* like the Arabs. And this guy's Russian accent was really outrageous! He looked funny too. They all did. His slicked-back hair was strange; his high-cheekboned face and pale eyes were strange; even his clothes, which were the same as everybody's, looked strange on him. Everything about him yelled "stranger." Nimrod turned his back on him to look down the road in hope of a car. There weren't many at this hour. He hoped he wouldn't be stuck with this Russki weirdo for long.

"You are hope for *tramp*?" asked the boy behind him.

Nimrod grunted again. What did he think, he was standing in the middle of an empty road for his health?

"You must to go back to kibbutz to work?" persisted the voice. Nimrod winced. His accent made him sound as if he were talking bad Hebrew through a mouthful of pecans.

"No," said Nimrod.

"I work after learn, in toy factory," said the boy. "Make much money."

"All right for some people," said Nimrod sourly. He knew only too well that the Russians, who were visitors to the kibbutz, not members, were allowed to earn money from their work. Kibbutz kids like himself, on the other hand, had to work for free, for the good of the community.

"You work in dates, true?"

Nimrod turned. "How do you know?"

"I see you. Dates very hard work. More hard than factory."

20

"I'll say," said Nimrod. But the compliment softened him.

"What you do in dates in this season?"

"Cut the thorns off the branches."

"You get up in tree and cut with big knife?"

"Yeah."

"You go up in big elephant lift? How is called?"

"Ephronim."

"Not fall?"

"One fell over, two years ago. The guy broke his leg."

"And thorns. Dangerous?"

"Sure. They're poisonous. If you get a scratch, it can become infected."

The boy looked at him with open admiration.

"I like to do man's work. Factory work is for old people." He did a passable mime of a toothless old person. "Very easy work." He gave an exaggerated yawn.

Nimrod grinned. "Boring."

"True."

After a pause Nimrod asked grudgingly, "What's your name?"

"Lev. And you Nimrod. True?"

"Yeah."

At that moment they both heard a van coming. They stuck their arms out and waved their thumbs. Nimrod, remembering that he wasn't supposed to be doing this, said hastily, "If it's an Arab driver, don't get in!"

"Why?"

"Dangerous."

21

"More than thorn?" said the boy. Nimrod looked back at him sharply. Was he teasing him?

The van drew up. Nimrod swore in his head. It was an Arab. What stinking luck, there weren't many around here. The Arab leaned out of the window and said in good Hebrew, "Where do you want to go?"

Nimrod hung back, but Lev stepped forward. He probably didn't know an Arab from a Jew! "Kibbutz Kfar Orde," he said.

"Get in, I'll take you."

"Don't, I told you," Nimrod muttered under his breath. But Lev ignored him. He got into the back of the old battered van and sat on the dirty floor. He grinned like a wide-mouthed frog out at Nimrod. Was he challenging him?

Nimrod dithered a moment while the Arab driver waited patiently. He was looking at him too, a neutral, guarded look. He probably knew perfectly well what was going on in Nimrod's head.

Oh, what the hell, thought Nimrod. *What can happen?* And he scrambled into the front seat.

By the time Lesley arrived at Ben Gurion Airport, her anger had subsided, and her excitement at the prospect of Nili and Glen's arrival had restored her to good humor.

Dov said he'd wait in the car park, and Lesley hurried to where she'd arranged to meet her husband, Ofer. He was waiting for her, not in the airport building—you weren't allowed in there unless you were traveling, for security reasons—but outside, where there was a kind of cattle run that the passengers had to pass along after they got through customs.

Holding Ofer's arm tightly, Lesley said, "How did the concert go?"

"It was good," he answered. He smiled at her. "You didn't hear the broadcast?"

"No, I had a teachers' meeting. Mom did. Full house?"

"Oh, yes." Ofer played with a major orchestra; their concerts were always packed. "Shula and Zion were there."

Shula had been—still was, though with difficulty because she lived far away—Lesley's very best friend since high school.

She had married a North African, who was definitely not into classical music, so Lesley exclaimed: "No! Shula got Zion to go to a concert!"

"He liked it too, or said he did." Ofer chuckled. "He said he liked my twiddly bits."

"Don't know how he could pick them out. I should think it would be one big noise to him."

"Shula's looking well."

"Is she back on her diet?"

"How should I know? Shula is always Shula."

"I wish she hadn't left the kibbutz. I sure miss her."

"Can you see Zion living the communal life?"

"Not much of it left," said Lesley. "He'd get on fine. We need a good carpenter." She sighed. It was a dream. To Shula's husband, the kibbutz, where you couldn't make money and "get on," was a joke. Shula, with her five kids and her mortgaged flat in Katamon and no job and difficult parents-in-law, was stuck. Luckily she didn't seem to know it.

Ofer looked at his watch. "Plane should have

landed by now. Miriam said three-fifteen—that's right, isn't it?''

"That's what she said Noah told her." Lesley looked around, faintly uneasy. "There aren't many people waiting. The barrier's usually lined three deep with families."

They waited a few more minutes.

"I wanted to bring Nimrodi, but then I couldn't," Lesley said.

She spoke in a certain tone he recognized only too well.

"Don't tell me. What this time?"

She did tell him. He heaved a sigh. Ofer didn't talk much, but he felt everything very deeply. Lesley was sad at having spoiled his happy mood.

"Oh, don't let's think about it now! Aren't you dying to see Nili and hear all her adventures?"

He squeezed her arm.

They waited.

At quarter to four a large number of people arrived and lined the barricade, and Lesley and Ofer joined them, expectantly. But when Lesley asked one of them, "Are you meeting the plane from London?" the stranger said, no, New York.

Ofer said uneasily, "Do you think your mother could have got the time wrong?"

"Let's ask."

They found an El Al official and asked.

"The London plane came in on time at thirteen-fifteen," he said.

Lesley and Ofer looked at each other aghast.

"Thirteen-fifteen!" They both instantly knew what had happened.

"Mom never could get the hang of the twenty-four-hour clock!"

"Maybe she just misheard. Thirteen-fifteen, three-fifteen—"

"We were two whole hours late! I should have checked! Why didn't I *check*? Where can they be?"

"Maybe they're waiting inside! If they've got any sense—"

They made inquiries. There was no one waiting.

"Let's phone home!"

They found, at last, a phone that was working. It took only telephone cards, and they didn't have one. There was nowhere they could buy one. It was nearly half past four. Lesley was getting agitated.

"There's nothing to worry about," Ofer kept saying.

Finally a taxi driver, realizing their problem, pulled his wallet out and offered them a battered telephone card.

"It's long-distance. We'll pay you back," said Lesley gratefully.

"No, no. On me," he said.

Lesley phoned her parents' number. "Oh, come on, Mom, Dad, come on!" But there was no reply. Then Ofer suggested they try the kibbutz office.

"Nili doesn't even know that number!"

"Well, who would she phone?"

"Let's try Yocheved!"

"Why should she phone my sister?" asked Ofer.

"Well, she might! It would be sensible. Yocheved lives closer to the airport than anyone else she knows. When we didn't show up, she might think to

25

ask Shalom to come get them." Shalom was Yocheved's son.

They called Ofer's sister in Jerusalem. She answered. She sounded upset, but then she was often upset; it didn't take much.

"Yocheved, it's Lesley."

"Lesley. Have you heard the news?"

"Have you heard from—" Lesley began at the same time. They both stopped. "What news?" asked Lesley.

"A child's been stabbed in the street."

"Oh . . . !" Terrible as this was, it had nothing to do with her present anxieties. "How awful! Listen, Yocheved, we—"

"The news just came over the radio. It just happened. It was in Gilo, right near here. Right out in the street in broad daylight! Can you imagine? Some dirty Arab murderer—"

"How old was the child?" asked Lesley, her skin unaccountably beginning to crawl. One always wondered . . . if one of yours was even out of your sight, and something . . . But it couldn't possibly be. They were here, somewhere. Here at the airport, not in Jerusalem. They couldn't be in Jerusalem.

"A teenager. That's all they said. Some teenage kid right here in our district! Lesley, what are we coming to, they're killing our children in the *street*!"

Lesley's mind was suddenly afire with foreboding.

"Killed?" she whispered.

"Yes," Yocheved answered shrilly. "That's what they said. Stabbed to death."

Nimrod

Nimrod and Lev got back to Kfar Orde quite safely ten minutes after the Arab driver picked them up. He even drove them right up to the gates before letting them off.

Nimrod, who had been in a hurry to leave school because he was bored and fed up, now didn't want to return home right away. He didn't want to walk through the kibbutz in case anyone saw him who might ask why he was home before the school bus. So when Lev suggested, tentatively, that he come with him to the toy factory—which was on this edge of the kibbutz—it seemed like a good idea.

The "toys" were actually educational games. The parts consisted of differently colored and shaped bits of plastic—red squares, blue triangles, yellow circles, and so on. In Lev's section there were machines for cutting the shapes off long bars of the colored plastic.

In the adjoining section, workers—mainly Russians—sat at big tables counting the pieces into drum-shaped cardboard containers while others stuck the labels on and packed them.

Lev went up to a man at one of the tables. He was a big, strong-looking Russian with slicked-back black hair and a heavy mustache.

"This my father," said Lev proudly.

The man stood up, towering over Nimrod, and put out a powerful hand to shake his. Nimrod thought he must hate doing this unmacho work. He'd obviously been some kind of manual worker back in Russia. A stoker or a dockworker, something like that.

"Good Lev got friend," he said in atrocious Hebrew.

Nimrod flushed. He couldn't very well say, "I'm not his friend," so he just said, "Do you speak any English?"

The big man's face broke into a smile of relief. "Yes!" he roared. "My English much better than Hebrew! You speak English? How come?"

"My mother's Canadian," said Nimrod. "We speak it at home."

"We need you!" said Lev's father. His meaty arm described a circle that took in all the Russian workers. "You teach us English! More easy than *ivrit*!"

"But we have to learn *ivrit*," said Lev, "Aba." At his use of the Hebrew for "father," they grinned, and the big man put his arm around him and kissed him exuberantly.

"I know, I know. Is hard at my age. But good to be in Israel!" he boomed heartily.

"You like it, then?" said Nimrod.

28

The man nodded hard and sat down again.

Not all the Russians liked it. There was always stuff in the papers about things going wrong for the thousands of immigrants now flooding into Israel and how they were complaining. Nimrod's grandfather called it the claim-and-blame syndrome. The Russians in town, he said, seemed to claim as many benefits as were going, and then blamed everybody from the government down because they weren't getting enough. Some of them were even turning around and going back to Russia.

The Russians in the kibbutz didn't complain much. Most of them thought they were lucky. The strange thing was, not many of them meant to stay. They were just here to learn Hebrew, earn some money, and then move on to live in town. Nimrod didn't think much of this arrangement.

Lev had moved to his cutting machine and taken over smoothly from the man who'd been at it before. It never paused in its work. The little red squares and yellow circles kept dropping off the long rods into baskets.

Nimrod had never really watched the process before. It was rather fascinating. He picked up the bright, light shapes and tried fitting them into patterns. Before long he became quite absorbed.

Under cover of the noise from the cutter, Lev was talking. "Is hard for the old ones to—what you say—"

"Get used to things?"

"Right! Before half a year, when we come . . . at airport . . . we not know what to do, where to go. Everyone want the city, make money, get house.

Then we see sign in Russian: 'Your first home in your new country.' Kibbutz woman talk my parents.'' Lev chuckled. ''At first, you know, my father shout. 'No more communism! Finish with that dirty way!' He think kibbutz is like Soviet Union! But he have three kids. No money. Soviets not give us to take any much out. We just got our furniture and something from our flat in Kiev.''

''You're not from Moscow?''

''No. Ukraine. Don't worry, not from Georgia.'' Nimrod caught his eye. Evidently Lev knew that some immigrants from Georgia had earned themselves a bad name. ''My father not gangster! Very good architect.''

Nimrod corrected his mistake. ''You mean a builder.''

''No, no! Arch-i-tect. Make plan for building. Others build.''

Nimrod looked again at the burly back of Lev's father, bent over his fiddly, undemanding work. He made some lightning reassessments.

He looked at Lev again. Somehow he didn't look so outlandish as he had at the bus stop, as they all looked in school.

''Can I help?'' he asked.

Lev said, ''Red basket full. You take to table there.''

As Nimrod lifted away the full basket, Lev swiftly moved another into its place. The red squares and yellow circles kept on dropping.

''Don't you eat after school?''

''No time.''

''When do you finish?''

"Three hour."

"Shall I bring you a sandwich?" Nimrod heard himself offer, to his own surprise.

Lev shook his head. Nimrod suddenly remembered that this factory worked around the clock, manned largely by these Russians. They must work very long hours. For them, every *agora* counted. A meal missed here or there wasn't as important as amassing money. Money to get out of the kibbutz.

"Why don't you want to stay here? Then you wouldn't have to work so hard," said Nimrod.

Lev smiled. "Kibbutzniks not work hard?"

"Well. Some do. Some don't. Either way they take their meals."

"Work okay. I like to stay, maybe. But parents want different life."

"They're just using the kibbutz."

"No!" said Lev indignantly.

"Well, what then?"

"Work hard. Kibbutz want our work. That's fair."

Nimrod wasn't so hot on kibbutz economics. He decided to ask his grandfather if the kibbutz was making anything out of the Russians' being here. Be good to know, in case he got into an argument with Lev.

He glanced at his watch. Okay, the school bus would be here in a few minutes. He could get off now and go have something to eat. He'd missed lunch at school through waiting for his mother.

"See you," he said abruptly to Lev.

"See you!" said Lev, hopefully.

Nimrod sloped off. *Not if I see you first, Russki,* he thought. It was a habit of mind. But from some-

31

where came an unexpected new thought: *Why not, though? He'd be okay if he weren't one of them.* But he was one of them, one of the strangers.

The school principal had told them they were supposed to welcome the Russians, be hospitable, make them feel at home. They'd had a rough time in the old Soviet Union, not just all the chaos and shortages going on there now, but anti-Semitism, all that. He'd reminded them how much Israel needed immigration.

Yeah, for sure. But who needed the immigrants? That was a local joke, but it was also true. Yah. They were too weird, too different.

Lunch was nearly over in the *hader okhel,* the big communal dining hall. All that was left were lukewarm scraps that Nimrod had to scrape off the bottoms of the big metal containers: fried rice, a tough old cottage cheese turnover, chicken soup, some bread gone dry. There was a big round salad bar for the health freaks, something Nimrod was not. He took some pickles and left the rabbit food.

He glanced about the big cafeteria to see if there was anyone he wanted to eat with, and at once spotted his cousin Yonatan, sitting alone at the far side. He was in army fatigues with his gun at his side.

Nimrod's face lit up, and he half ran between the tables with his loaded lunch tray swaying perilously. When he reached Yonatan's table, the tray was awash with chicken soup.

The two greeted each other with nods, and Nimrod sat down opposite his cousin.

"Hi. When'd you get home?" Nimrod asked, hiding his happiness. He hadn't seen Yonatan for the

32

month of his reserve service. He laid a slice of bread in the spilled soup to sop it up and then picked it up and ate it. Then he began sawing at the turnover, which was tougher than a bit of tractor tire.

Yonatan said, "Just now. Got a lift from camp."

"I got one from school. With an Arab," mentioned Nimrod carelessly.

Yonatan looked up.

"He was okay. Brought us right to the gate."

"Are you stupid or what? I've told you. You can't trust them. Oh well. You'll learn when you get into the army." Yonatan wiped his mouth on a paper napkin. "They'll have that *kuku* off you as well," he remarked. "The army barber'll stuff a cushion with it."

Nimrod stroked his tied-back hair fondly. "Two cushions," he said. Even Yonatan wasn't going to get to him about his hair.

Yonatan gave him a look, then stood up, hung his duffel bag and gun over his shoulder, and picked up his tray. Nimrod gazed up at him, his grin vanishing.

"Hey, what's your hurry?"

"I haven't been home yet."

"You mean you haven't seen Ilana," muttered Nimrod. Ilana was Yoni's girlfriend.

"Right," said Yonatan, and started to go. Nimrod felt he must hold him somehow, keep him for a little while before he vanished again into his impenetrable grown-up life.

"You know Nili's coming home today. She's bringing Glen."

That stopped him.

"Glen's coming? What about—" He stopped, and

his eyes shifted away from Nimrod. It was as if he had to pause, to make sure his voice came out casually. "Is my dad coming with them?"

"No. Just them."

"Letting them travel alone, eh? Just too busy, I guess. Wal, if that ain't my pa all over." He said the last part in English, Canadian English, the "secret" language he and Nimrod had used when they were younger. He stood for a moment looking through the window. Then, without another word or glance for Nimrod, he strode off to the kitchen with his dirty dishes.

Nimrod ate, his head down over his tray.

Yonatan was, next to his parents and grandparents, and perhaps lately even ahead of them, the most important person in his life. And Yonatan practically ignored him.

Well. He was nearly twenty-four. Why should he bother with a kid of sixteen? He was a man. He'd seen and done plenty. He knew about Arabs. Boy, did he know.

It was one thing to sit beside one in an old van—a friendly Arab, one of "ours." Even that could make your neck prickle. But if you'd stood in a street in Gaza and had them running at you in waves, with masks covering their faces, hurling stones and curses at you, if you'd patrolled in Nablus and never known when a rock was going to drop on your head, if you'd driven in an open jeep through the streets of Hebron or the roads of the West Bank and not known when you might get hurt or even killed . . . then you knew.

Nimrod cursed himself for being an idiot. Bragging like that. He shouldn't have ridden with that Arab. He shouldn't have let Lev do it. Nimrod broke rules on principle, but not if they made sense to him. When Yonatan had said, "You can't trust them," and called him stupid, Nimrod had known he'd never do it again.

When he'd put his tray and dishes on the washing-up carousel, he went outside. The sun was warm, not as it would be in high summer, so hot you could melt, but warm enough. He stood for a minute by the bicycle rack. There weren't many bikes in it just now. His, of course, was at school. He thought of the walk—five minutes at least—along the concrete paths to his grandparents'. Too much trouble.

He picked out a bike that he knew belonged to old Dov, the driver. Well, he was nearly at the airport by now, he wouldn't be needing it till he got home, and Nimrod meant to have it well back by then. He swung his leg over it and pedaled off at full speed down the wide concrete path that led away from the center of the kibbutz toward the far perimeter facing the river, where his grandparents still lived.

They'd lived there for twenty-five years, ever since they came to the kibbutz, though their house had been enlarged and remodeled a few years ago. It was nice, now. His grandmother had designed the inside herself, open plan. She said she'd got claustrophobia from the little room and a half they'd had at first. Now they had two big rooms opening off each other. One was a kitchen–living room, and one was a bedroom-study. They even had a tiny spare room. That was where Glen would stay.

Nimrod's grandfather was sitting in a lounging chair reading the *Jerusalem Gazette.* Just as Nimrod entered, after a token knock, Nat Shelby gave a furious exclamation, crumpled the whole paper into a ball, and hurled it away from him. It caught Nimrod on the nose as he came around the corner of the tiny passage.

"Nu, Saba, what's wrong?" asked Nimrod, reaching down to pick it up. He knew his grandfather would want to smooth it out later. The pro-government, right-wing policy of the paper maddened him, but for someone who couldn't easily read Hebrew, there was no alternative.

"Idiots! Fascists! Religious maniacs! Why doesn't that piano player go back to his wine bar!" This was a reference to the current editor, who had not had a lot of previous experience as a journalist.

Nimrod put the paper ball on the table and went to the kitchen part of the room to switch on the kettle. "Can I make some *botz,* Saba?"

"You'll clog up your stomach with that muck. Put some proper coffee in the percolator!"

"Takes too long." Nimrod found the fine-ground coffee in a tin. His grandmother always got some for him from the *col-bo,* the kibbutz store. He put two heaped teaspoonfuls of the thick fragrant brown powder into a mug and poured boiling water on it, producing *botz,* which meant "mud." Then he added lots of coarse white sugar. "Want some?" he asked.

"No, thank you! ... Oh, all right, might as well if you haven't patience to make me a proper drink."

"Where's Savta?"

"She's gone to get some fruit for Glen's room."

"What's wrong with this?" Nimrod asked, indicating a bowl of oranges and dates. His dates, the ones he'd helped grow last season. He picked one up and sampled it expertly: big as a man's thumb and gluey sweet, with a dry papery skin that he carefully peeled away. One of these was a meal in itself.

"Your grandmother would like to line the room with silk and tile it with gold," Nat was muttering. "You'd think some young pasha was coming to stay."

Nimrod put a second mug of mud-coffee and a package of cookies on the table beside his grandfather and sat near him.

"Of course, Glen's our grandson," Nat said after a minute. "Nobody wants him to be happy here more than I do. But the way women carry on, you'd think nothing was good enough."

"Don't you like Glen?" asked Nimrod curiously.

His grandfather turned his head sharply, his mouth a little open.

"What kind of fool question's that? Not like my own grandson?" he barked. Nimrod said nothing, and after a moment Nat said more quietly, "I've never met the boy. How could I dislike him?"

"I just thought, because he's Uncle Noah's son."

There was a silence, and Nimrod, who liked to provoke interesting responses, thought he'd gone too far. But his grandfather loved him so much that he didn't provoke very easily.

"Don't get things wrong, Nimrod. I don't dislike your uncle. He's my son, I love him. I just disapprove of him in some ways, that's all." He gulped down some coffee and made a face.

"Why?"

"I guess you know why."

"Because he left Israel?"

"Because he left his family and ran off with another woman."

"A Jewish one, at least."

Nat gave him a look. "Oh. So you know all about that."

"I know you were furious when he married Donna, because she was a Catholic."

Nat sat frowning. Eventually he muttered, "I saw things in black and white when I was younger. In Canada, if a Jew marries out, you feel as if he's . . . breaking faith with the past. Helping the Amalekites."

Now it was Nimrod who frowned. The Amalekites meant anyone who wanted to destroy the Jewish people. That seemed a bit strong for Donna! But his grandfather was an extreme sort of person. Nimrod had learned long ago to add a little water to some of his more off-the-wall pronouncements.

"But you're okay with Donna now."

"Yes."

"Why?"

"She's a beautiful person and the mother of my grandson."

Nimrod swigged his *botz* contentedly. Despite his grandfather's frequent outbursts, there was something peaceful about being here. He liked this apartment, with all its little comforts and what his mother called its Canadian accent.

She'd pointed out that as people got older, they often looped back to what they'd come from. This place, with its cheerful fabrics and light-colored woodwork, its framed prints, paintings of pine-fringed lakes and wheat fields by Canadian artists, its pretty ornaments and its fridge full of goodies, was so different from that of his other grandmother—his father's mother—while she'd been alive.

Everything in her apartment had been dark and heavy-looking, with lots of thick embroidery and painted plates, the taste of Eastern Europe. She too had made him snacks, pastry cakes full of poppy seeds and rich custard, but somehow around her he had always felt sad. Poor old Savta. First, Grandpa Samuel dying so young from long-term health damage from his time in the concentration camp. Then losing her son-in-law, his aunt Yocheved's husband, in the Six-Day War. And then that bad business with Nimrod's uncle Adam, whom he'd never known . . . Some people had such lousy lives, just one terrible thing after another.

As he sat there ruminating, it struck Nimrod as strange that his parents, who'd met in school, here in the kibbutz, should have come from such different sorts of people, from such different countries and backgrounds. If they hadn't been Jews who'd come to Israel, how easily his parents might never have come together, how easily he might never have been born!

"Can I look in Glen's room?"

"Sure, go ahead. The prince's parlor."

The room was small, but it had a built-in desk and bed, the lighting was just right, and there was a little radio. And lots of books.

"How does she know he likes to read?"

"Well, if he doesn't, he's no grandson of mine!"

"I don't like to read. Does that mean I'm not your grandson?"

This was an old tease, but this time his grandfather merely grunted and said, "Your organ of imagination is rotting in your head. It's a pity."

Nimrod came back into the main room. "Nobody's perfect," he remarked.

"Far from it, in some cases! For instance, why were you home so early from school? And why did you take a *tramp* when you know perfectly well it's forbidden?"

Nimrod choked on a date. "Hell, Granddad! You must have spies everywhere!"

"I do. Come on, let's have it."

In the nick of time the door flew open and his grandmother Miriam came hurrying into the room, carrying a bag of fruit and a bunch of wildflowers.

"Talk about forbidden!" crowed Nimrod, pointing at them. "Savta! Those are protected!"

"I only picked five," she said defensively, and then, as if this excused everything: "They're for Glen." She found a little vase for them and arranged them. "There! He'll like those. Did you look at the room, Nimrod? Is it all right? I mean, would a boy of fourteen feel comfortable in it?"

"Apart from all the books," said Nimrod, winking at his grandfather.

She looked at the clock over the sink. "They've landed by now! No phone call, by any chance?"

Nat said, "Someone rang while I was in the bathroom. By the time I got there they'd hung up."

"When will they be here?" asked Nimrod.

"Let's see, it's nearly four. They'll have cleared customs by now. Then two hours' drive home . . . Say six o'clock."

"If nothing goes wrong."

"Wrong! What could go wrong? Don't say that!" said Miriam Shelby sharply.

"Hey, Savta! You're superstitious!"

"Who isn't?" she said, busying herself arranging kiwi fruit on a dish.

Nat straightened up from flattening out the newspaper on the table and picked up the TV remote control.

"Time for the news," he said.

FOUR

On the Edge

The kibbutz car found the steep hill leading through the wadi up to Jerusalem too much for it. Dov, the old driver, feeling the engine cough and give up, managed to steer it on momentum into the side of the busy road, while cars swerved around it, honking unforgivingly.

Lesley and Ofer stumbled out. They hadn't told Dov anything, except that the children had arrived early and possibly gone to Jerusalem. Dov had known then that the car probably wouldn't make it up through the hills.

Now the old man got out the tools and disappeared, muttering, under the hood while Lesley and Ofer stood on the curb, waving their arms desperately at every car that approached.

At last a taxi drew up. Dov emerged from the oily depths of the failed motor.

"What, leaving me to it, are you? What's your hurry? I'll get you there. Give me a chance!"

"I'm sorry, Dov. We have to go. We're—we're worried. You understand."

"Stupid kids," muttered Dov. "Why didn't they stay put? I don't know." He stood watching gloomily as the taxi pulled away.

They sat in the back, holding on to each other and not talking at all. At last, after nearly an hour of picking their way through rush-hour traffic from west to east, they reached Yocheved's apartment block in the Gilo district, at the far side of the city. Ofer paid while Lesley stood shivering in the early dusk.

"Maybe we should keep him on?" she said between chattering teeth. "We may—we may need him."

She heard a cry and looked up. Her sister-in-law was leaning over the balcony of her apartment, three floors up.

"Don't come up! We're coming down! Shalom says you should go to the central police station. We'll go with you!"

The taxi drove off. Ofer and Lesley stood on the sidewalk. After a few moments they heard Yocheved and Shalom clattering down the tiled stairway.

Yocheved rushed out first. She looked distraught. Her gray-streaked hair was uncombed. The clothes on her bulky body were askew, her blouse collar half tucked inside out. She embraced them both with tears running down her unpowdered cheeks.

Shalom, her twenty-five-year-old son, put his hands on her shoulders. "Ima, don't. We don't know anything yet."

"I know!" Yocheved cried. "I know! I feel it!

43

Just like with your father—just like with Adam—I feel it! Oh, God! Is it never to end?''

The weight of her against Lesley's body was almost pushing her over. Lesley couldn't respond or say anything. The fear had made her mind and body numb. But she felt a swift relief when Shalom detached his mother.

"Please try to be calm, Ima. This doesn't help. Come on, the car's right over there."

They hurried through the deepening twilight to the car parked on the wide, quiet street.

This was a new district. Not all the blocks were complete. It was one of the so-called fortress suburbs, constructed to make sure this sector southeast of the city would always be part of Jewish Jerusalem. The blocks, tall and close together like pale sentries, were rather beautiful with their arched windows and white-gold stone. But Lesley didn't like coming to this part of the city, which had been open country in Jordan before 1967. Unlike Yocheved, she felt it didn't belong to them.

A few hundred meters beyond the last house in this street was an Arab village. The tall blocks of Gilo were like a phalanx of giants bearing down on it.

"That's where he must have come from!" cried Yocheved, throwing out an accusing finger. "The accursed murdering monster!"

"Shh, Ima. We don't know. We don't know anything yet. Please. Get in the car."

Shalom was so kind. Lesley felt with gratitude the touch of his hand cupping her elbow as he helped her in, neither too brusque nor too sympathetic. Through her numbness, her absolute unwillingness to

44

be part of *now,* she retreated into the past: Shalom's birth on the first day of the Six-Day War, his father's death in battle on the last. Brought up by Yocheved, who had never remarried, he had been cocooned by love. It had not spoiled him but made him (as Ofer had once said) male outside and female within, strong but with a sensitive and tender heart.

He loved Nili. Everyone loved Nili. *If anything—* Lesley clamped down hard. *Don't. Don't. Don't. It can't be her. It can't be her.* But when nobody met them when they got off the plane, what was more reasonable, more *typical,* for her to do than to get the minibus to Jerusalem and then head for her aunt's? Where else would she go if no one answered the phone at home?

She knew the way. All those family visits. And two years ago, when there'd been a national youth movement camp in the hills near the city, she'd taken it into her head to visit Yocheved before coming home. . . . She'd been in trouble over it. But she did things like that. She was so open and free; warnings just rolled off her. She had the courage of someone who has never known anything but love and security.

And now, today, even more confident after her week abroad, Nili would take Glen in hand. *This is my home, I know what to do!* Showing off a little to the stranger cousin, finding her own way competently through the crowds at the bus station, buying the tickets, knowing the right bus, knowing the right stop, beginning to walk through these thinly peopled streets, past the ghostly, half-built blocks, so near the edge of the town, the start of open hilly countryside, apparently so peaceful, that cradled the ancient village. A village that could hold hatred and menace under its disguise of simple, timeless beauty.

They drove to the central police station in the bustling heart of Jewish West Jerusalem. Here they would know. The awful uncertainty would end—one way or the other.

Ofer was thinking: *We could have phoned from the airport. From Yocheved's.* Why had they come here? Was it because the very notion of hearing such news through a machine was unthinkable? No. It was just to put it off. To put it off, however dreadful the not knowing was, until the last possible moment.

Dusk had turned into near darkness, and the streetlights were ablaze. The shops had opened after the one-to-four P.M. siesta break. The crowds jostled thickly on the uneven sidewalks; the roads were full of honking traffic. Buses, taxis, cars, motorbikes, all ridden by people whose lives were not on an edge of catastrophe. It seemed to Ofer he was looking at people in another world. A world of blissful happiness, of innocence, where fear didn't exist.

Shalom led them through an iron gate and into a big building with double doors.

"Wait here," he said. "I'll ask." He started to go toward the desk, then hesitated and turned. He held both hands out to them, as if begging. "Listen, I'm sure it's all right. I'm sure—"

"I'll come with you," said Ofer.

He left his wife and sister holding each other's hands near the entrance, and he and his nephew walked to a big desk. Ofer had trouble putting one foot ahead of the other. It was like walking toward his execution. It was not that he believed his sister had supernatural powers. Or if she had, he had them too, because he too felt a certainty of something fatal and terrible up ahead of him.

Yet it was absurd. How could it be that out of all the teenagers in all the city, he could be so afraid that his child, who shouldn't even have been there, was the nameless victim?

The two men stood at the desk. Neither could speak. The officer on duty didn't speak either. He was looking, not at them, but over their shoulders at the women. His face was full of surprise.

"Is that your wife?" he asked Ofer abruptly.

He nodded.

"You must've come about your daughter," the man said.

Ofer felt a jolt inside his chest and gripped the edge of the huge desk. "Yes."

"She was brought in two hours ago. I saw her. . . . She's just like your wife, isn't she?" He shifted his eyes back to Ofer and said hastily, "Oh, she's all right, *adoni,* don't be afraid! She's in shock, but she's unharmed. We took her to the hospital; she's being treated there. We've got her under guard because as soon as possible we have to interview her."

Ofer forced his voice out past relief that was all but choking him. "About—what?"

"About the boy, *adoni.* The boy she was with. I'm sorry to have to tell you. He's the one who was killed."

The Notice
on the Door

"A terrible thing," muttered Nat, shaking his head as he switched the TV off after the news. "It just shows you what the Occupation has brought us to."

"Brought *them* to," said Miriam. "We only do what's necessary."

"Ah. You mean, if only the Arabs would lie down and be quiet, there'd be no need for us to repress them?" said Nat sarcastically.

"We don't repress them," said Miriam tautly.

"Yes, we do, Savta," said Nimrod. "We have to."

"Well, I don't believe it. The newspapers—"

"Miriam! The only newspaper you ever read is this rag, and even they can't deny—although they play it down—that our troops are shooting demonstrators in the streets of the territories every week!"

48

Miriam didn't answer at once. She just sighed heavily and stuffed a date into her mouth. It was an old, old argument. She would not and could not ever accept that Israeli soldiers were doing a single thing that was not "necessary." And although Nat argued with her, he couldn't bear to rub her nose too hard in the facts.

He'd never told her, for example, what their grandson Yonatan had confessed to him about what had happened with him on the West Bank three years ago. Nat knew that it would have broken Miriam. He often wondered if Donna knew. How did you cope with your son's coming home on leave and telling you a thing like that. . . . He didn't know how *he* had coped with it. Not too well, if he remembered rightly.

"Anyway," said Miriam defensively, "it's one thing to shoot in self-defense when they're throwing rocks. Rocks are as lethal as bullets—"

"Oh, yes? Which would you rather face?"

"It's another to set out deliberately to stab a child to death. That's absolutely barbaric."

"Perhaps we've had something to do with driving them to it," said Nat with great sadness.

"No Jew would ever dream of doing such a thing!"

Nat reached for his pipe. As Miriam ate for comfort, Nat smoked. Each tried to control the other's little vice. But Miriam grew fat and Nat's cough got worse.

"At this very moment," Miriam said in distress, "some poor family is getting the news. Can you just imagine it! News that will break their hearts. God pity them!"

49

"Evidently He didn't," said Nat shortly. "His pity for this part of the world seems to be wearing thin. Who can wonder?"

Nimrod was getting restless. He stood up and moved toward the door. He was thinking. Three hours, Lev had said. Maybe he'd mosey back to the factory and pick him up after work and see if he'd like to mess around on Yonatan's computer with him.

If Yonatan agreed, of course. And he just might, if Nimrod brought one of the Russian kids. He was pretty strong on being welcoming to the Russians. He was disgusted when Nimrod had made a few rude remarks when the Russians'd first come.

"You going, Nimrodi?" asked his grandmother, turning over her shoulder. "You'll come back later, to help me settle Glen in?"

"At six," he said. "See you." He turned in the entrance. "Shall I take the newspaper, Saba?"

Nat fell for it. "What for?"

"To save your blood pressure!"

Nat shook his fist at him through his pipe smoke, and Nimrod went out.

Old Dov's bike was waiting for him. He felt a mild unease as he mounted it. He'd better get it back pretty soon. He needed a second bike of his own, really.

As he whirled along the path under the trees, he saw a little posse of people walking toward him. Three of them were strangers—two men and a woman. The fourth person in the group was Yoel, the kibbutz general secretary, the nearest thing to a "chief" in the kibbutz.

In the few seconds he was facing them, before he

swerved off the path to avoid them, it struck Nimrod that they all looked pretty serious. He turned back over his shoulder to look after them. One of the strange men was in uniform. Not army. Police.

Nimrod thought, *Someone's in the* botz. *Glad it's not me.* It felt definitely good not to be the one in trouble, just for once—though, hell, he'd never been in that sort of trouble! The kibbutz very seldom brought in the cops. If there was anything, which was very seldom, they usually preferred to deal with it themselves. The only time Nimrod could remember cops in the kibbutz was when that lunatic Ari, from two grades higher than Nimrod, had swiped one of the teachers' cars for a joy ride at night and ended up in a ditch.

Ari was crazy, but he had some great ideas for fun things to do. It was Ari who'd started the "pub," a meeting place for the seniors where there was some actual alcohol. At first it had been secret and "illegal," and when the kibbutz found out about it, there'd been an outcry. But by that time too many kids wanted it. The kibbutz was so afraid they'd go off drinking in town if the pub were banned that they "legalized" it. Ari became a hero. . . .

Nimrod, passing the parking space near the dining hall, saw the car the strangers must have come in— a police vehicle, sure enough. Interesting! It made up Nimrod's mind. He had to tell someone, and Lev was the only person whose whereabouts at this moment he could be sure of. He veered to the right and bumped over the dried-out mud ruts toward the factory.

The scene was exactly as he'd last seen it, with

all the same people and Lev fitting another red bar into the cutter. Nimrod had a sudden insight into his boredom. How could you do that for three hours straight? Your brain would shrivel up!

"Hi," he shouted over the screeching cutter.

Lev looked up. He looked really pleased to see him.

"How much longer?" asked Nimrod.

"Twenty minutes."

"You want to come to my cousin's place and play computer games for an hour?"

Lev's face split open in a wordless grin.

"Okay, I'll just go ask him if he agrees," said Nimrod. "By the way, the cops're here."

"What you said?"

"The police."

Lev straightened up and, for the first time, let go of the bar. His wide face had lost color. "They came to take someone?"

"Dunno," said Nimrod. "I'll try to find out!"

Only when he was back on the bike did he remember someone saying that most Russians were afraid, in a very deep place, of the police.

"Come in!"

Yonatan was not in his room, but his mother, Donna, was. She was working with the computer herself. *Hell!* Nimrod had forgotten that Donna did quite a bit of word processing, writing her medical reports.

She looked around at him through her rimless glasses. She wore her hair very short; when she teased Nimrod for looking girlish with his long hair, he told her she looked like a guy. "Oh, it's you, Nimrod! Hi there, kiddo. What can I do for you?"

Like her parents-in-law, she usually spoke to him in English. Her Hebrew was fairly good, but she never used it if she didn't have to.

"Yoni around?"

"He came and went. Oh, I know what you want! Give me a few minutes to finish this, and it's all yours."

"Sure he won't mind?"

"It's not only his, you know, this. His father sent it to both of us. That's my story, anyway. . . . Don't worry, pal. Yoni's with Ilana. He won't be back for hours—if ever!" She rolled her eyes comically and turned back to her work.

"Can I bring someone?"

"Whoa! Who? Not one of your dreaded classmates? 'Cause one crackpot messing with my favorite toy's enough."

"He's one of the Russkis."

"You know they hate being called Russkis," she said, pattering away furiously on the keyboard.

Nimrod said nothing. The principal had said to think how they'd feel if they went abroad and got called yids or kikes. Since Nimrod had never heard either name, he hadn't been very impressed.

He sat in the most comfortable chair and ate some nuts. Donna worked away busily. After a while he said, "The cops're here."

"Hm?"

"There's a cop car in the car park, and I saw them. Yoel's with them. Do you think they've found

53

out that when Grandpa works in the dairy, he snitches cream to feed Tuli?''

''I wouldn't put it past him,'' said Donna. ''He'd make off with a whole cow for that mangy old cat of his.''

''Grandma won't even let it in the house.''

''I told her not to! It's eighteen years old. It stinks.''

She hit the Exit button with finality.

''There! Finished. Now I should go see if Miriam needs any help.''

''What do you feel about Glen coming?''

She looked startled. ''Me? Nothing. I mean, I'm glad. It'll be real interesting for Yoni to meet his half brother.''

''Funny they've never met before.''

''Yeah. Very funny,'' she said with an edge.

''You'd think Uncle Noah would have brought him and Dale to meet us.''

''You would think so only if you didn't know my ex-husband.''

''What do you mean exactly?''

''Nimrod, you're worse than Nili—questions, questions.''

''It's family stuff. I'm interested.''

She sighed. ''Well. You know your dear uncle Noah brought me here to Israel after Yoni was born, telling me how desperately important it was for me to like it and settle here, and I did my darnedest— oh, you know all this.''

''Tell me again. As I grow up, I listen better.''

''Ho-hum, put on the old tape. So. We got a place in Tel Aviv, and your uncle got a good job with a construction company, and as soon as Yoni was in nursery school, I got work, too. I went to language school and struggled with Hebrew and studied to pass my nursing exams all over again and watched my little Canuck growing up as a wild Israeli. . . . Nimrod! Take that grin off your face! You were born here. You didn't ever have to get used to it. For me it was hard. Hard, hard, hard.''

Nimrod pretended to play soulful music on a violin. She threw a nut at his head.

"All right, have your fun! It *was* hard. And then came the Yom Kippur War in 1973. And that time Noah was drafted. It was what he'd always said he wanted, to really be part of it, what he'd lacked so badly as a volunteer here in the Six-Day War. And he went, and he was part of it, and oh, boy. It turned out being part of it that way, being a number and following orders and risking your life and having to shoot at people, just wasn't for him.''

"You mean he was a *muglev*.''

"We can't all be heroes, Nimrod,'' she said sharply. "It wasn't exactly that, anyhow. He was finding a lot of things about life here—I mean, in the town—not up to his standards. He came up against lots of monkey business in the construction industry. Arabs were doing all the actual building, and they were being well ripped off by the contractors, and Noah was expected to go along with it. He hated that. He actually made a fuss about it, and they fired him.''

Nimrod was listening closely now. "Well, you must have agreed with him about that. You always side with the Arabs.''

55

She gave him a straight, narrow-eyed look. "No, I don't, Nimrod. Only when they're right."

"Did you hear what they did today?" Nimrod digressed suddenly.

"No?"

"Some teenager in East Jerusalem was stabbed."

"Oh, God," she said loudly. There was a silence. She stared at him, as if trying to take it in. "Who was it?"

Silly question. "Well, it can't have been anyone we know, can it? They won't tell the name till the next of kin are informed. Go on. What happened with Uncle Noah?"

She heaved a sigh as if trying to shake off the awful news.

"Well, he was thoroughly turned off the whole country by then. He just never stopped finding things that were wrong. And I—you know, me, the Catholic, the non-Jew, the one who hadn't wanted to come, who had no connection—I found myself defending it."

"Why?"

She stretched her long legs into a V. "I don't know exactly. Something about it I really began to like. Perhaps it was just that it was so gutsy, so alive. Such a *challenge.* Oh, I grumbled a lot, but it was the kind of grumbling people do about their own place. And Yoni, of course—well, he just was an Israeli kid, for all my efforts to make him a little Christian, and after a while I realized he was far more Jewish than not. And I kind of gave in."

He saw her put her hand up to touch her throat. A tiny crucifix hung there on a chain. A lot of people in the kibbutz would like to have seen her stop wearing it, but she always wore it.

"And then, of course, there were your grandparents. Miriam and Nat. They were so wonderful. When Noah left, I came here. They could easily have sided with him against me, but they didn't. Apart from Miriam's trying to get me to convert for Yoni's sake, they have been just like my own family."

"When did he leave exactly?"

"In 1975." Her flow of talk dried up suddenly. She looked down at her hands in her lap.

"Go on," urged Nimrod.

"That's all. There were quarrels. He wanted me to go back to Canada, and I—I wanted him to stick it out here. I thought the change would be too hard for Yoni. And then Noah met—" She dried up again.

"Valerie."

"Right. The Terrible Tourist from Outer Toronto. *She* was going back all right. She hated it in Israel, couldn't wait to get out! And next thing you know—"

She stopped. Nimrod suddenly jumped up.

"Donna, I have to go fetch this Russki. I'll be back."

"Sure. I'm going home now, but you know where the key's kept." She looked up at him and gave him a bit of a grin. But he saw her eyes and he fled like a rabbit. Stories were one thing. Emotions were another.

He rode at full speed on the creaky old bike back to the center of the kibbutz. *Must leave Dov's bike now,* he thought. *He'll be back any minute.*

The dining hall was all lit up for supper, and people should have been drifting in to eat, but something was wrong.

There were groups standing on the big veranda outside the main doors. The young kids, who were usually out there playing ball, were just standing silently. And as Nimrod rode past, he saw something else. There was a square of white paper on one of the double glass doors.

He braked and nearly went over the handlebars. Suddenly the little group of people he'd seen before, the kibbutz secretary, the woman in civvies, the uniformed police officer, added together with this unusual gathering and the paper, spelled something worse than some high school kid in trouble.

Something really bad had happened.

Nimrod stood facing away from the lighted building, braced with his feet on either side of the bicycle. He stared unseeingly at the distant lights of the factory. His brain was racing. Well, it couldn't be Yonatan anyway. Yonatan was safe; he was here. But there were plenty of other men doing their reserve duty and younger kids doing their initial three-year stint in the army. It must be one of them. An accident during training or on maneuvers, maybe, or infiltrators might have killed a soldier. Things like that happened.

But in that case, why was the man in police uniform? When something happened with a soldier, it was always an army officer who came.

To his own great surprise, Nimrod rode on. He didn't know why, because the obvious thing to do would be to turn back, join the crowd outside the *hader okhel* and just ask. But something stopped him from doing that. Instead he was going to the factory to pick Lev up first.

Lev the Russki. Nimrod, for no reason he could have explained, wanted Lev with him when he heard.

SIX

Nili's Nightmare

Nili knew it was a nightmare when she began to wake up. She was able to draw away from the face, to see it wasn't a real face.

What it was, was a dream of a big white building with window holes for eyes and arches for eyebrows and a horrible sharp-cornered oblong mouth, opened in a silent scream. Only now she realized it wasn't a mouth; it was really only a vacant doorway. But still, as it lingered behind her eyelids, there was something there, something too frightening to know.

She opened her eyes to get away from it. And saw her mother.

Her mother was sitting beside her, holding her hand in both hers. Her face was terrible, worse, in a way, than the building-face in her dream. Nili immediately felt something solid inside her breaking down, and tears burst from her eyes without any warning.

Her mother bent over her and gathered her in her arms. She held her and rocked her, and they cried together. Nili thought she was crying because her mother was. After a while she pulled away. Only then she saw that her father was there too, on the other side of the bed. And he was crying too!

"Ima! Aba! What's wrong?" she cried out sharply. The sight of her father's tears frightened her worse than anything. She had seen him cry before, and it was always about something terrible, like a death.

A death . . .

She stiffened. Her eyes glazed. Her hand, still in her mother's, clenched in a sudden spasm.

Out of the oblong cave of that empty doorway had come two men.

They came so quickly; they skimmed silently over the empty road. There was no chance of dodging or escaping. In a split second, it seemed, they were upon them.

What happened next, as it replayed itself in Nili's memory, was so swift, so unnatural. . . . In a way, she felt as if it hadn't involved her; it was something she'd watched from afar, through a screen, on a stage.

One man caught hold of Glen from behind, and suddenly he went stiff and there was a look of surprise on his face. He hadn't seen them coming as she had; he knew nothing about it. One second he was walking along the curved empty street beside her, talking to her quite excitedly, and the next he had turned to face her. He gave a sharp gasp and his eyes widened and then . . . he dropped down.

Dropped down onto the sidewalk, and the man behind him stood there with a bloody knife in his hand, looking at her.

And that was the worst, worse than Glen's lying there—because she was next. She was going to be killed. The man was stepping over Glen and reaching for her—

Nili screamed.

A nurse came running into the room. She almost pushed Lesley aside and took Nili by the shoulders, looking into her eyes.

"It's all right now, Nili," she said commandingly. "It's all over. Just keep saying to yourself, very strongly, 'I'm safe. I'm safe.'"

Nili didn't hear her or notice her. She was back there in Gilo. The man was reaching for her. She saw his eyes, black in a fierce young face, dark with hatred. She was going to feel that knife in her body. She was going to die—now—now!

But something happened to stop it. What happened?

She didn't feel the prick of the needle in her arm. She found herself lying back on the bed with her mother's arms around her. Her clear, agonizing memory had become reduced to little weak, flashing images. Another face—an arm—a swift movement, tugging her aside. A fierce push, and then a jolt as the hard pavement came up to meet her. Two voices—short, angry words. The sound of running feet. Silence. And a feeling of indescribable, almost heavenly relief.

She was not going to die. She had been saved from dying.

As her eyes closed on the present, they opened on the past. She saw Glen in his red checked jacket lying still, a few feet away. The bag he'd been carrying was under him, pushing up his body into an arch. His knees were bent. His pale, freckled face was against the stone sidewalk. His eyes were a little bit open. As if he were just waking up in the king-size bed that morning when she had tickled his neck and said, "Come on, you lazy, wake up!" But now he would never wake up again, and she knew it beyond a shadow of doubt. Her cousin was dead.

Nevertheless, she called him, fiercely, desolately.

"Glen! *Glen! GLEN!*"

Nothing moved.

The image of him drifted farther and farther away.

Lesley and Ofer watched her eyes drooping closed, hiding the glazed look of terror. The anguish in their hearts died down a little. At least she wasn't feeling it now. The needle had given her a little rest from remembering it.

"It's good," the nurse was saying. "She was reliving it. If she can do that so soon, it means it's not going to sink down into a very deep place in her mind where she can't reach it, where it can do a lot of harm."

There was a knock on the door of the private room. The nurse went to see who it was. It was the plainclothes police officer who had already introduced herself to Lesley and Ofer.

She was waiting for Nili to be ready to talk to her.

"She'll sleep for several hours," said the nurse. "Come back in the morning."

"But she was awake. I heard her scream," said the policewoman.

"Do you want to upset her even more?" asked the nurse severely. "You must wait till she recovers a little. How would you feel if it were your daughter?"

"If it were my daughter, I'd want to catch whoever did it, even more than I do now," she retorted.

But she left. Ofer said, "Thank you," to the nurse, who had returned to the bed and was staring down at Nili. She reached out her hand and brushed the thick bangs off Nili's pale forehead.

"*Miscainah*," she said. "Poor little thing. Animals. They're just wild animals."

"Why do you think he didn't kill her too?" Lesley whispered.

The nurse shrugged. "Disturbed in the act. Only thing I can think of. Nothing's bad enough for whoever did this."

In Kibbutz Kfar Orde the news spread like spilled water.

Yoel, the general secretary, had been at home when the police came. When, hampered by shock and reluctance to perform the awful duty that lay before him, he had slowly put on his jacket and set off with the others to tell Nat and Miriam, he left his wife white-faced and shaking. She sat still for a long time, her fists clenched in her lap, her head bent, her eyes screwed shut, hardly breathing.

At last she got up, went to her desk, and wrote a

notice on a piece of plain paper. Then she hurried to
the dining hall and stuck it on the glass double doors.

> *Glen Shelby*
> *grandson of Nat and Miriam*
> *is no more*
> *murdered by terrorists*
> *in Jerusalem today.*
> *Our Nili will return to us.*

Nobody in the kibbutz, even his own relations, had
known Glen. But everyone, every last person, felt his
death as a personal loss.

Partly this was because it could have happened to
any of their children. Such was the basic insecurity
of their lives. Everyone felt frightened, outraged, di-
minished by the loss of this Jewish child. And partly
it was because Glen had been the grandson of Nat
and Miriam, the nephew of Lesley and Ofer, the half
brother of Yonatan, the cousin of Nili and Nimrod.
This made him part of them all.

Miriam lay on her bed covered with a blanket. She
was curled up like an unborn child. Her hand lay
over her face as if to shield it from a bright light.
The kibbutz nurse had given her something, and it
was beginning to work. Still, every now and then a
sob, left over, gathered like a wave inside her and
blubbered out through her open mouth.

Nat sat beside her with his hand on her hunched
shoulder. His pipe of consolation lay neglected. His
eyes were fixed on the blank wall behind his wife's

head. His heart was numb and cold, and he was shivering.

Only his lap was warm. An aged cat sat on it, a cat that was normally banned from the neat and spotless apartment. Almost as soon as the news had sunk in, as soon as Miriam had collapsed in a storm of weeping and been put to bed, Nat had crept to the door. His cat, Tuli, had been there, as if waiting. He had picked it up and brought it in.

Now his free hand stroked its bedraggled fur. In bliss at this unusual treat, it sank its old claws into his leg every now and then. Nat didn't mind. It was good that he could still feel that little pain through the monstrous pain of sorrow and regret that was overwhelming him.

After a long time he remembered. There was this terrible thing that he had to do. He had undertaken it to save Noah from hearing it from anyone else. He had said he would phone him. Phone his son and tell him that *his* son was dead.

How did a father do that? he asked himself. A father so long estranged, a father no longer even close to his boy. But he had to. It was a duty.

He lifted his cat onto the bed, where it curled up in the bend of Miriam's knees. He went to the phone. But no, he couldn't do it here. Not where Miriam might hear him.

He walked out into the warm night. He didn't use his bike. He was thinking that every minute's delay meant another minute of peace and happiness for Noah. False peace and false happiness, but what did that matter? Noah would look back on this time and be grateful, perhaps, for every moment of it.

Oh, my poor little boy, Nat thought brokenly. *My poor little boy!* It didn't seem strange to him that he was thinking of Noah as if he were still a child whom he was going to have to hurt cruelly.

He walked slowly through the sweet-smelling, lamplit darkness to the house of his daughter-in-law Donna. At least he didn't have to break the news to her. Yoel had done it, with the help of the policewoman. What would it mean to her, the death of this son of her husband's with the woman who had taken her place?

He knocked gently. Donna knew his knock. Her clear Canadian voice answered, "Come in, Nat."

They stood and looked at each other, the old man and this woman whom he had once hated. Yes. He was ready to admit it now. He had hated her for taking his son from the faith, for trying to turn him into a Roman Catholic. For refusing to convert and make his grandson a Jew. But that was long ago. In these years when she had chosen—chosen, against the strongest pressures—to share their life and bring her son up as an Israeli, he had learned to respect and then to love her. Not least because she loved him, as if he had been her own father.

She came and put her arms around him, and they stood together silently.

"He didn't suffer," she said. "They swore to it. Tell Noah that."

She knew, as if by instinct, why he had come.

"Stay with me while I do it," he said.

He sat by the phone, took out a small address book fumblingly, found the place, and dialed the long number. Then she took and held his hand. The ringing sounded in his ear, amplified by the thudding of his blood.

"Hello?"

It was the bright, expectant voice of Valerie, his other daughter-in-law. Nat said, "Hello, Valerie. This is Nat. Noah's father."

"Oh, hello, Nat! How kind of you to call me. They've arrived, then?"

"Is—is my son there?"

"Why, no, he's still in London."

Of course. Of course. *Idiotic old fool!* Still in London.

He swallowed, and looked at Donna. She had heard. He tried to speak, but his voice wouldn't come out. Into the long silence his son's wife, four thousand miles away, was saying, less brightly now, "Are you still there? There's nothing wrong—is there?"

The phone dropped into Nat's lap. His face crumpled. He shook his head. He couldn't do it. Donna saw he couldn't do it.

She gently took the instrument from him.

"Valerie, this is Donna. I've got something very bad to tell you. I'm so sorry it has to be me."

Much later that evening Dov, worn-out and smudged with motor oil, limped home in the wretched car that had broken down twice more on the way. He had patched it up as best he could, but he knew it was done for. It gave up finally at the far end of the drive. He had to walk the last hundred meters to the gates.

They were closed and locked for the night. He

picked up the phone to summon the night watch with the key. He was a long time answering and a longer time coming. Dov stood there in the light of the perimeter floodlights on aching legs, longing for his bed.

The night watch at last arrived and unlocked the side gate. "Did you hear?" he asked at once.

"*Nu.* What?" mumbled the old man, for once indifferent to news good or bad.

"The kid you went to meet at the airport, the little Canadian. He was the one those murderers killed."

There was no radio in the old car. Dov had heard nothing till now. He couldn't take it in. He stood staring with his mouth open.

"Terrorists, man! In Jerusalem! Don't you know about it? The whole country's up in arms!"

Still Dov didn't take it in. "Nili—?" he asked at last. He had no picture in his head of the boy. But a picture of Nili, bright and dazzlingly alive, came leaping.

"Thank God the swine didn't get her. She's okay."

Dov said no more. He stumbled through the gate and along the rest of the drive. It seemed a very long walk to the dining hall, where he had left his bike that morning. His mind, unwilling, unable to take in the news, concentrated on just one thing, one morsel of comfort: that his bike would be there, waiting, to take the weight off his legs and take him home.

When it wasn't, he couldn't believe it at first. Incredulous, he paced up and down along the bike rack on his aching legs. *Someone in the kibbutz had taken his bike. . . .*

He sat down heavily on the bench where the bus stopped and put his face in his hands. He tasted absolute despair. After a long day, and a long life full of troubles, he found himself wondering what the hell it had all been for.

Questions

"Now, Nili. You've been through an awful ordeal and I'd like nothing better than to leave you in peace, but you understand we have to try to find these men."

"Okay."

"Two men, you said, right? Did you see them clearly?"

"One."

"Which one? The one who—"

"Yes."

"Describe him to me."

"I have."

"Please, *motek,* tell me again. You may remember something new." Nili shifted uncomfortably. She wasn't in bed anymore but sitting up in a chair in her pajamas. She'd had to put up with a lot of this in the last forty-eight hours, and she was sick of it.

"He was an Arab."

71

"How do you know? Was he wearing a *k'fiyah*?"

"No. But they spoke Arabic."

"Ah! And you learn Arabic at school, don't you, Nili? Did you understand anything they said?"

She replayed the short, angry words in her head. Only a few came clear, the ones she had understood. "One said, 'Why not?' and the other said, 'Enough.'"

"Where were you?"

"On the ground."

"How did you get there?"

"The other one pushed me."

"Not the one who—"

"No. I said. The other one."

"The one you didn't see."

After a moment Nili, screwing up her eyes, said, "I did see him, sort of."

"Can you describe him?"

"I—I don't know." Suddenly she said, "He had a mustache."

"The second one."

"No. The young one with the knife. He had a black mustache."

They'd already shown Nili some outlines of faces: long ones, squarish ones, ones with low or high foreheads, and others with long or wide jaws. She had done her best to pick out the bits of faces that agreed with her memory of the face with the dark, hate-filled eyes. There was a man sitting in the corner, drawing on a pad. He was putting the bits together into one face. Now he got up and showed it to her. He'd just put the mustache in.

She looked at it a long time.

72

"He was younger."

"Younger than the picture? Or younger than the other man?"

"Both. He was much younger than the one who pulled me aside."

"*Pulled you aside?* You said he threw you on the ground."

"He pulled me aside first. He—pulled me behind him."

"What?"

"The first man, the young one, was coming at me with the knife." Her voice wobbled, but she steadied it. "The other man pulled me behind him."

There was a silence.

" 'Why not?' and 'Enough'—what do you think those words meant?"

"One of them wanted to kill me, and the other one didn't," said Nili immediately.

"Are you sure about that?"

"Yes," said Nili.

The artist had been making some adjustments. Now he showed the picture to Nili again.

"That's getting right," she said. "But there's something not right about his eyes. They were more—mad."

The policewoman signaled the artist to move away. She leaned toward Nili.

"Nili, this is important. Why do you think the second man pulled you aside?"

"How can I know?"

"Please, try to remember more about him."

Nili tried. "Nothing else. He was staring at me. Then he kind of jerked me by the arm."

"You noticed this second man looking at you?"

"Yes. I think I—sort of glanced at him. He was staring at me."

"Was he standing next to the other man?"

"Yes. No. Not right next to him. A bit to one side."

The policewoman handed Nili a pad and a pencil. "Show me again where everyone was when—when the thing actually happened."

Nili drew circles. "This was me. This was Glen. This was the first man—behind Glen." Nili swallowed. "This was the second man. The three of them were facing me."

"Nili. If this second man was staring at you, and you saw him staring, you must have seen his face."

Nili's mother smoothed the screwed-up wrinkles off Nili's forehead with a gentle hand. "Please, give her a rest!" she said.

"In a minute. Nili?"

"Yes. I saw him. But I—I can't remember."

The policewoman looked at Nili's mother. "She must have a picture at the back of her mind. At a moment like that, everything is recorded. It's just a matter of triggering the memory."

She stood up. "You've been wonderful, Nili. A real heroine. We're all proud of you. Now you rest, and then I'm coming back and I'm going to show you some photographs. I shall ask you to look at them very carefully and see if you can pick out either of the men."

"When can we take her home?" asked Lesley.

"It would help us if you could let her stay here

74

in Jerusalem until tomorrow. I know it's a lot to ask. But we need to have her close at hand.''

"Can you wait another day, hon?''

"I want to go home, Mom," said Nili in English.

"Just one more day, Nili," said the policewoman. "You want them caught, don't you?''

"Only the one who killed Glen," said Nili.

There was an odd silence in the room. The police-woman was frowning. "Not the other one?''

Nili felt impatient. She was very tired. "Of course not," she all but snapped. "He saved me.''

"Nili. He was one of them. He stood by while Glen was killed. When I show you the photos, don't forget that!''

Then she nodded to Lesley, and she and the artist went out.

Nili relaxed a little. She put her face against her mother. "I want to go home, Mom," she said again. Suddenly she was nearly crying.

Lesley stroked Nili's long hair and said nothing.

"If they want me to be in the city, why can't I be at Auntie Yocheved's?''

"You don't mind—going back to Gilo?''

Nili shook her head.

"Well, Nili, do you know," said Lesley slowly, "I think I would.''

Nimrod came to see Nili that evening by bus. He came into her private room cautiously, on tiptoe, peering nervously around the door first.

"Come on in, stupid, I'm okay!" she said loudly.

He came in. She didn't look okay. He was shocked

by the black circles under her eyes, her pale, strained face. Her hands made little jumps for no reason.

He sat on her bed and tried to grin. There was so much to say he couldn't think of anything, so he blurted out: "They've put Jericho under curfew, and all the Arab towns on the West Bank. The bus had to go the long way around. They're rounding up lots of Arabs."

"What do you mean, rounding them up?"

"Arresting them. Taking them in for questioning."

"They think the men came from Jericho?"

"Everyone's saying they came from the village near Gilo. And when the settlers heard what happened, they went crazy—crazier than usual. They went after the nearest Arabs with guns."

"Was anyone killed?"

"Dunno," said Nimrod. He did know. It was all over the news. But he didn't want to tell Nili the details.

But Nili wouldn't let it go at that. "Are any of *them* being arrested?" she asked.

"No. Course not. Arrest the settlers?" asked Nimrod sarcastically. "What an idea!"

"Even when they shoot at people without even knowing if they did anything?"

"The settlers are Jews, aren't they? They can do no wrong." He was quoting his grandfather. But it seemed bad to him too that Jews, religious fanatics many of them, who'd settled that area illegally because they thought God had given it to them, should have guns and be able to blast off at people, seriously injuring a boy of his own age, and beat up on Arab shops and cars, and for nobody to do a thing about it.

Nili wanted to know everything. Nimrod told her about their uncle Noah's sending a message to ask if Glen could be buried in the kibbutz cemetery. Nat and Miriam had put in a special request. There'd been tremendous surprise about it, and a lot of discussion. Everyone had taken it for granted that Glen's body would be flown home for burial in Canada. But in the end the kibbutz had agreed.

"Did you go to the funeral?" Nili said.

"Of course. Half the kibbutz went. You'd have thought he was a *ben-kibbutz.*"

"Did Saba and Savta go?"

"Yes. Savta lost it completely when she first heard. But she pulled herself together. She's being very strong now."

"She didn't even know him."

"That's part of why she lost it. She told me. She didn't ever have a chance to know him, and now she never will."

"I'll tell her all I know. Maybe that'll help."

Nimrod said nothing. He didn't have the least idea how to help or what to do. His own anger had to be dealt with somehow. At first it had been completely swamped by his relief that Nili was okay. But within hours it had risen to the surface like some awful monster that was eating him up inside. *Those murderous Arab pigs. Killing a little kid. Killing my cousin. I'll kill them. I'll catch them and kill them.*

He pushed this stuff away for the moment and told Nili more news. Valerie and Noah had flown in for the funeral, she from Toronto, he from London.

"Valerie brought Dale."

77

"*Dale!* How could she? She's only eight! How awful!"

"It was awful. Poor little kid, she doesn't know what's going on."

"What's she like?"

"Like her photos. Fair-haired. Fat. Weird fussy clothes like a doll. Doesn't talk."

"Why not?"

"Probably just shocked ... You could see Uncle Noah didn't think Valerie should have brought her. But Valerie said she had no one to leave her with and she should have a chance to say good-bye to her brother."

"How's poor Uncle Noah?"

"Bad. But he sent his love to you."

"I hope everyone's treating him nicely."

Again Nimrod said nothing. He didn't know how to answer.

Noah and Valerie had actually met for the first time since the tragedy, at the grandparents'. Nimrod had been there and seen their meeting. Harrowing as the scene at the graveside was to be later, that meeting, and the meeting of the whole family in mourning, was worse.

Nimrod remembered—along with every other single thing the evening that he heard the news—how he had fled from Donna's sad eyes. Emotions ... He had always steered clear of them. Steered clear, steered clear—and suddenly he was in a sea of them, over his head. He was sinking and drowning in feelings, his and other people's, raw, undiluted, too strong to hide or control.

Valerie had shouted at Noah, shouted at him in

front of everyone: "I told you not to send him here! You would do it, and now he's dead!" That had been absolutely terrible, nobody had known what to do or where to look. Grandma had interfered, trying to soothe her and be on Noah's side at the same time, but it had only made things worse.

And it wasn't just about Glen. There were undercurrents, though with a strange taut skin over them, as if everybody were holding everything down except grief and compassion. But Nimrod was watching—not because he wanted to but because he was in the midst of it and couldn't avoid it.

There were bad feelings. Uncle Noah and his grandparents. Uncle Noah and Donna. Uncle Noah and Yonatan. And Donna and Valerie ... they weren't even talking. But perhaps it was just that there was nothing to say.

And in the midst of it his cousin Dale, a little fat, bewildered, overdressed kid, clinging to her mother, not crying, looking from one person to another as if waiting for someone to tell her the world wasn't collapsing. Of all the people Nimrod felt sorry for, he felt sorriest for her. But he was out of his depth and couldn't do anything.

"Listen, Nil. There's someone outside who wants to see you."

"Not the cops again!"

"No. He's a pal of mine. He came with me. Wanted to say hi to you."

"Who?" Nili knew all his pals.

He looked sheepish. "He's one of the Russ—Russians. Can I bring him in? He's okay."

Lev had been more than just okay. He'd been Nimrod's best help.

It was weird. He'd wanted it to be his father, but his father had hardly been around because of Nili. Even more, Nimrod had wanted it to be Yonatan. But Yonatan had no time for him either. And not much sympathy.

"We're at war with them," he said shortly. "In wars people get hurt and killed. Be glad you didn't know him. Next time it could be someone you know."

Nimrod had turned to his grandfather, the person who had never, ever failed him. And he was some comfort. At least he found time to sit with him for a while before the funeral.

"Nimrodi," he said, "what's happened is, we've been wounded. All of us. As if we'd been in the line of fire and we'd all got bullets in our flesh. But wounded people mustn't hang on to their injuries, make themselves into invalids. We have a duty to heal. Your uncle may not be able to, because if your child dies, well, you don't get over it. But as for you, you must shake it off as soon as you can. It's not a big grief for you. So you must help your sister, because it'll be much, much harder for her."

Nimrod had wanted to stay with him, to listen to him talk more about healing and getting on with life. But there wasn't time. The funeral was only forty-eight hours after the thing happened, and there was so much to do.

But Lev stuck with him from the moment they had gone back to the *hader. okhel* that night and heard the news, right through the horrific hours that followed. He had even stayed the night with him at home because Nimrod's parents were in Jerusalem and he would have been alone.

He talked and let Nimrod talk. Not just about what had happened but about their lives. Nimrod found himself spouting on and on about all kinds of things. Things he never normally talked about. Like how Yonatan didn't seem to care about him anymore. He even told Lev about how his uncle Adam had died in a horrible accident with his own gun and how his father had almost flunked out in the army and didn't do annual reserve duty like most other men. He'd never said a word before to anyone about how he felt about that, but the shock of Glen's death had unlocked something in him.

But oddly the thing he was most grateful for was that in the middle of the night when they were all talked out, and Nimrod just didn't know what to do with the anger-monster that kept surfacing inside him, Lev suddenly said: "Let us go and play some games on your cousin's computer."

Yonatan was sleeping over at his mother's, so his room was empty. It was also locked, but Nimrod knew where the key was hidden. Somehow the thought of playing computer games seemed the one thing he had to do. He let them in, and they played for two hours. Nimrod concentrated furiously, but he didn't shout and get excited because he didn't want anyone to hear them.

"We shouldn't be doing this," he said to Lev once.

"Yes! Why not? You use what you have. It is like alcohol if we were drunkens," he replied seriously.

His funny mistake even made Nimrod laugh. He felt very guilty for laughing. But when his grandfather later told him he had a duty to heal, he felt that had been all right.

Now Lev came shyly into the hospital room. Nili looked up at him. He was tall and thin and funny-looking in her eyes, with his slicked-back hair and thin, sallow cheeks. He put his hand out, and she shook it and felt his knobby knuckles and smelled his smell. It was rather a nice smell, but funny too, somehow. Different.

"This is Lev," Nimrod said.

"Hello." He suddenly brought out a bunch of wilted flowers from behind his back and thrust them at her.

"Hey. Thanks. They're . . . beautiful."

"They are, as a matter of fact, dead. I'm sorry."

"They'll be okay. Put them in that vase over there."

Lev obeyed, then sat down on the chair beside her bed. "You feel more good?"

"Yes, thanks. Much better."

"The cops given you a hard time?"

"A bit. It's not their fault."

"Cops always like to given you a hard time. Once in Soviet Union they given me."

"Yeah? What happened?"

"It is because we want to come to Israel. They break in our place and turn over everything. Not only once. But one time they turn over my books, tear them, break my records. I got very mad and I say something. They give me one."

"One what?" asked Nili, fascinated.

"One *sbeng* on my face," he said, demonstrating a slap. But he was grinning as if it were not very important.

"What a scandal!" said Nili indignantly.

"In Soviet Union was no scandal, was usual for refuseniks like us."

"How long were you a refusenik?"

"Ten years."

"Ten years!"

Lev nodded. "Ten years since my father apply to leave, to emigrate, and get refused. He lose at once his job. My mother lose her job. My father get job mending radios. Then boss find out he's a refusenik, and he lose that too. Take job do anything, dig snow, janitor, many thing, dirty and hard work. Very bad money. Ten years."

Nili was staring at him. She had, for the moment, completely forgotten herself.

"And what happened to you?"

"Me? Nothing so bad. I am child. Just, in school the teacher tell class my parents no-good traitors for want to leave."

"That's not nothing!" said Nili. Lev shrugged. "Didn't the other kids tease you?"

"No. Just not talk me. Parents say them to not talk me, teachers too."

"That's horrible," said Nili. "Were you the only Jewish kid in the school?"

"Only Jew kid with refusenik parents, yes. Other Jew kids also not talk. They frighten teacher point to them too."

Nimrod sat quiet. He had heard all this that night.

He watched his sister's face, no longer pale and passive but full of life, aglow with indignation. He wondered if she was thinking what he was. About how the kids at the high school weren't acting much better than those kids back in Kiev.

"And when they let you go, when they told you you could go, how did you feel?"

He grinned at her, that wide-mouthed frog grin that Nimrod now knew well and no longer thought was comic or strange.

"That best day," he said. "Best day in my life. My parents make party. All Jew we know comes. Bring food, vodka, wine. Everyone eat and drink and sing. They say us, 'You going, maybe we get out too.' They kiss my father, hit his back. Say he is hero."

Nimrod said suddenly, "Bet they never said that before. Bet they kept away like the kids kept away from you at school."

Lev gave his shrug. "Some, yes. They frighten. What can you do? When people frighten, they do strange thing."

"And now they're all flooding out."

"True. Since is no more Soviet Union, many come. Come and grumble and want to go back!"

"Don't you ever grumble?" asked Nili.

He looked serious. "No. Only I don't have friend here I can trust."

Nimrod stiffened.

"How do you know when you can trust someone?"

"Easy," Lev said. "You trust friend when he stand up with you in a fight."

"But we don't fight in the kibbutz."

"True!" said Lev. "That's why I don't have friend I can trust!"

Nili looked at Nimrod. They both looked at Lev. He was deadly serious. He looked absolutely amazed when the other two burst out laughing.

EIGHT

Dale's New Name

Yonatan stole a look at his little half sister Dale. She was sitting on the bed in his room, doing absolutely nothing.

He'd offered to play computer games with her. She had shaken her head. He'd suggested a walk. No good. In desperation he'd given her some papers and pencils to draw with. These lay neglected on the crumpled coverlet between her plump, bare knees. She was staring at him. She'd been staring at him like that for half an hour.

Maybe his mother was right, and she wasn't all there. Or maybe his grandmother was right. She'd said the shock of the sudden cataclysm in her life had been so great that she had "gone into retreat." She hadn't cried yet. Everyone seemed worried about that.

Now Yonatan had been asked to look after her for a couple of hours while her mother had a nap. Not much to ask, under the circumstances. But he wasn't used to kids, certainly not little girls in frilly dresses. He didn't know what on earth to do with her. He couldn't concentrate on anything while she sat there looking at him like that with those huge, unblinking eyes.

"What do you want to do?" he finally asked desperately.

"I don't know," she answered in her tiny, whispery voice. He'd hardly heard her speak properly, aloud, since she'd arrived with her mother three days ago.

"I should be working on the tractor," he said, trying not to sound resentful. He'd got off work easily enough, but there was no one to replace him in the fields, and he was itching to get on with it.

For the first time a flicker of interest brought her blank blue eyes into some kind of focus.

"Can I ride with you?"

He thought quickly. It was absolutely forbidden to take little kids on the tractor, but rules were being bent all around because of what had happened.

"Have you got some jeans?"

She was off the bed in a moment. "I'll change. Take me back to Mommy," she said.

He put her on the crossbar of his bike and rode her back to the spare apartment the kibbutz had assigned to Noah and Valerie. When they got there, Dale opened the door and rushed in. The curtain between the living room and bedroom was drawn. Valerie must be sleeping. Yonatan motioned Dale to be quiet. She nodded, and fished a pair of big-waisted jeans out of a suitcase and put them on under her trilly dress. Then she peeled the dress off and put on a T-shirt. She turned around, and Yonatan sucked in his breath.

The T-shirt said, "My brother went to London and all I got was this lousy T-shirt."

Yonatan stared at it. His mouth had gone completely dry.

"Where did you get that?"

She looked down at it as if she'd never seen it before. "Oh, Mom gave it to me. Can we go now?"

She put her hand in his, and they went out quietly. Yonatan was shocked. The T-shirt must have been in Glen's luggage. His suitcase and Nili's had been left at the airport, and El Al had had them delivered.

Yonatan wasn't strong on projecting himself into other people's feelings, but now he found himself trying to imagine Valerie's as she had unpacked. Awful and terrible. She must have found Glen's present to Dale and given it to her without comment. What a weird thing to do. But everyone was doing weird things. Even him.

He rode Dale, now sensibly and "kibbutzicly" dressed, to the tractor shed. He climbed up first onto the big John Deere and started the engine. As he felt it vibrate into life, an awful thought came to him that almost made him switch off and climb down again.

What if there were an accident while he was in charge of Dale, what if—?

A pang of imagined horror shot through him, but he shook himself clear of it. Stupid. What was happening to him—all these fanciful notions? As if a few skins had been peeled off his tough inner self, making him soft and get-at-able again, as he used to be, and had stopped being.

"Come on. Climb up."

Dale came, willingly but awkwardly. She put her knee on the metal step. He reached down and hiked her the rest of the way up and sat her on his lap.

"Put your hands on the wheel and help me steer."

He backed the heavy tractor out of the shed, went into forward gear, and began to drive out of the yard toward the fields. The vegetable area was quite a long way off—nearly a kilometer. Once clear of the kibbutz, he changed gear.

"Do you mind if we go faster?"

"No!" she said at once. "I want to! Go fast!"

"Tell me in Hebrew. Say, *'Mahair! Mahair!'* "

"Mahair!" she said, not whispery anymore.

The tractor jerked into top gear, and the empty fields flew by. She began to bounce on his knees.

"Mahair! Mahair!" she shouted, playing the wheel a couple of inches each way under his hands.

They bounced over a rut and she shrieked with excitement.

When they got to the right field, he had to lower the harrow at the back to begin work.

"We have to go slow. You'll be bored now."

"I won't! Just let me steer."

"Okay. Keep straight. Whoa, straight, I said! That's better. Good. You are doing very good." He drove slowly and carefully, his hands hovering close to the wheel, letting her try. They went from one end of the field to the other.

As soon as they'd begun the turn, "Take your hands off, Jonathan!" she ordered him loudly. He did for a second, then put them back. *"Jonathan! I'm* steering!"

"No. I can't risk it. You could turn us over."

She said nothing. He took the wheel. Her hands were limp now. He thought her feelings were hurt. Suddenly she said, "Let me off."

He braked, and she slid off his legs and scrambled to the ground.

"What's wrong?" he asked over the engine's noise.

She looked up at him, her blue eyes again unreadable.

"If we turned over, I might die," she said.

He felt a jolt like an electric shock. It was his exact thought, back there in the shed—exact, as if she had caught it from him. They stayed in the same position, looking at each other.

Then he leaned down quickly, stretching out his hand. "It's okay," he said. "It's okay. Come on up. I'll take care of us; nothing will happen."

She hesitated, then climbed up slowly. When she was standing alongside him, without warning she threw her arms around his neck.

He felt he couldn't bear it, but he had to. He switched off the engine and put his arms around her. He held her till she pulled back. It was he who had to swallow down a painful ache in his throat, and for the first time he thought, with a sense of it being real: *This is my little sister and our brother's been killed.* The thought caused a sort of cracking in his chest, a softening of something hard and shell-like.

He put his hands on her shoulders and cleared his throat.

"I'm going to give you a kibbutz name," he said. "Dahlia. Do you like that?" She nodded solemnly. "Okay, Dahlia, we've got to work. That's the ignition key. Turn the engine on—that's right. Grab the wheel. Let's go."

They worked together for over an hour. Dale didn't get bored. Nor did she say, *"Mahair!"* and play the wheel like a baby. She concentrated and tried to help.

In the end he could see she was getting really tired, so he took her back to the kibbutz.

"You work like a real kibbutznik," he said.

"I never worked before," she said. "It's fun."

"It's not all fun," he said.

"I guess. That's what Daddy says."

"His kind of work is different," Yonatan said. He was feeling very fond of her. He put his arm around her to steady her on the bike and felt flattered when she took his hand as they walked up the path to the apartment.

Valerie was up and had put some makeup on to cover the ravages of crying. She thanked Yonatan with distant politeness for looking after Dale and offered him tea or coffee. He refused. He could hardly bear to be in the same room with her since he had had that flash of empathy about her unpacking Glen's case. He could feel her pain even when she hid it.

"Lesley and Nili are back from Jerusalem," she said with a fixed smile.

"Oh. I'll go see them," he said. He turned to Dale. "So long—Dahlia." She smiled at him and he ruffled her fair hair.

After he'd gone, Valerie said sharply, "What did he call you?"

"Dahlia. That's my kibbutz name. I'm hungry, Mom."

Her mother gave her some cookies that had been brought to the room by strangers. Valerie tried to think of these unknown kibbutz women as kind—she knew how sorry they were for her in her loss, how hard they were trying to help her. But to her they were all just part of this monster place that had killed her son.

"Where did he take you?"

"To the fields. We drove a tractor. I worked."

"You *worked*?"

"Yeah, Mom, real hard. You ask him if I didn't. I steered the tractor all by myself."

Her mother stared at her, her face gone suddenly white. "How could he!" she breathed, almost too angry to get the words out.

Dale swallowed what she was eating and said, "He took good care. He's neat. He wouldn't let anything bad happen."

Valerie turned sharply away. After a moment she said, "Just the same. You can't go again. I can't . . . let you, Dale. And—and I don't want you to have . . . a kibbutz name."

"But I like it, Mom!"

"There's no point," she said in a hard voice. "We won't be staying long enough."

Dale went to the window and looked out through the screen at the kibbutz gardens, so lush and exotic and different from home.

"It's nice here," she said wistfully.

Behind her she heard her mother say in a strangled voice, "Nice? Glen died here."

"I know. But it's not the place's fault."

"Yes, it is! This country eats people. I knew it the first time I was here. I couldn't wait to leave then, and I can't wait to leave now."

Dale had overheard her say the same thing to her father earlier in the day. He had said quietly, "If you feel so strongly, why did you agree that he should be buried here?" And she had almost screamed: "Because you wanted it! I don't know why. I was crazy! I wish we could take him home!" But then she had said dully, "But what for? What do bodies matter? He's gone."

Now she said, "Tomorrow we'll go see Glennie's grave. We'll say good-bye to him and then we're going home and I hope I never hear the word 'Israel' again."

Dale didn't say anything, but she had a strange thought. *I'm glad he's buried here, with the palm trees and the big white birds and the fish ponds. He can hear the tractors working and see the planes fly over.* She knew with part of herself that he couldn't, but the thought made her feel quite happy.

Yonatan expected Nili to be resting in bed, but when he reached his aunt Lesley's house, his cousin was watching television with Nimrod.

"Hi, Nil," Yonatan said awkwardly. *"Ma shlom'ekh?"*

"I'm okay. I'm fine. I'm glad to be home."

"I bet. Where's your mom?"

"She's gone for a walk with Uncle Noah."

Yonatan sat down and helped himself to salt sticks and watched the TV for a few minutes. He was thinking about his father.

He hadn't seen him for five years, or for uncounted years before that. He had been so deeply angry with him, for so long, that he just hadn't known how to behave to him, how to receive him when he showed up now in these horrible circumstances, in which Yonatan couldn't show his anger.

But when he saw Noah's face, he couldn't even feel angry. He'd actually hugged him; they had stood embraced for a long, long moment. He kept thinking back to it, wondering if he had faked it, if he'd hugged his father only because the situation forced him. But it wasn't quite like that.

And at the funeral, which Valerie hadn't been able to face, they had walked together in the procession to the graveside. His cousin Shalom and his aunt Yocheved had driven up from Jerusalem. Yocheved had cried aloud almost all the way through; she seemed in a worse state than anyone. After the service, which was nonreligious and almost unbearably poignant, with readings of children's poems and some beautiful singing, his father had put the first shovelful of earth into the grave, onto the coffin, and then handed the spade to Yonatan, who had done the same.

He looked down as he turned the spade. His little half brother, who would never be anything more to him now than a photograph, lay under that harsh rain of soil. He had felt a long, powerful pain, made of regret and fury, so strong that all resentment against

94

his father seemed to break up and flow away with the earth, down into Glen's grave.

There'd been no need to take Noah's arm as they stepped back to let Nat, Ofer, and Nimrod take their turns. But he had. And his father's suffering face had glanced at him in surprise and gratitude.

They hadn't talked yet. Yonatan knew they must talk before the family left, and he dreaded it. He didn't want to think about it.

"Why did you stay in Jerusalem so long?" he asked Nili.

"The cops. They were all over me. Enough already."

"Were you able to help?"

"Yeah," said Nili, her eyes on the screen.

Yonatan turned his head. "You were? How?"

"They showed me photographs of terrorists. Men they know, that've done stuff before."

"And you picked one out?"

"Yeah," said Nili.

Yonatan got up. His breath was suddenly coming short with excitement. "But that's terrific! That's great, Nil! Who was he? Did they tell you anything about him?"

"No."

"You don't seem very excited about it! If you picked him out, they'll get him, for sure! They'll get the murdering—"

"He wasn't the one, though," said Nili.

"What do you mean?"

"The one I recognized. He wasn't the one who . . . did it."

"I don't get it," said Yonatan blankly.

Nili gave a tutting sound of impatience. "What is there to get? There were two of them, a young one and an older one. The young one did it, and the older one saved my life. It was *that* one that I recognized."

"Oh, what's the difference? They were both in it! Saved your life—*shtuyot,* he couldn't have meant to! Pair of cold-blooded killers, like all of them are in their hearts!"

"I didn't want to tell them I recognized him," said Nili. "But they kind of saw from my face that I did, and they got it out of me."

"Very good!"

"No, it wasn't. If they get him, they'll hurt him."

Yonatan gazed at her in bewildered astonishment, almost with disgust. Nimrod was gazing at her too. She looked around from watching the screen and saw their faces. "What are you two staring at? What's so strange?"

Yonatan looked at Nimrod, who shrugged and made a she's-nuts face.

Yonatan crouched down beside Nili's chair.

"Listen, daughter-of-my-aunt," he said. "You don't know the Arabs. I do know them. Believe me. No one tried to save your life. The man you picked out—don't give him a thought. Just hope they catch him before he kills someone else. Catch him and beat the hell out of him and lock him up forever." He stood up. "And if I could help them to do it, all of it, I would."

She looked up at him in dismay. But suddenly she smiled.

"You wouldn't really, Yoni," she said. "Not you, you're not like that." Then she went back to the TV.

He found he had taken a step backward. His mind had gone blank as if she'd hit him on the head. If she *knew*—! But she couldn't. He hadn't told his secret to anyone except his grandfather. She couldn't know. That's why she'd said that.

Nevertheless, the guilt and confusion he had felt three years ago came rushing back, overpowering him. He went out without another word.

Flowers
on the Sidewalk

Ofer's nephew Shalom left his mother's apartment in Gilo, went down the stairs to the street, and just started walking.

He loved his mother, but there was no denying that she was getting sorely on his nerves. He didn't exactly blame her. The tragedy that had happened so close to their home, and so close to their family, was reason enough to weep and wail. It was just that Shalom couldn't take any more of it for the moment.

"If only they'd telephoned from the airport ... You could have gone for them ... they'd have been safe ... it would never have happened ... !" Shalom had listened patiently for hours, days, to the "if onlys." He'd thought of a few of his own.

If only Miriam hadn't got the time of the plane wrong. *If only* Noah had traveled with the kids from London. *If only* Nili had had sense to stay in the airport instead of taking it into her head to bring Glen to the city ... What must those directly concerned with the disaster be feeling? How must they be weeping and wailing and accusing themselves?

Shalom found it difficult to stand the thought. He shook himself, lit a cigarette, and walked on down the newly tarmac'd street, sucking the numbing toxin of nicotine into his lungs. Despite his mother's continual nagging, he couldn't stop smoking.

He paused where the town ended. The last, unfinished block stood on the edge of the bare hills. The road petered out. Beyond, not far away, lay an Arab village.

It was a place he knew firsthand, not just from a distance. He was doing postgraduate studies in psychology, but he worked nights in a restaurant, and several Arabs worked there too, doing the menial kitchen work. Finding Shalom treated them as equals, they gradually lost their sullen wariness. One boy called Ali in particular had become friendly. Once, when the boy had been in a jam, Shalom had lent him some money. And in return Ali had invited him to his home. And he happened to live in that village.

Shalom could make out the very house from here. It was a poor enough place, but he knew how much of a compliment it was that he had been trusted so far. He had met Ali's mother, who looked quite old enough to be his grandmother but couldn't have been much over fifty, because there were two other kids at home, the youngest no more than eight.

She had treated Shalom to a sumptuous Arab meal, far more than this family could properly afford. He

99

remembered especially the big potatoes, roasted to perfection and spilling a delicious stuffing of cumin-spiced minced lamb and pine nuts. . . . The wonderful food had eased the difficulties caused by language, since the mother spoke no Hebrew.

His own mother had thought he was mad to go, but when he got home, she demanded to know every detail. She had become very quiet when he described the dinner. This had secretly amused him. She didn't like it when other women fed him good meals.

Now he could see army vehicles and police cars, uniformed men moving about the streets. No Arabs showed themselves; the village was under twenty-four-hour curfew. Every house was being searched. Fifty men from there had been rounded up for questioning. Shalom's Arab workmates, including Ali, had not shown up at the restaurant for three days. He wondered where they were, what was happening to them.

After a while he flung his cigarette butt away with a tense movement and started back by another route.

A hundred meters from the spot where Glen had been killed, he stopped again. There was a bright hillock there. He approached slowly. It was flowers. The sidewalk was blocked with flowers, in bunches and sheaves. He bent down and looked at the cards.

"In memory of a brave boy." "In memoriam." "Pity the children." One said, "Sleep easy, son. We will avenge you."

He turned the bunches over gently, reading card after card as if they had been meant for him. He stopped at one that had been among the first to be laid there. The card, lying innocently among the beautiful scented roses, said simply, "Death to the murderers."

Shalom's hands tightened on the flower stems until the thorns pricked him. Then he put the bunch back, straightened up, and walked on.

Death to the murderers. An eye for an eye.

The media were playing up Glen's death. Some of the popular papers were calling him a martyr. Letters and editorials were accusing the government of "letting our children be slaughtered in the streets of the capital."

Only yesterday Shalom had been walking in King George Street and seen a man pacing up and down with a sign that read: KICK THEM OUT BEFORE IT'S TOO LATE! EVERY ARAB WOULD KILL A JEWISH CHILD IF HE DARED!

Shalom had stopped and said quietly, "That's a lie."

The man had turned on him, showing his teeth in a snarl. "Arab lover! Jew hater! Go to Arafat! Go to Saddam! Filth! Scum! Traitor to your people!" He looked as if he would like to tear Shalom to pieces.

"You need a psychiatrist," Shalom had said, and walked away, but his blood was beating in his ears, and he had burst into a sweat. He feared such people. The man was quite mad, of course, but there were plenty who weren't who had the same ideas.

When he'd first heard about Glen, blind anger had spawned the same thought in Shalom's brain: *Kick them out! Death to the murderers.* But he'd gotten over that.

Shalom had been born in June 1967, on the first day of the war that had resulted in this hellish situation—his people holding down another people and occupying their land.

Five days later his father had fallen in battle. He'd given his life for a famous victory that some had called a miracle. *What a black joke,* thought Shalom. A miracle then that had saved the State of Israel. A curse now, twenty-five years later, with Israelis and Palestinians alike still paying in blood for the result of that victory—those accursed territories. The Occupation.

Shalom, during his yearly stints of army service, had so far managed to avoid going into the territories. But that couldn't last. Sooner or later every soldier had to do his part in controlling the *intifada,* the Arab uprising. Next month Shalom was due to go back into uniform for another month. . . .

Perhaps his anger about Glen's death, and the grief of his family, would help him toughen up. But he didn't think he could shoot into a crowd, however menacing, much less aim at a child even if it threatened him with a stone. If there was one thing he was sure of, deep down, in this whole morally confusing situation, it was that you mustn't touch kids. But until you'd faced their ferocious anger, how could you be sure what you'd do? Thinking about this was keeping Shalom awake nights.

His mother didn't help.

"Shoot them if they threaten you! I don't care what the orders are! Your clear conscience won't comfort me if they brain you with a rock!" She too lumped all the Arabs together as the ones who had killed her husband. But Shalom knew, had always known, that was wrong, as wrong as that madman with the sign.

But he would have to defend himself, and he was torn between two fears: that he would do something shameful that went against all his principles, and that he might be weakened by his feelings, knowing how those young men felt behind their masks, the women who screamed abuse and shook their fists, the old men with their hate-filled eyes. And the boys who'd been told that throwing stones at the soldiers was the way to be men.

Were those Palestinian boys, many of whom had been killed in the streets, so different from Glen?

Shalom wouldn't dare ask this aloud. He could imagine his friends' reaction, his mother's. Why, how could he compare? Glen was no threat to the Arabs! He was not even an Israeli, not even involved. He was *innocent*. . . . But what did that mean? He was here because his father had sent him. Just as those boys in the streets who threw stones and risked being shot were doing it because their fathers and brothers had told them to.

Either way, those Palestinian children who'd been killed were no less dead than Glen. And, surely, no less mourned.

Shalom lit another cigarette to dull the edge of his thoughts.

When he got back from his walk, he found his mother had dried her tears, combed her hair, and put some makeup on. She had a meal waiting for him.

"Wonderful news!" she said, bustling out of the kitchen with a dish of meatballs.

"Nu?" said Shalom wearily. What "wonderful news" could there be? That Glen had woken from the dead?

"Your uncle phoned. Nili was able to pick out one of them from a book of photographs of known terrorists. They'll soon find him, the rabid dog."

Shalom nodded and sat down to eat. "Fine," he said. "Good for Nili."

It was good. Justice would be done. Now no more suspects would be rounded up; they'd know whom they were looking for. Perhaps the settlers would calm down, and the people who'd been picked up already would be allowed to go home. Ali and the others would come back to work.

Shalom always hated it when the wrong people suffered. It had happened so often, on both sides, and it did no good; it only bred more hatred. The bible said, "If they are coming to kill you, get up early and kill them first." Fine. But it didn't say, "If an innocent is killed, kill another innocent. Or two. Or a hundred. It doesn't matter. One crime justifies others."

The meatballs were good, and his mother was smiling. Shalom promised himself that he wouldn't have another cigarette tonight.

TEN

On the Tel

On the eastern edge of the kibbutz there was
a tel, a hill formed of countless ancient towns
built on top of one another over the ages and
gradually smothered by earth. A path with
built-in wooden steps led to the top, and up
this Lesley and her brother, Noah, climbed
in silence.

When they got to the top, they sat down on
a crude bench and looked east toward the hills
of Jordan beyond the tiny, trickling river, the
fabled River Jordan. From this vantage point
they could just make it out in places, twisting
and looping amid scrub and palm trees
below them.

Lesley's only thought was to help Noah
somehow. But how to do it? Just, perhaps, by
distracting him for a few minutes from his
pain.

''You can't see it from here,'' she began,

"but the word 'peace' is written in Arabic on the side of the tel, in huge letters, made of stones. It faces Jordan. Our resident sculptor did it with help from—" She stopped. She'd been going to say, "From all our kids." You had to think before you said the simplest word to Noah now.

"What's that, some sort of sick joke?" asked Noah in a muffled voice.

"No. It's a nice message," said Lesley.

"What's the use of 'nice messages' that nobody receives? All those stones stuck in the hillside could have had better uses."

"Like what?" asked Lesley unwarily.

"To build walls between us and them."

Oh, Noah! she thought. "But I like that word being there."

"Dear old sis. Always the optimist. Do you still believe in it?"

"I do. It must happen, or we're lost."

He smiled sadly. "After the Six-Day War you told me, little teenage hopeful that you were, that there'd soon be peace, that the Israelis and Arabs would help each other, that we'd be able to travel to Amman and Damascus and Beirut—ah, Beirut! Not much left of that! Not much peace there, or tourism. . . ."

They were quiet.

Lesley could see how every time he came near to the bitter red-hot core of his thoughts, he sheared away. It seemed only a very strong thought, a painful thought, could counter that core of misery, because he suddenly said, "What do you think of me?"

"Noah! I love you! What do you mean?"

"No. Be truthful, Les. What do you think of me for what I did?"

"I don't understand. When?"

"When I . . . ran away."

She turned her eyes from the view and looked at him. His poor face! He was eight years older than she was, but he looked far more. The mourning beard he was growing was grizzled with gray, and his eyes behind their glasses were pitted in shadow and red from weeping. Her heart was a hot ache in her chest. She took his hand in both hers.

"Noah, do you really think I could even *think* reproaches for the past at a time like this? Anyway, I got over all those kinds of thoughts long ago. I don't judge you."

"You're the only one around here who doesn't then," he said.

"How can you bother about that now?" she asked gently.

"How can I not? You're the people I come from, the ones whose judgment matters most."

"You should worry only about your own judgment," she said.

"Sure. But what if mine is the same as theirs?"

"And is it?"

He took his hand away from her and bent down to pick some blades of dry grass.

"I know I should never have left here. I know I shouldn't have left Donna and Yonatan. Do you think I don't judge myself for doing that, for being weak and a failure, as an Israeli, as a soldier, a husband, a father—everything?"

She turned back to the hills. She didn't bother to

mention that as the world judges, he was a dazzling success.

"We can't all be heroes," she said, unconsciously echoing Donna. "Ofer was no more suited to be a tough, ruthless soldier than you or his brother."

"No. All the more credit to Ofer for coping," said Noah. "As for poor Adam . . ." Everyone said "poor Adam." But then he suddenly noticed the quality of her silence and turned to her. "Was his death really an accident?"

She hesitated. She could tell Noah, surely. . . . "No. He made it look like one, the while-cleaning-his-gun sort, but he left a note—just one. He left it where only Ofer would find it. Ofer's had to keep that secret from everyone but me, all these years. Even Yocheved doesn't know, and his mother never did, of course."

After a long time Noah said, "I suppose that is worse than what I did. Except he didn't have a family."

"He had his first family. I've always wondered whether Ofer might not have hated the army so much if that hadn't happened with Adam."

"What did the note say?"

"It was very confused. He was obviously having some kind of breakdown. He went on about some Syrian boy he'd killed face-to-face in a bunker on the Golan Heights. And some stuff about the Occupation destroying us. But it was mostly about how he couldn't stand the noise anymore."

"What noise? A noise in his head?"

"No, no, a real noise. It was near the end of those terrible years of the shelling."

"The shelling of the kibbutz, you mean?"

"Yes, you remember. After the Six-Day War, Palestinians who'd fled to Jordan mounted attacks on us from just down there"—she pointed—"in 'the jungle,' as we called it, all that scrubland just across the river. They had their mobile launchers hidden there. It was really ghastly. We slept in the shelters for three years. Day or night we never knew when a shell would land. One Passover one landed on the terrace behind the culture house. The Seder was over, and we were just getting ready to leave. It was a miracle no one was killed. If it had come two minutes later . . ."

"I remember," said Noah, "standing with you on the balcony of that culture house, where you used to go 'to look at the neighbors,' as you called it. Some neighbors . . . Why in God's name did the kibbutz hold the Seder there in the first place? It must be about the most exposed building in the entire area!"

"Don't ask me. We were crazy stubborn. Determined not to give in to them or change our arrangements for them. Well, we did, after that, you can bet! It was the beginning of the end of my old view-the-neighbors culture house as a community center."

"I noticed it was looking a bit run-down."

"We never go there anymore." She smiled a little, wryly. "Who needs culture now that we have television in our rooms instead?"

Noah looked at her in a puzzled way, as if he were bemused to find himself thinking of anything outside himself and his pain.

"And what brought it to an end—the shelling?"

"Oh, not us. King Hussein of Jordan, dear little

109

Hussie. He'd had enough of the Palestinians being trigger-happy in his kingdom, so he set his crack Bedouin troops on the Palestinian fighters, killed three thousand of his Arab brethren, and chased many of the rest into Lebanon. The shelling stopped overnight. In fact . . .'' She gave a little chuckle.

''What?''

''I was just remembering how Ofer went out in the fields one morning to open the irrigation and found two terrorists huddled in a furrow. They'd crossed the river in the night to get away from Hussein's revenge, which evidently they feared far more than they feared us! Can you imagine? After making our lives a misery for three years, they ran into our arms crying, 'Save us, save us!' We had a good laugh over it.''

''Meanwhile, there was brother Noah safe and sound in Tel Aviv, and later, safer and sounder in Toronto.''

''Come on, Noah. Quit beating yourself over the head.''

They sat silently for a while. Down below, the kibbutz fish ponds reflected the sunlight like mirrors, and the white herons spread their wings in graceful slow motion.

''Do you think Yoni hates me?''

''Has he acted like it?''

Noah shook his head. ''He's a great kid,'' he said. ''And . . .''

Lesley gave his hand a convulsive squeeze. Yoni was now the only son he had. She couldn't bear to hear him say it, and he didn't. He stared across the hazy landscape and swerved on to another topic.

"I remember you pointing out that Arab village over there. I see it's grown—more than the kibbutz has."

"Well, at least we're still here. Them and us."

"And there was a bridge you showed me. Away to the right."

"You can still see it. What's left of it."

He turned his head. "Those bits of stick? Is that it?"

"Yes, that's my bridge. . . . It doesn't cross the river anymore. I suppose that's symbolic. I couldn't cross it now."

"What do you mean, 'now'—as if you could *then!*"

Lesley smiled to herself and said nothing. But a half-submerged memory of a wild childish exploit surfaced to challenge her. What would Noah say if she were to tell him about it? If she were to link it with what she counted as the most vital thing in her life now, her voluntary work? The seeds for that had been sown then—when she was fourteen, a new immigrant, alienated from her classmates, and had set herself to learn Arabic better than any of them.

With her good Arabic she was able to join a special organization that worked for human rights. Working for human rights in Israel often meant fighting to improve Arabs' rights. There were people, even in the kibbutz, who were not too happy about what her organization investigated and exposed. She thought, *This is not the moment to talk to Noah about my basic belief that Arabs have the same rights as Jews.*

But oddly, something seemed to communicate it-

111

self to him, because he suddenly said, "You used to write to me in Saskatoon about some Arab living in that village."

"Ah, yes. My 'boyfriend.' "

" 'Boyfriend'?"

"That's what the other kids called him to tease me. He was actually just a young Arab field-worker that I could see from the culture house balcony."

"Of course, you never actually met him."

"Yes. I did. Twice . . . The second time was after the war, when our class went on a trip to the newly conquered territories. Boy. When I think of that now—how happy we were to have won! We thought it was the end of everything bad, the beginning of a new age. . . . Why didn't we realize—" She heaved a deep, sad sigh. "Anyhow. This Arab boy, Mustapha his name was, he was in Tubas, an Arab town that his father had run away to."

"Run away?"

"Well, look. Look at their village. Right next to the border. When war broke out, the man thought it would be safer to move to a town farther away from Israel. How was he to know we'd conquer the whole West Bank? He took Mustapha along and made him work as a street peddler. I bought some nuts from him . . . no . . . he gave them to me. And we talked. He said—"

Noah stood up abruptly. "I don't want to know what the little Arab swine said!"

But Lesley sat still, a sudden sharp memory, like a videocassette, playing itself in her head.

"You can say 'peace.' You won. But when you lose, it is different. You can't think of stopping. You

must think only of fighting, till you don't have to feel—'' And the gesture that said, more clearly than words, *''ashamed.''*

''Then it will go on forever. Because someone must always lose.''

''It will not be us. Not at the end.''

She could see herself, standing there in the noisy, bustling street. She could smell again the Arab coffee, the unknown spices, the dung and dust. And over all, another smell, the smell of shame and defeat.

Twenty-five years ago. A quarter of a century. She, just fifteen (that very day had been her birthday), full of life, full of hope—*like Nili, just like Nili.* When she looked at Nili, she often saw her own young self as if she had never gotten older, as if she were watching herself growing up all over again.

And Mustapha, whom she thought of as her friend but who saw her as his enemy, standing there with his tray of almonds, his bitter black-olive eyes and black hair, and his face full of—

Something clicked in her head.

Her thoughts, her memory tape, stuck and froze, midframe. His face! She was not aware that she had gasped.

Noah said, ''What?''

She didn't even hear him. That face. *That face.* It was impossible. No, it couldn't be. All those years! But the eyes . . . and the eyes in the photograph that Nili had picked out for the police in Jerusalem . . .

They were the same.

ELEVEN

News
of a Capture

Dale woke up early to a gentle tapping on the window above her bed on the hard old sofa. She knelt up. Nimrod and Nili were outside, gesturing to her.

"Do you want to come to breakfast in the *hader okhel* with us?"

Dale knew what the *hader okhel* was. She knew quite a few words in Hebrew already. She didn't bother answering but nodded, jumped up, and pulled on her jeans. She didn't wear the T-shirt. She had seen the way people looked at it. She found a blouse of her mother's, which hung down nearly to her knees, but other kids in the kibbutz wore big, floppy tops. She moved quietly, not wanting her parents to wake up. She felt much better when they were asleep.

When she got outside, she thought at first that Nili and Nimrod had run out on her, but then she saw them far up ahead along the wide path that led to the middle of the kibbutz. They were bent over, and she could just make out what they were doing: making some mark on the concrete path. They pointed at the ground from a distance, and she looked down and saw a chalked arrow at her feet, pointing the way. She gave a gleeful skip and ran, her eyes down, following the arrows.

When she reached the dining hall, she felt she had got to it practically on her own. It was so much fun here. At home she wasn't allowed out of the house by herself, but here it was safe. In the last few days she had roamed freely. Yoni at first, and lately Nimrod and Nili, took her around, showed her things, and then sometimes she went back alone, feeling very daring and grown-up.

She'd seen the calves in their little square pens and stroked their noses and let them suck so strongly on her fingers that at first she screamed and thought they would swallow her hand! She'd visited the toy factory, and Lev, Nimrod's friend, had given her a handful of plastic shapes for herself and a leaflet showing patterns you could make with them and how they could help you with fractions.

She'd stood in the henhouses among hundreds of white hens all milling around her feet and watched the eggs going by on a belt. She'd learned how to make all the turkeys gobble at once. She'd sat in a real small airplane that couldn't fly anymore, but she pretended it could, and Nimrod showed her how to play at being a pilot.

And today Nimrod had said she could play on the big jungle gym that the kibbutz had built for the kids, a big one made of wood and ropes and metal tunnels and slides.

People in the dining hall greeted her. Some of the women touched her hair, put an arm around her, and pinched her cheeks. The men nodded and smiled. There was something in their smiles that was sad, but she knew they liked her. She'd never had so many friends before. At first she'd been shy, but with Nili and Nimrod she wasn't. She felt good here.

She didn't think about leaving today, going home. She hated thinking about that, so she pushed it away.

Breakfast was interesting. At home Dale ate a lot but only certain foods. Here you had to choose among mainly unfamiliar things. She chose the hot gluey cereal and a hard-boiled egg and dark, chewy, tasty bread, quite different from the light white stuff at home (and nobody cut your crusts off here or would have cared if you'd fussed). Then Nimrod and Nili took her to the jungle gym.

It was so much fun. She was usually scared to go on slides and swing on bars and stuff, but with Nimrod and Nili doing it with her, she found she could do lots. She wasn't even scared to climb up and walk cautiously across a swaying, slatted path high above the ground, holding on to ropes and pretending she was on a ship at sea.

Of course, Nimrod had to spoil it, sort of, by asking her teasingly, when she puffed, why she was so fat.

" 'Cause I eat too much," she said, quoting her father.

"Well, don't," he said. "I don't like fat girls."

"Don't be mean," said Nili. She put her arm around Dale. "You be as fat as you like," she said.

"Aren't there any fat kids in the kibbutz?" asked Dale, looking stricken.

"Of course there are! My mom's best friend, Shula, is as fat as a butterball and everyone just loves her, and her kids are fat too."

"But they're not in the kibbutz," corrected Nimrod. "If you want to be my girlfriend, you have to diet," he said sternly.

"*Shtok,* Nimrod," said Nili. "Don't mind him, Dale."

"My name's Dahlia," said Dale. "Yoni said."

"Nice name. Dahlia means a flower," said Nili.

"A very thin flower," said Nimrod.

"*Shtuyot,* it's a round fat flower!"

"What's '*shtuyot*' mean?" asked Dale.

"It means 'stupid rubbish,' like he always talks," said Nili.

"*Shtuyot, shtuyot,* Nimrod talks *shtuyot!*" crowed Dale.

"*Bo-i,* Dahlia, let's go up the commando net!" Nimrod said. "Beat you to the top!"

Her parents had to come and get her, and her mother was almost mad at her for not remembering to come back on time for them to go visit the grave. Dale felt guilty. She shouldn't have gone on the jungle gym or be having a good time, and she wasn't dressed for going to a cemetery.

"Can Nimrod and Nili come with us?" she asked.

The others were all silent, and she knew she shouldn't have asked that. Nili said, "We have to go to school. And you should go just the three of you.

But don't worry. When you've gone home, we'll go visit Glen and keep his grave nice.'' Valerie made a little sound in her throat, but Dale wasn't listening. She was looking at Nili, thinking how cute she was, wishing she had that long dark hair and those neat bangs instead of being all frizzly and blond.

After the visit, Dale and her parents walked back from the cemetery.

Dale walked in the middle, but she didn't hold their hands. She hadn't felt anything very much, looking at the grave. She'd said, ''Good-bye, Glennie,'' when her mom told her to, but she felt funny about it, as if she were in a play. She hadn't been at the funeral, and she didn't really believe he was under the pile of fresh earth.

And she hated seeing her parents cry and hold each other that way, and try to hold her. She wriggled free of them, and now she was walking along, swinging her arms and looking around her at the hills and fields and trees.

A strange bird with barred wings, and a crest that nodded forward and then sank back, landed on the path in front of them.

''Look! What's that?''

''It's a hoopoe,'' said her father dully.

''Isn't he neat!'' she said. ''I saw a real colorful one this morning, all purple and blue-green. The birds here are all so neat! Have you seen those big white ones?''

Her parents didn't answer. Dale ran ahead to the house. She knew her way now, and she liked the independent, confident feeling. But when she got indoors, she stopped, and her good feelings died.

There were half-packed suitcases lying about the room.

Shoot, she thought, *we're really going to leave!* She tried to think of something good about it, like Pollyanna, and her next thought was: *Still, it'll be fun telling Glennie all about the—*

Her thought struck a barrier that suddenly sprang up in her head and stopped her cold. A huge wall that reached right to the sky and to the edges of everything. For the very first time she understood that Glennie wouldn't be there.

Home without Glennie. The house, the yard, the street, playing, fussing, watching TV, eating meals, going to school. Without Glennie.

Her parents found her on the bed crying as if she'd gone crazy. But before her mother could even start to comfort her, she had jumped up and was yelling at the top of her voice.

"Mom, I don't want to go home! I don't want to go home! It's better here! Please let's don't go home. Let's stay here, please!"

Valerie stroked her hair. "Honey, we can't stay here. We don't belong here."

"Yoni says all Jews belong here! We're Jews, aren't we?"

"Yes. But Canada's our home."

She looked up at her father through her tears. He was looking at her strangely. Then he sat down by her on the bed.

"You know, your aunt Lesley was kind of like you but the other way around. When our parents

119

wanted to bring her here from Canada, she made the same fuss you're making. She felt she belonged in Saskatoon, that everything good was there. But she found her parents knew what was best, like we do now, for you.''

Dale threw herself face down on the bed and howled. She couldn't bear it. "I won't go. You can't make me!" she sobbed.

"Come on, pumpkin, you wouldn't want to stay here without us?" her father said in tender, almost joking tones.

"Yes, I would! Mom cries all the time, and you act so funny, you don't seem to like anybody here except Aunt Lesley! I could live in the kids' houses with them and learn *ivrit* and go on a diet and get thin, and I want to be called Dahlia, not Dale. I hate Dale, I won't answer if you call me Dale!"

Her voice rose and rose, and they couldn't get through to her. One part of her, a small part, knew she was talking *shtuyot,* but the wall was there in front of her, and it seemed to her as if only by climbing to the top of the commando ropes with her cousins at her side could she maybe get over it.

An hour later the luggage was all packed and ready when a knock came on the door. Valerie supposed it was someone to tell them that the taxi had come early; they hadn't said their good-byes yet. She opened the door. It was Nat.

"Can I talk to you both?" he said.

She beckoned him in and offered him the sofa to sit on, but he chose an upright chair. "Where's Dale?" he asked.

120

Valerie nodded at the curtained-off bedroom alcove. "She's sleeping. She was a little upset."

"No wonder."

"I don't think it was so much about Glen. She—she doesn't want to leave."

"Of course it's about Glen," said Nat at once. "It's just coming out that it's about something else because she can't face it yet."

"I'm not so sure," said Noah. "She's kind of different here from at home, like the kibbutz suits her. What did you come to say, Dad?"

"I came to say they've caught one of them."

Valerie and Noah looked at each other and then, breathlessly, back at Nat.

"The one Nili picked out in the rogues' gallery. They got him within forty-eight hours. He's in police custody in Jerusalem, and they're questioning him now."

"Is he the one who—"

"No. I gather he's the older man who was with him. But they were together. Don't worry. They'll get the name and whereabouts of the actual murderer out of him."

"How?" asked Valerie unexpectedly.

"They know their jobs, Valerie. They'll get him. Don't worry."

Noah, who had been sitting on the sofa, stood up, sat down, then stood up again. His hands were jumping. Valerie sat very still and stared at Nat. She seemed to be frozen.

Nat felt he had to go on talking. "You'll be able to go home with . . . knowing. . . . It should be easier for you."

"How do they know for sure?" said Noah.

"They're pretty sure. But they want Nili to go back to Jerusalem and—"

"My God, you're not—"

"—identify him."

"They can't! Poor kid! They can't ask her to—"

"Oh, she's a tough one. Don't worry."

"You keep saying that, Dad! 'Don't worry! Don't worry'!"

"Sorry, son. Sorry. This has been hard for all of us. It's hard not to say the wrong thing at a time like this."

Noah was pacing up and down. Suddenly he stopped.

"When is she going?"

"Tomorrow. They're sending a car for her."

"I'm going with her."

Valerie cried out, "You're *what*?"

He looked at her. "I've got to," he said.

"She's got her father! What are you—"

"Val—"

She jumped up and faced him.

"We're going home. *Today*. The flights are booked. You promised. *You promised.*"

Noah looked at Nat, who got up at once and left the apartment. Valerie didn't even see him go. She said, keeping her voice down, but with passion, "We have got to get away from here, Noah. This hateful place—I want to go home—"

"Do you, Val? Do you really want to go home?"

She bit her lips. "I've got to face it sometime."

"Could you go alone? I mean, with Dale?"

"No!"

"Then you'll have to stay awhile, Val, I'm sorry."

She looked as if she might fly to pieces. But she reined herself in, and after a few moments she said, quite controlledly, "Just tell me. Why are you doing this?"

Noah tried to take her hand, but she was as stiff as a tree.

"Because I want to see them."

She just stared at him, waiting.

"I want to see the men who killed my son. I want to look in their eyes. I want to know who they are, why they did it. That above all. I have got to know why I had a son a week ago and now he's gone."

Valerie said, "They did it because they're terrorist murderers. Because they're evil."

"I don't believe in evil," said Noah. "I believe in stupidity. I believe in anger and the urge for vengeance. I believe in a mind-set of blind obedience and patriotism. If it's any of those, at least I shall be able to comprehend it. But not evil. People aren't born evil. These men were once boys like Glen."

"Of course they weren't like Glen! Do you think if Glen had lived to grow up"—she clenched her teeth but forced herself on—"he could ever have gone out and stabbed an innocent child?"

There was another knock on the door. Noah went to it at once, opened it, and said, "Oh—the car. I'm sorry. We've changed our plans; we're not going now." He took out his wallet and gave the driver some money. Then he closed the door and turned to look at his wife. There was a look on his face she had never seen before, a look of absolute, unshakable decision.

All the fight went out of her.

She slowly unclenched her fists. "Well, at least Dale will be pleased," she said with surprising calm. "Help me unpack."

TWELVE

Mustapha
in Prison

Mustapha lay on a hard bed in a cell in Jerusalem.

The boy whom Lesley remembered was no more. He was gone as surely as Glen was gone, leaving only remains—a baffling yet solid trace, like Glen's body in the grave overlooking the Jordan.

The trace still left of Mustapha the boy was in his head. It puzzled Mustapha the man, Mustapha the fighter. It puzzled him and made him very uneasy. It was as if some other person were lurking there, another being occupying a secret place in his skull. No. Not a person or a being. A power. One that could suddenly leap out and cause him to lose control, to act like a stranger. A stupid, heedless stranger, ruled by his emotions.

He had thought—been sure—he had destroyed it, left it far behind in the past. It troubled him a great deal to have had proof, so recently, that it was still there, a contradiction of all the rest of him, of all he had made of himself. A weak spot.

He was aching. The men who had burst into the house where he had been hiding had not cared to treat him gently; he would have been astonished, and perhaps even contemptuous, if they had.

He had killed one of theirs.

Not he himself—his nephew Feisal had actually struck the blow—but he might as well have done it. He had taken part in a number of actions against the Jews. He had not killed a child before, but it didn't make any difference. From their point of view he was guilty.

So when they took hold of him and slammed him against a wall, it was no more than he'd expected, and in any case it was not so bad. What affronted him were the names they called him, degrading, humiliating names. They cursed him as a child murderer. As if there were something especially bad about that! As if they were above that!

Arab children were being killed every week in the streets of their towns, and before the *intifada* there had been the bombing of refugee camps where the Arab freedom fighters had their headquarters. Who knew how many children had been killed by Israeli raids on Beirut? What was special about children? Or women? Or old people? If they were not dangerous now, they would be, or they had been, or they would like to be. The enemy was the enemy.

But the Jews liked to think they were different. They let themselves think killing a child in the street, with a knife, was somehow worse than killing from the air or with guns.

Mustapha lay still to ease his bruises. He let his mind wander, so as not to feel too much fear of what his interrogation would be like. He had been interrogated before, when he was young, in the seventies, when they had taken him in before he had even taken part in any actions. It had been very bad. He had talked then. This was a chance to redeem himself.

He knew that Feisal was hiding. Feisal, his sister's son, was only seventeen. He had never experienced arrest and what came after. He must be very afraid. Especially if he knew Mustapha had been taken. He would be afraid that Mustapha would talk. But he wouldn't. Not this time.

The girl kept coming into his mind. He kept thrusting her away.

He couldn't understand himself. Why was he thinking of her? Why hadn't he let Feisal kill her? It had been stupid beyond stupidity to let her live to identify him.

They'd called him a mad dog, a wolf.

During his time as a youth in an Israeli prison he had read a book in which the wolves were the heroes. The story told about the laws they had among themselves. One law said that no wolf was allowed to kill a man because it brought trouble upon the pack. It was only allowed if a wolf was teaching its children how to kill.

He had been teaching Feisal. Feisal wanted to be part of the struggle—part of the pack. That was *their* law: To be worthy, to prove yourself, you had to kill.

When Mustapha had been sent abroad for training, he was made, among other things, to bite the heads off live chickens to toughen him up. Not that he'd needed it—not after what he'd been through. Each time he had told himself that the chicken was the Jew who had interrogated him. . . . But Feisal was not so strong and tough as Mustapha thought he needed to be.

The night before the thing was to be done, Mustapha left his sister and her husband and went up on to the roof of the house. There he found Feisal sitting by himself, smoking and trembling. Getting up his nerve.

He sat by his nephew. At first he didn't talk to him, but soon the boy's shaking started to alarm Mustapha. Feisal was his family and also his candidate. He had told the leaders, "He can do it. Name a day, a time, and he'll go out and do it."

Now he doubted. The first time was always the worst. It went against something soft and weak that was in you because you were young and the anger and hatred were not yet strong enough to overcome your childish feelings. It went better if, the first time, you felt threatened, but to kill then proved nothing. The point was to do it because it had to be done, because you'd decided, because you could obey any order.

He said, at last, "This time tomorrow you'll have done it."

The boy looked at him. He had a new mustache. It was a good one. Mustapha remembered himself at that age. He had not been able to grow a mustache, not then. He had thought this signified a weakness.

He had been ashamed of the skimpy black caterpillar over his upper lip.

Of course, what he had really been ashamed of was the fact that he'd talked. It was easier to worry about the mustache and forget the moment when he had screamed out the names. After that he had been in prison a long time. By the time he got out he had as good a mustache as any man could want, and other signs of manhood, too, like big muscles and a tough, thick skin. It had some scars on it, healed scars to remind him that pain was not so bad. Pain you could bear and recover from. It was shame that stayed unhealed forever.

He said that to Feisal, there on the roof. "Don't think about the deed. That's just something to be done. Don't think about being caught. I'll be with you to see that you're not. Just think about how ashamed you'll feel if you fail. If you're sitting up here tomorrow night and you haven't done it."

Feisal had nodded. But he hadn't looked at his uncle. When he put the cigarette to his mouth, it jiggled wildly so that he took one drag and threw it away, hard and angrily, as if it had betrayed his weakness.

Mustapha sought in his mind for something to put fire in the boy.

"Remember last year, how we danced?"

The boy looked at him, and a slow smile came over his face.

Last year they had stood up here on the flat roof of their house—the house of Mustapha's sister's husband—and watched as the Scud missiles came over, all the way from Iraq, heading for Tel Aviv, the heart of Jewish-occupied Palestine. Saddam Hussein was sending rockets to kill the Jews! For all anyone knew, rockets with gas in them, enough to lay whole towns to waste. Perhaps the warheads were even nuclear. Perhaps the whole of Israel and every Jew in it would be blown to dust! If they had looked to the west and seen the mushroom cloud rise from the seacoast, they would have cheered the louder.

Saddam cared nothing about the Americans, or the British, or the Israelis. Saddam did what he liked, and to hell with all those imperialist-Zionist pigs! Saddam was for the Arabs. Under the Prophet, Saddam was king, Saddam was saint, Saddam was brother, father, avenger, god, hero, and conquerer!

As the huge deadly missiles flew through the sky over their heads, blotting out the stars for a fraction of a second and leaving a trail of sparks like a heavenly comet, the men of the village shouted and leaped in the air, chanting, "Sad-dam! Sad-dam! Sad-dam! Kill, kill, kill the Jews!" in an ecstasy of triumph.

They were drunk with it, careless of the consequences. The entire West Bank was under strict curfew. No one was allowed out at all; at any moment a patrol could appear and fire up at them or break into their houses to arrest them. Who cared? This was their hour! The greatest, most intoxicating hour any of them could remember, the hour of deliverance and vengeance!

But an hour was only an hour, however glorious. It ended. They had to come down off their roofs, sober after their intoxication. The fierce, joyous hysteria petered out when it became clear that the Scuds were merely destroying a few apartment blocks—mainly empty; the Jews ran away at night—killing a few, injuring a few.... The mass devastation the Arabs had dreamed of simply didn't happen.

What happened to *them* was that they were punished.

They were forced to stay in their houses. They weren't allowed to go to work or to the shops or to school. Their many children, shut up like animals, got on the adults' nerves. The women struggled to feed their families until they ran out of food. The men were the worst. The confinement, the disappointment, the frustration made them crazy. Shut up in their overcrowded rooms, families quarreled and fought. It went on for weeks and weeks.

Later Mustapha heard that a lot of Jews had protested against this harsh punishment, but that the government was relentless. "They danced," they said. "As the Scuds came over, they danced on their rooftops." It was enough to justify any punishment.

And the war was lost.

The Americans came to Kuwait with so many weapons, so much technology, so many men, Saddam's brave troops hadn't a chance. They were slaughtered in scores of thousands. Some were simply buried in sand in their bunkers by advancing earthmovers. Even when they were retreating to Basra, they were strafed, killed, and burned. It was always that way. The West had the money, the technology; there was no justice, no real hope. It was like fighting some giant from another world, armed with weapons that couldn't be stopped.

There was nothing to do, when the curfew finally

ended and the backlash of disillusion came, but to go back to what they had before. The struggle. The struggle to survive and to fight back, any way they could.

And their secret leaders grew strong and bold and ruthless.

You want to be part of it? You want to be a man, a Palestinian brother? You want to hold up your head, get your own back? You want us to know you're not a traitor, because if you are a traitor, we'll kill you? Then do as you're ordered. Don't go to work when we tell you to strike. Shut your shops when we say so. And if you want to be a true hero of your people, kill whom we tell you to kill. A Jew, an Arab collaborator—death to the enemy!

That was what they had told Feisal. Kill a Jew. Old or young, it didn't matter. *The more you kill, the more frightened they'll get. Yes, we'll be punished, all of us, not just the blow strikers, but it's always been that way. Houses will be bulldozed; people will be arrested, beaten up, imprisoned. Maybe even killed. It's worth it not to let them think we can be treated like dirt. And one day, one day, if we kill enough of them, they will be driven out.*

When the morning of the appointed day came, Feisal lay in his bed and curled himself up and said his head ached like a beating drum and he couldn't move. He was sick. He would do it tomorrow.

Feisal's father, who owned a bakery and was a small, pathetic creature in Mustapha's estimation, raised his voice for once. "Leave my son alone," he said to Mustapha. "You're a thorn in the flesh of my family! Why is it your business, hothead? Are you trying to get us all arrested? Are we to have no rest from all this endless trouble?''

But his wife turned on him and said, ''Go to work,'' in a tone of quiet authority that he could never resist, and he banged out of the house.

Then the woman stood over her son's bed with her arms akimbo, and her dark eyes in her dark, lined face narrowed.

She was Mustapha's older sister, Fatma. When they were children, they had often fought, but when he was released from prison that time and had no-where to go—his father would have nothing to do with him after his arrest—his sister had found a place for him in her home even though her husband was against it.

She was a strong woman. Now she took hold of the bed her son was lying in and tilted it sharply so that he fell on the floor. He lay there looking up at her, begging her with his eyes, but she was relentless. She looked at Mustapha and made a gesture he couldn't mistake. It said, ''Get him out of here and make him go through with it.''

Mustapha hiked Feisal to his feet, and before his nephew knew what was happening, they were outside the house. There Feisal did not dare allow people to see that he was being dragged or led. He straightened up, shook off his uncle's arm, and walked ahead down the narrow, unpaved road.

They took a bus into Jerusalem with other villagers who worked for the Jews. When they got to the bus station, they took another bus. Then they got off and walked in silence. Mustapha led the way now. He knew where they were going; he'd planned it—to that quiet, semipopulated district near the edge of the city.

Feisal spoke for the first time since he'd fallen from the bed. "I forgot the knife. You didn't give me time."

"I've got it. Here. Take it."

He handed it to him stealthily. Feisal took it at once and slipped it into his pocket. There was a briskness to his movements that reassured Mustapha. The boy was not trembling now. Perhaps the crisis of his fear was over. He was walking erectly, looking straight ahead, his face set, his eyes narrowed like his mother's.

Mustapha almost smiled. If this boy had his mother's will! Fatma could have done it and not thought twice. She believed in hatred translated into action. *Women,* he thought, still surprised at the recent change in his ideas. He had always despised them, looked down on them as inferiors, but since the uprising started, they had changed, shown their strength. Some of them had proved themselves as tough and reckless as any man.

When they arrived at the district of Gilo, Mustapha took Feisal by the elbow. "See that doorway. We'll hide there."

They went into the empty entrance of a half-finished block. As they entered, Mustapha noticed how beautifully the building was made. When finished, it would be luxurious. The pale golden stones on its face were all shaped and dressed, each one an example of the stonemason's craft. Nothing but the best was good enough for these Jews, and the best workers in stone were his own people.

How could they! he thought bitterly. *Building palaces on our land for the enemy to live in!* But he knew quite well how they could, how they had to. A man must work and earn bread for his family, and the Jews, though they paid as little as they could get away with, did pay. His own village had grown in size and prosperity since the Occupation, on money earned in Israel. It was this that turned some Arabs into traitors, made them accept the Jews, fawn on them, collaborate, even inform. . . .

Mustapha spat on a slab of white-gold stone at his feet. A car went by.

"What are we waiting for?" said Feisal impatiently.

"The first lone person who passes."

But the first person who passed was a hulking soldier with a gun on his shoulder. They ignored him. There was no need to take stupid risks.

They waited. Feisal was growing restive, groping for a cigarette. Mustapha stilled him with a look. Feisal, sulky, turned away.

Suddenly he saw them, stiffened, and moved his head to draw Mustapha's attention. A boy and a girl, carrying a bag each, walking on the sidewalk alongside the newly planted trees.

The two men stood perfectly still in their shadowed hiding place, watching like leopards in the grass as the deer move unsuspectingly nearer.

When the children were exactly opposite, Mustapha gave the signal, and together they sprinted across the road. The older man sensed rather than saw the knife emerging from the pocket, tensed his own arm, and sent his will boring into his nephew's brain.

Then they were upon them.

Feisal grabbed the boy first because he was nearest. He threw one arm around his shoulders, across his throat to half turn him. Mustapha instinctively made a thrusting movement with his hand, as if it controlled Feisal's, and as if Feisal were a puppet on his fingers, the knife was in, and it was done.

The boy dropped the bag. It hit the sidewalk a moment before he went down. It was done!

But the girl was there. The girl . . .

For Feisal she was just another target. He was excited, keyed up. He had killed once, it was easy, he wanted to do it again! She was standing there, stunned, defenseless—open. He reached for her.

But that was when the strange power from the past took possession of Mustapha and made him do the thing that so disturbed him when he thought of it, lying days later in his prison cell.

It was the face, he thought now, forcing himself to relive the moment in order to understand it, so it could never happen again. It was something about her face. Her hair. It was a ghostly head from another life, come back to undermine and weaken him.

He didn't think. That was the trouble. His brain was bypassed. The power moved his arm, making it thrust her behind him, push her onto the ground. It made him stand between her and Feisal's knife. And when Feisal half snarled at him, balked of his prey, "Why not?" the same power opened Mustapha's mouth and made him say:

"They said 'one.' Enough. Let's go!"

THIRTEEN

The Lineup

Nili was sitting on one of the little kids' swings, feeling a whole lot better.

She was swinging herself gently, heel and toe, waiting for the school bus. She could just get to it in time to be the last to scramble on board if she left the swing the second she heard it honk.

It was a beautiful May morning, hot and going to be hotter, but Nili liked the heat. Being sweaty and sticky wasn't nice, but heat meant a lovely contrast when you jumped into the swimming pool or even just got under the shower at the end of the day. It made drinking cold drinks and eating ice cream all the better. There were other good things. Fewer clothes, just a sleeveless, scoop-necked T-shirt and shorts, sandals that you could kick off in class and feel the coolness of the tiles on the soles of your feet . . . And the long vacation, only a month away!

She wasn't thinking of Glen and the awful thing.

She had at first. It had obsessed her, not just the thing itself but her part in it. Over and over again she'd relived the fateful moment, outside the airport building, when the crowds of welcomers—which had so dismayingly *not* included her parents—had all met their travelers and gone away, leaving her and Glen standing there alone.

Glen had said ironically, "Hey, welcome to Israel!" and she had jumped into the breach without thinking.

"Oh, there's been some mix-up. I know what we do. We go to my aunt in Jerusalem!"

"Shouldn't we phone your folks first?"

"You need a phone card."

"Someone might lend us one. We should phone before we leave here, see what's happened."

And Nili had dithered, feeling forlorn and let-down but rallying strongly at the prospect of leading the way efficiently to Aunt Yocheved's, of her aunt's delight at seeing them unexpectedly, plying them with kisses and food and taking over responsibility. . . . Shalom might run them home. . . . She'd even thought how proud her parents would be that she'd managed so well on her own. She'd overridden Glen's objections, swept him off to the minibus. . . .

Stupid! Stupid! Stupid!

She'd lain awake night after night, going over in her head those moments, those headstrong, babyish thoughts and actions, struggling to find a way to unsay and undo them—to go back, unlive what had been, and relive it all differently.

No way. Never had that hackneyed phrase seemed

more grimly true. No way could she change it. The guilt grew. She cried until she had no tears left, and no one could comfort her.

Until her grandmother Miriam came to her.

"It wasn't your fault, darling! Not one bit of it! It was mine. Of course it was! *I* got the time wrong. I was responsible. How can a little girl all alone possibly be to blame? You only did what you thought was sensible. How could you know it would go wrong?" She had cuddled Nili in her arms, rocked her, and spilled her own tears of remorse on her, tears that seemed to wash away at last Nili's own terrible guilt.

And after that everyone had told her to try to push it out of her mind. Nimrod had said she had to. Saba had said she had a duty to get better from it. And Yonatan had given her a trick to do every time it came into her mind: She had to think, *Out out out!* And usually out it went.

Even being with Dale didn't remind her anymore, because Dale was separate from Glen in her mind. She'd never seen them together.

Dale had rushed up to her in the *hader okhel* this morning with her face shining.

"We're staying, we're staying!" she cried, and threw her arms around Nili's waist.

"Hey, that is terrific!" Nili hugged her. "I'll tell Nimrod to stop his tears. He was crying *all night* because you were going to Canada."

Dale had looked up at her, her mouth open, believing it for a moment. Then Nili grinned at her and went, "Boo-hoo-hoo, my girlfriend Dahlia is leaving

139

me!'' and Dale got it, and laughed. She had a really good sense of humor.

"Now show me what to eat that won't make me fat," she said.

"You must eat TCP."

"*TCP!*" shouted Dale. "That's disinfectant. It smells yucky!"

"Well, still you must eat it. Come, I'll show you."

Nili solemnly led her around the salad bar and heaped her plate. "*T* for tomatoes, *C* for cucumber, *P* for peppers, TCP!" she explained. Dale didn't look much happier, but Nili showed her how to cut everything up small and put oil and lemon juice on it from the bottles and mix it all with hard-boiled egg. "You see how pretty colors?" she encouraged. "Now you eat with bread. No margarine."

Dale crunched an obedient mouthful.

"Is that so bad?" asked Nili.

"Yes," she said. "But I'll do it. I'll get thin. You'll see."

It never occurred to Nili to ask why Uncle Noah and Valerie had changed their minds about leaving.

Now, on the swing, she leaned back to the length of her arms, holding the swing chains, closed her eyes, and put her face up to the sun shining through the leaves high above her. Her hair hung down, so she could feel a little breeze on the back of her neck. Summer. What a *keff* . . .

Suddenly it was shattered, all her peacefulness and trickling-back nice feelings.

"Nili, there you are! I've been looking all over for you!"

It was her mother. Nili jerked the swing to a stop

and felt as if she'd been rudely woken out of a lovely dream.

"What, Ima?" she asked crossly. And then: "There's the bus! I must run!"

Lesley stopped her. "You're not going to school today, hon. We're going to Jerusalem."

She froze. "What? No. Why?"

"We have to. Come home and put some other clothes on."

She began to lead her toward their house. Nili hung back, instinctively resisting.

"Why didn't you tell me this morning?"

"I wasn't sure when they'd be coming for us. They've just phoned to let us know they're on their way. They'll be here in about twenty minutes."

Nili balked, digging her feet in like a stubborn pony. "It's the cops again! I don't want to go back there! What do they want me for *again*? It's not fair!"

Her mother turned to face her. "Nili, I'm sorry. Do you think I like you being caught up in all this *go'al nefesh*? I'd do anything to spare you, but I can't."

To her own shame, Nili began to cry. "But what do they want?"

Lesley put her arm around her comfortingly, but Nili pulled away.

"Listen, Nil. They've caught one of the men. They need you to identify him."

Nili stopped crying abruptly. "Which one?"

"The older one."

Nili started to say something but stopped. She walked on with her mother, who put her arm back around her shoulders, and this time Nili let it stay there because she was too busy thinking to notice.

The police car was quite big, and that was just as well, because to Nili's surprise, Uncle Noah was coming too.

He said he was going instead of her dad, who couldn't come. His orchestra was giving a big concert in Jerusalem that night. There'd been talk about it. With the family in mourning, shouldn't he cancel? But Uncle Noah had told him, "Go." And Saba had said, "Life has to go on. Our work is what holds us together." So Nili's dad had gone to Jerusalem the day before—before they heard about the man.

In the car the grown-ups wanted to talk to the police driver about the latest developments, but to Nili's secret relief, he didn't seem to know anything. Then her mother tried to make conversation with her uncle, but he didn't want to talk, so they traveled almost in silence. When Nili had done all her thinking, she was able to go to sleep. She slept most of the way.

They had to shake her a bit to wake her up. The car was in a courtyard in front of a big old stone building with bars on all the windows.

"Is this a prison?" she asked.

"No, Nili. It's called the Russian Compound."

"Russian!"

"That's just an old name for it. It's like a police station."

They got out. The air smelled different here, very piney, and it was much cooler. Nili was glad her mother had made her put on a blouse with half sleeves and long pants, especially when they climbed the satin-smooth stone steps and went inside. There it seemed very dark after the bright sunlight outside, and the air was definitely chilly. She shivered.

They were put into a little room to wait.

"What will happen? Will he come in?" she asked fearfully.

"No, hon, of course not!" said her mother.

Her uncle said: "What they'll do is, they'll put him in a lineup with a number of other men. You'll stand behind a glass screen—he won't be able to see you—and you'll look at all the men very carefully, and then you'll tell us which one is him."

"If any of them is," said her mother.

"What?" asked Nili, confused.

"They'll ask you to pick out the man if he's there," said her mother. "You must be very sure it's the same man before you pick him out."

"Well, of course she knows that," said her uncle.

"You make it sound as if it were quite certain that he'd be among them," said her mother.

"Aren't they sure then?" asked Nili.

"They can't be quite sure until you've identified him. That's why they need you, why we had to come."

Nili understood. She'd seen lineups in the movies. She did some more thinking, but it was the same thinking as before, only with a clearer picture of what would happen. She sat quietly. She knew she had to be very calm inside, not excited and wound up as she had been when they showed her the book of photographs.

After what seemed like a long time, a woman police officer—the same one who had questioned her in the hospital—came in. She bent over to bring her face level with Nili's, which annoyed her because it made her feel she was being treated like a child. The policewoman carefully explained the procedure again.

"I know, my mother and uncle told me," she said.

"All right then, are you ready?" Nili nodded. "Let's go." The woman straightened up.

"Us too?" asked Noah. "Can we be with her?"

The policewoman looked at Nili. She didn't bend down this time.

"We'd prefer her to be on her own, without you," she said. "What do you say, Nili? I'll be with you. Would you mind not having them?"

"No," said Nili at once. She noticed Uncle Noah's face change.

"But I want to see this man," he said.

"Perhaps later," said the woman firmly.

She led the way through the corridors, down some steps into the basement. It was chillier than ever here.

"Are you cold, Nili?"

"I'm okay."

"Are you scared?"

"No."

"I would be. I think you're a brave girl."

Nili said nothing. She knew the policewoman wouldn't have been scared, she was just saying that. There was a sort of buzzing going on in Nili's stomach, as if there were bees in there. It got more intense as they went into a darkened room with a glass panel. There was light on the other side, as if that were a stage and they were in an audience.

The policewoman motioned her to sit down and not to speak. After a moment or two a door opened beyond the panel and some men walked in. Nili watched them as they walked across and formed a line. She couldn't hear anything, but there must have been an order, because they all turned at the same time to face her. She noticed there were numbers over their heads on the wall, the number one for the man farthest to her left and ten for the one on the far right.

Something deep inside her gave a little jolt before she even knew that she'd spotted him. He was number seven. All the men were dark and about the same age, but she couldn't have made a mistake; it was him. She remembered how he had stared at her, but not as he was staring now, just looking blankly ahead of him. Then his eyes had burned with something like astonishment, shock almost, with—well, as if he had recognized her. She hadn't realized that before. Yes. Seeing him again, she remembered better. He'd looked as if he'd suddenly seen someone he knew.

The men stood still. The policewoman was watching her. Nili let her eyes move along the row.

She felt a secret excitement. No one knew for certain except her. If he could see her now! Yet he must know she was there. He was waiting in suspense for her to pick him out. He must be quite sure she would.

The policewoman said, "Well, Nili? Do you see him?"

"No," she said. "He's not there."

The woman turned her head sharply. Nili looked up at her. She looked surprised and not at all pleased.

"Nili! Are you sure?"

"Yes," she said simply. Her tongue started to come out to lick her lips, but she tucked it back again.

"Look at them all again. Look at each face, Nili. Look very carefully."

Obediently Nili looked again at each face. There was a sort of similarity. They were all dark-haired, dark-eyed, with sallow skin, but their faces were quite different shapes, their hair grew differently, and though they all had the same blank, waiting stare, there were differences about their eyes.

She let her eyes rest for a few seconds on number seven. He was clean-shaven, but his chin was dark. His hair was rather long and a little bit wavy. He was handsome. . . . She tried to see something in his eyes, some kindness or goodness, something special that would fit with his having saved her life. But he just looked like an Arab waiting for something to happen.

Well, it wasn't going to! Wouldn't he get a surprise! He had done something wonderful for her, and now she would pay him back. Nili hugged herself without knowing it.

"Nili, you are cold. Just once more, are you one hundred percent sure?"

"Yes," said Nili. "He's not there."

Nili had thought that would be the end of it, but she was wrong.

There was a terrible lot of fuss and bother before they were allowed to go. The police were alarmingly upset, although they tried not to let her feel they were upset with her.

The book of photographs was produced again, and she was shown the photograph she'd picked out before. It gave her a shock to see it, because although it had been taken when he was some years younger—little more than a teenager—it was quite obviously *him*. She had to lie again, and it was far more difficult this time.

"I made a mistake," she said. "This isn't him."

"But you said it was."

"You sort of made me say it."

"We made you say it? What do you mean, Nili? We didn't force you!"

"No, but—well, when I first saw it, I thought it was him for a second, and then you all kept on at me, but I wasn't absolutely sure, and if that was him in there, I'm sure it wasn't the same one."

They grew crafty.

"Which one in there was this one?"

"Num— He was . . . sort of on the right. Not quite at the end." She thought if she said the exact number, they would know she had specially noted it.

"So you did notice him!"

"Yes. Because he looks like the photo. And the photo looks a bit like the real man. But it isn't him. It's someone a bit like him."

They seemed exasperated, or worse. One of the policemen, a big, tough-looking one, leaned down and put his face close to hers across the photo book. He smelled of cigarettes like her cousin Shalom, but he wasn't like him in any other way.

"How can you be so positive that it isn't him?"

There was something in his voice that scared her. She thought: *He could get nasty if he found out I'm*

147

fooling them. She felt glad she had lied, because if this man got hold of number seven, he might hurt him to get him to tell about the other one.

When that thought came to her, she did *Out out out!* quickly, because she knew that if she thought about *that,* she would soon be thinking about Glen, and then she would stop being sure that what she was doing was right.

After a lot more business, including private little talks that the police had with her mother and uncle (who were both looking very strange), they were allowed to go. But when they got outside the building, there was no police car to take them home.

Uncle Noah went back in to ask about it. While he was gone, Nili's mother was silent in a way Nili didn't like. It made her feel tense and uneasy.

"What's wrong, Mom?" she said rather too loudly in English.

For a while her mother didn't say anything. She just looked at her very piercingly. Nili turned her face aside without being able to stop herself. Her mother knew her so well.

"Nili," she said in the most serious voice she ever used, "the man they're looking for is a heartless murderer who killed your cousin."

Nili said nothing. She thought of saying, "He didn't," but that might sound too much as if she were on his side. She didn't want anyone to know that. They would never understand. She could never explain that moment of total relief when he got between her and that mad-eyed killer with the knife.

"They'll have to let him go now. Did you realize that?"

Nili still said nothing. In her heart she was glad.

"And if a murderer is let go, he may kill someone else. Anyone who had a hand in letting him go is partly responsible for that."

Something sharp and unpleasant jumped inside Nili's chest. But she clamped her jaws and said nothing.

FOURTEEN

Noah's
Spending Spree

Noah came out again looking angry. But then he'd been looking angry ever since he found out that Nili had not identified the man.

"It seems they only provide cars for cooperative witnesses," he said.

"Did they *say* that?" asked Lesley in astonishment.

"Of course not! They said they were very sorry but they don't have a car to spare. Tried to give me money for a bus. But we're obviously being punished."

"I don't believe that," said Lesley flatly.

They all stood for a moment. Then Noah shook himself. "Well, whatever. Let's go find a taxi."

"All the way?" exclaimed Lesley. "It'll cost—"

Noah gave her a look, and she didn't finish her sentence.

Suddenly Nili didn't want to go home. She said, "Why don't we go visit Auntie Yocheved?"

The grown-ups exchanged glances. There was a long silence. At last Lesley said doubtfully, "Well, it would be a nice thing to do. Then maybe Shalom would drive us home."

"Doesn't she live in—" began Noah slowly.

"Mom! Why don't we go to Daddy's concert?"

The minute the words were out of her mouth, Nili felt sure she'd said the wrong thing. Her uncle was staring at her as if she'd hit him.

"A concert!"

"Oh, Mom, please! Can we? It'd be so nice! Daddy'd be so surprised to see us!"

Lesley's eyes narrowed. Nili felt a sort of panic. What was her mother thinking? Was she thinking Nili was trying to distract them? It was sort of true, but could her mother have guessed it?

Lesley looked at Noah, whose face had gone suddenly hard.

"A concert!" he said in a strange, almost sarcastic voice. "Great. Good idea, Nili. Let's go for it. And afterward we'll all spend the night at the King David—your dad too."

Both the others gawked at him. The King David Hotel! Was he joking? How could he *joke*? No, whatever this was, it wasn't a joke.

"But we've got no luggage," said Lesley faintly.

"We've got the whole afternoon. Let's go buy ourselves some pajamas and toothbrushes," said Noah.

*   *   *

Lesley began to be frightened almost at once after that.

To begin with, she thought, *Grief takes people different ways.* Shula, her old friend who now lived among North African immigrants in a poor sector of the city, had told her about a neighbor who'd lost her son in Lebanon, and all she did for weeks after the funeral was go into town and buy things she didn't need and hadn't money to pay for. Well, that was one thing. A woman might shop frenziedly to stop her thoughts. But a man?

It seemed Noah couldn't get enough of spending money. Nothing could stop him. If was as if he were trying to wear out his credit card.

Nili grew hyper to match him. She greeted every purchase with almost hysterical squeals. The pile of packages grew. Lesley tried to hurry them past windows, but every time Nili even glanced at something, Noah said, "You like that? Let's buy it!"

And he bought things neither of them had even looked at, things they wouldn't have dreamed of wanting. A huge oil painting of Jerusalem he spotted in a gallery window, a Persian rug, and an antique lamp with a copper base and a parchment shade, plus a whole set of Armenian hand-painted dishes, to be sent on. Not to his home in Toronto. To the kibbutz.

Lesley began to panic. "Noah. Enough. Please. Enough!"

"I haven't even started yet. Where do they sell sofa beds in this town?"

"*Sofa beds!* What in heaven's name do you want with a sofa bed?"

"That old wooden thing Dale's sleeping on is like

a rock. I'm going to get her a really comfortable one.''

Lesley stopped dead. ''Noah, this is madness. You're not staying long enough to start buying *furniture.*''

He stopped too, and stood on the bustling sidewalk facing her.

''Who says I'm not?'' he said dangerously.

''You're not, that's all. You've got your work, your home. Your life. None of it's here.''

''None of it's anywhere if it's not here.''

''What are you talking about?'' she almost shouted.

He looked at her, or he seemed to, but the sinking sun caught his glasses and they flashed at her so she couldn't see his eyes. A danger signal. He was out of control, a stranger, lost in some weird state of mind where she couldn't reach him.

She grasped his arms. ''Noah. Don't. You're scaring me. Stop it.''

For a moment she thought she'd reached him. But Nili, who had wandered on when they'd stopped, suddenly came rushing back.

''Mom! I've seen Shalom. He's in that restaurant. That's where he works!''

Noah immediately pulled free of Lesley's hands. ''Good,'' he said. He took Nili's arm and turned her back the way she'd come. ''Let's go see what Shalom would like for a present. And we'll get his mother something too—two hundred fancy handkerchiefs, perhaps, or a year's supply of Kleenex!''

Lesley was appalled. She understood the crack— Yocheved had cried too much at the funeral; she had

153

upset everyone with her crying—but she had been crying for Glen. For Noah to make cracks about *that* was simply unbelievable.

She followed the others slowly. She must do something. But what? Oh, if only the damned police had given them a car! They'd have been home by now.

Noah and Nili had turned into a little restaurant that served Middle Eastern food. Shalom was waiting tables there. He greeted them when they came in, kissing Nili and Lesley quickly and shaking Noah's hand. Obviously he was astonished to see them and didn't know what to say.

"The boss has his eye on me. Why don't you sit down and I'll bring you a cold drink?" He showed them to a table near the window.

Noah hesitated. But then he shrugged. "Good, let's keep it in the family—what's left of it." Lesley jumped. This was horrible. She felt as if she were on the edge of a volcano.

They sat down, putting their packages under the table.

Nili was still on her high. Her face was flushed, and she was avoiding everyone's eyes.

"Uncle's bought us so many things, Shalom! Can I show him my Levi's, Mom?" She was already rummaging in the bags.

"Maybe not now, Nil, Shalom's busy."

Noah glanced at the menu, then put it down. "Let's eat. We'll have the best you've got. Whatever it is. I know—one of those huge hors d'oeuvres, humus and tehina, and the eggplant salad that tastes burned, the whole *gesheft*. And after that we'll have

154

steak and fries. And wine with it, lots of wine, and Coke for Nili.''

He didn't notice the silence, how they were all, even Shalom, looking at him, how other people in the restaurant were beginning to look because of his strange, loud voice.

''We're going to a concert afterward, Shalom. Did I mention that? Music hath charms, you know. And charms are just what we need. Ofer's playing—where is he playing, sis?''

''At the Jerusalem Theater,'' whispered Lesley.

''The Jerusalem Theater! There's a funny thing! I took Yoni to a show there once when he was a kid. Puppets, it was great. They do a lot of children's shows there. I was planning to take Glen to Jerusalem one day, take him to shows, show him the sights, take him to the Wall. But he got here ahead of me—''

He stopped abruptly. Lesley reached out her hand to him, but he stood up sharply and walked out of the restaurant on stiff, wobbly legs.

After a moment Lesley changed the direction of her hand and put it around Nili instead. They sat silently with their heads together. Both of them were trembling, and Nili, who had understood at last that everything was terribly wrong, began to cry silently.

Shalom leaned down to them. ''Shall I go after him? Try to bring him back?'' Lesley couldn't talk. She just shook her head, not ''no'' but ''I don't know.''

Shalom took off the small apron he was wearing, left it and his order pad on the bar, and went out into the street, ignoring a surly shout from his boss.

He spotted Noah almost at once. He was in an alley alongside the restaurant. He was leaning against the stone wall with his hands up to his face. Shalom, after hesitating, walked to him and put his hand gently on his shoulder.

"The bloody swine," Noah said, his voice shaking with fury. "The filthy butcher! She wouldn't identify him. Got a glitch in her head somehow. Kids—"

Shalom, who couldn't follow this, stood quietly, waiting.

"It was him." Noah went on, his voice shaking. "The police are almost sure of it. He has a bad record. He was hiding out when they found him. They were sure they could nail him. Now he'll go free. And they'll never get the other one, the one who stabbed my little boy to death."

He straightened up and looked around. He didn't know Shalom very well—Shalom had been a small boy when Noah had left Israel and they'd met only a couple of times in the years between. But there was something about Shalom that made people open up to him.

"I wanted to slap her at the police station. Make her admit she was lying. I wanted to slap her hard in the face. What do you think of that?"

"It's in all of us," said Shalom.

"Think how I feel," said Noah. "Being so angry at her. I love her. That must be why I bought her all that junk."

Shalom watched him take out a clean handkerchief and wipe his glasses and his eyes. *You're probably angry at her for being alive,* he thought.

What he said was, "Let's go back in. They're waiting."

"I'm sorry. I'm half mad."

"*Lo hashuv.* Never mind."

"But why did she do it, do you think?"

"I don't know the story. Maybe it really wasn't him."

"It was," said Noah. "I know it was. And now I'll never, never know why he killed my son."

Noah went back and apologized. They had a meal. Nobody talked much or ate much. The packages were now an embarrassment, but they had to take them along to the theater in a taxi.

"We'll check them in the cloakroom," said Lesley.

"And forget to collect 'em," said Noah ruefully.

"*No!*" protested Nili, and then hung her head. Lesley and Noah's eyes met, and they managed some kind of smile. For a moment everything seemed normal.

The theater was a beautiful building on one of the hills that held the city. The golden stone still glowed in the twilight.

In the high, expansive foyer, concertgoers of all ages crossed the smooth marble floor and went up the wide staircase. There were works of art decorating the walls and landings. Everyone was well dressed, talking quietly to one another, behaving beautifully.

Noah was thinking, *This is all so civilized. People seem normal and even happy. But this is Israel. Probably nobody here tonight hasn't known tragedy.*

Some even worse than mine. How can all this fit together? A few miles from this—this temple of culture, there's violence and barbarism. Ours as much as theirs.

As a matter of habit, he'd bought the best seats in the vast theater. The three of them sat with Noah in the middle. He put his arms along the backs of both Lesley's and Nili's seats, but he didn't touch them, though he wanted to, suddenly—to hold and protect them against the dangers that, it seemed to him, might snatch them away from him without warning, as they had snatched Glen.

For a cruel moment he remembered how he had tried to put his arm around Glen, that last morning in London, by the elevator. How Glen had twitched his shoulders as if he didn't want him ... He clenched his teeth and closed his eyes in pain. *What am I doing here? How is it that I am going on with my life? Why am I not roaring like an animal with pain and rage and banging my head against stones because you are dead, my little son? Forgive me, oh, forgive me!* It was like a prayer.

The musicians filed onto the enormous stage and took their seats. Nili bounced a little and pointed into the woodwind section.

"There's Daddy, see?" she whispered solemnly.

"Yes, I see him."

"They're going to play Brahms. Brahms is Daddy's favorite."

"Mine too," said Noah, fighting back his tears lest he spoil her pleasure. *Brahms, of all composers ... Brahms ... can I bear it?*

The mere thought of Brahms's music seemed to

158

flood him with emotion. He squeezed Nili's shoulder. *A brand saved from the burning,* he thought. *She, at least ... I'm glad for her father—for us all. I swear I am fully, unreservedly glad. It could have been both of them.*

And as the music swelled out, a moment of understanding came to him. He knew, suddenly, why Nili had done it. Her innocent compassion had told her that she owed that murderer her life, and she had paid her debt with a dangerous, difficult lie.

But that flash of understanding didn't help the clawing hunger in his heart to penetrate the minds of his son's killers.

Shalom was washing dishes in the restaurant kitchen. It wasn't usually his job, but he did it uncomplainingly. The boss, a big, black-haired Jew from Morocco, put his unshaven face in.

"Sorry, my friend. But cheer up. The kitchen slaves'll be back tomorrow."

Shalom looked over his shoulder. "That's good."

"I'm not so sure! Listen, do you think I like employing a bunch of *arabushim*? You think I trust 'em as far as from here to here?" He held his finger and thumb close together.

Shalom said nothing, his hands moving automatically in the soapy water.

"If I could get Jews for the same wages I pay that lot, I'd kick them all out of here tomorrow! Look how they've left us in the lurch this last week!"

"Not their fault," muttered Shalom.

"What do I care whose fault it is? So they're under curfew, and for my part I feel safer! Maybe one of 'em actually did it. How do we know? If they didn't do it this time, they'll probably do it next. Every one of them would kill one of us if he dared. We should throw them all across the cursed border, if you want my opinion.''

Shalom felt a little shiver run down his back. The same thing that was written on the board of that crazy fellow in King George Street. And his boss, whatever else he was, wasn't crazy.

FIFTEEN

Conscience

Because of the concert, it wasn't until they were all in the hotel that Nili's conscience, which had been lying dormant in her head, woke up and began to give her serious trouble.

It was the room that did it. The hotel room. It brought back to her the last time she had been in a luxury hotel bedroom, the morning they left London, the morning she and Glen had had a fight.

She had not allowed herself, even once, to think about that. But as soon as she came into the room she was to share with her parents, a room even more beautiful than the London one, with its golden stone walls, vaulted ceiling, and glorious paintings, it all rushed back to her.

Noah and her mother had told her father right after the concert what had happened at the police station.

161

They were brief about it. ''Nili wasn't sure enough,'' was the way Uncle Noah put it. Nili's mother had corrected him. ''She was sure,'' she said, ''that it wasn't him.'' Then there was this awful silence when nobody looked at her except her father, and when she glanced up at him, the pleased-to-see-her look had gone from his face and been replaced by one that was puzzled and unbelieving, as if he weren't sure he knew her.

Nothing was said then. But when her mom was in the bathroom at the hotel, her dad spoke to her. ''Nili, were you very, very sure at the police station that it wasn't the same man?''

She had to keep it up now, of course, but it was more difficult somehow, with her father looking at her in that penetrating way as if he could see into her brain.

''Yes,'' she said, but she didn't sound as sure as before.

''Daughter, a mistake in this case would be very serious. It would be a great responsibility for you.''

She didn't know what to say. He looked into her eyes. And suddenly he frowned and said, ''And if by any chance you'd told a lie, whatever the reason, that would be one of those lies you would have to take back very quickly before it did a lot of damage.''

The panicky feeling was back, stronger than before.

''Daddy, don't, it wasn't a lie, it wasn't!'' She was already nearly crying because her conscience had woken up the minute they'd walked into the bedroom and she'd seen the king-size bed. For just a second she'd almost seen Glen in it, and it had given her a terrible shock. She wasn't feeling strong in her lie anymore.

He kept that piercing look fixed on her for what seemed forever. Then her mother came out of the bathroom.

"Bed now. We've got to get home early tomorrow," she said.

Nili was glad enough to get into her single bed, in her new pajamas, and turn her back on her parents. She pretended to sleep, but her mind was active, looking ahead to tomorrow. The bees she had felt at the lineup were back, in her stomach and in her head, buzzing around angrily, only now they seemed to be stinging her too. She curled up tighter in the bed in little spasms as the stings came.

Her mother was speaking quietly on the phone, explaining to Nili's grandparents why they weren't home. After telling them about the concert, she mentioned the police station. "Nili said it wasn't him. . . . Yes. . . . No. . . . No, they weren't very happy at all. . . . Yes, I think they did. I don't know. We don't quite know what to think. . . ." Chills passed over Nili's body under the bedclothes. The whole kibbutz would probably know by tomorrow. Know—what? Not about the lie—would they? Just that, somehow, she had failed.

What would Nimrod think about it? And Yonatan? How would she be able to keep the lie up when they began probing and questioning? The thought of facing them all made her shrivel up inside.

She didn't let herself think about Valerie and Dale. That was a huge *Out out out*. If she thought about

163

them, she would have to know that this lie was forever. Because if they ever found out, it would be, more than before, as if she'd been part of killing Glen. All the horrible guilt she'd felt at first would rush back, ten times worse.

The lights went out, and her parents settled down. Nili wanted to sleep—she was deeply tired—but every time she sank to the very brink of sleep, a bee in her brain stung her and woke her up again.

In the middle of the night, weary and half sick, she got up and walked silently past the end of her parents' bed to the balcony. She stood out there in the dark, with her hands on the stone railing, and looked far out across the valley behind the hotel.

No people. Just the night city, forsaken by its sleeping inhabitants. Jerusalem the golden, only now it was black and starry like the sky seen up close.

The long golden band of the lit-up walls of the Old City was like the Milky Way, and there were thousands of other lights. There were big black hole–shaped patches, too, which were parks, with just strings of lamps winding across.

Nili imagined herself flying off the balcony and down into the valley. There her flying power deserted her, and she dropped down into one of the black, empty places, only it wasn't a park now. She didn't land softly on grass; she dropped into a bottomless hole. She fell down and down and down with her arms at her sides and her eyes closed, and she wondered why it felt better to be vanishing deep into the earth than to be lying safe in bed with her thoughts endlessly buzzing and stinging like bees.

*   *   *

Instead of getting a taxi to take them home, Noah rented a car.

"Which way are we going?" asked Ofer uneasily as Noah, after consulting a road map, took off to the north.

"The short way. Through the West Bank."

"I hope it's safe," Ofer said, as they left the well-peopled roads of Israel proper and dipped down toward Jericho. "Maybe we should go around."

"It's so much farther. . . . The car rental people said the curfew's still on. Let's just see how it looks."

It looked strange. Strangely empty. The places where the fruit sellers and other traders usually set up their stalls near the bus stops were bare. The few people they saw in the town, mainly women, were hurrying along with plastic shopping baskets, their veiled heads down. If the shops were doing business, it was behind closed shutters.

Once they passed a young man on an old bicycle. He teetered nervously as they drove past him. Noah, glancing up to the rearview mirror, saw him halt and gaze after the car with an unreadable expression. Noah found he had stopped the car and was staring into the man's face in the mirror. Ofer, when he spoke, seemed to wake him from a sort of trance.

"This town's okay, but I don't like the idea of going through Nablus. The car has an Israeli license plate, not a West Bank one." With a jolt Noah remembered such cars could be targets for stones or Molotov cocktails.

He shook himself and started the car. He must have been crazy, coming through here. What if anything happened? He did a U-turn, and they drove back out of Jericho in a cloud of dust.

But the young Arab's face in the rearview mirror stayed with him.

As soon as they turned into the kibbutz and parked in the central car park, Nili slipped out and took off for the sanctuary of her room in her parents' home, not waiting for the others. She got there well ahead of them. She reached for the key in its usual place under a flower pot. It wasn't there, and when she tried the door, it was unlocked. She entered cautiously.

Nimrod was there, watching TV with Lev.

They both looked up at once as she came in. Lev looked nervous. He said, "*Shalom*, Nili," in an odd voice, as if he were trying to warn her. Nimrod said nothing and zapped the remote to switch off the set. There was something about the way he did it—a kind of spasm in his arm—that made her realize she was in for it.

"Where are the parents?" he said sharply.

"They'll be here in a minute."

"Do you want to talk in front of them or just you and me?"

Nili was shocked. So direct! And the way he was looking at her!

"What do you mean?"

"You know."

She did know. But she couldn't let him see that she knew.

"No, I don't! What's wrong with you?"

He got up. "Lev, *l'hit', beseder*?" He was dismissing Lev, in a friendly way, telling him to get lost. Lev took the hint and started out. When he reached the door, he stopped, and Nili thought he might turn and say something, something—she sensed it—to soften Nimrod. But he must have decided it wasn't his business, and left.

Nili heard her parents and Uncle Noah outside, speaking to Lev. Nimrod said, in a voice of command, "Come on."

"No, I—"

"Come on, I said."

He took her arm in a hard grip and almost frog-marched her to the door just as their parents came in.

"Hi, Mom. Hi, Dad . . . Uncle. See you," he said tersely, and before more could be said, he had Nili outside and was walking her swiftly along.

"Where are we going?"

"Somewhere no one can hear or interrupt."

He led her to the old culture house. No one went there anymore, and it was dilapidated and sad-looking. The outside steps that led up to the balcony were roped off, and there was a faded sign that said BALCONY UNSAFE, but Nimrod simply ducked under the rope, and Nili had to do the same.

They mounted the steps onto the balcony, which faced away from the kibbutz, across the Jordan River to the hills beyond. There Nimrod stopped and faced his sister.

"Okay," he said in English. "What the hell happened?"

"Wh-what do you mean?"

"It was him, wasn't it? They wouldn't have

brought you in if they weren't sure. Why did you say it wasn't?''

A long, long silence followed. Nili felt caught, trapped in her lie. Her mind flew this way and that in a panic. He couldn't know. He couldn't. So why was he looking as if he did know, beyond a shadow of doubt, about her lie?

She could not admit it was a lie, but looking at Nimrod, she found it impossible to reaffirm it either. Perhaps it was because he *knew* her that no denials would work.

''You wouldn't understand,'' she said at last.

He gave an exclamation under his breath and took a step backward, away from her, as if she'd changed before his eyes into something repulsive.

''Do you know what you've done?'' he said furiously.

She said nothing. Inside her everything was melting and burning, and she could feel the burning echoed in the skin of her cheeks. She was trembling, and she knew he could see it, like a sign proclaiming her guilt.

''You don't understand,'' she whispered again.

''I understand you're an ugly traitor,'' he said in Hebrew. ''I understand I don't want you for my sister.''

He gave her no time to answer. He pushed past her, around the curve of the building, and she heard him running down the steps, vaulting over the rope. She was alone.

Nili stayed on the balcony for a timeless time. She had no spirit to climb down, no courage to go home and face her people.

When Nimrod first left her, her legs went wobbly. She sank down on the concrete behind the balustrade and just huddled there in the shadow.

She played it all over again in her head, the lineup, the moment when she could have pointed and said, "There he is!" Why hadn't she? Oh, why hadn't she? What did she care about that Arab man compared with her family, who loved and believed in her? If they had beaten him on the spot, in front of her eyes, if they had shot him dead, she couldn't have minded as much as she minded Nimrod's calling her an ugly traitor and not wanting to be her brother, as much as she minded her father's doubting her. She couldn't have been as frightened as she now was, too late, at the prospect of living with this terrible lie forever.

She sat there in shadow with her head on her bent knees. She couldn't even cry. It was too bad for that.

At last, shivering all over like a wet animal, she pulled herself to her feet. She held the rail as she had at the hotel the previous night and stared out across the kibbutz fence, the rough ground, the line of green in the river valley, to the Arab village beyond, the pale hills behind that. Arab land. Arab village full of Arabs, who hated the Jews, hated her, wanted to make her not be here, to make all Israelis not be here. Arabs who only wanted to make the Jews' lives like the balcony, precarious, crumbling, unsafe; who wanted the whole kibbutz to become like the culture house, abandoned, run-down, empty.

She had grown up pushing this knowledge away so she could be happy. But she had always known it deep down.

Was it because she had wanted just one Arab not to hate her that she had lied?

Had she really thought that the Arab who had stood there while Glen was murdered would think better of the Jews because she had refused to identify him? Had she thought she could soften his heart, change his mind, show him that all Jews were not his enemies?

With Nimrod's face, full of anger and contempt, still sharp in her memory, she couldn't dredge up a single reason why she had done it. Or why she should ever go back down to face the consequences.

After a long time of just leaning there, swamped in misery, she heard the grating of feet on the steps. She tensed. They were slow, a man's steps, reluctantly coming to find her. Her father? Her uncle?

Her grandfather?

But it was her cousin Yonatan who came around the corner.

He stopped and looked at her for a while. She looked fearfully for anger in his eyes, but they weren't angry. She couldn't read what was in them.

"Nimrod told me," he said. "He should never have said that to you. You know he didn't mean it."

"Yes, he did," she said. Her voice choked in her throat as the tears came.

He closed the distance between them and put his arms around her. He had never done that before. Now he just held her, and she sobbed against his shoulder, and he let her.

"We shouldn't be up here," he said after a while. "This balcony's a death trap. Come on."

"I can't!"

"You can come to my place. You don't have to see them yet. We'll talk."

They went down. He led her around by a less frequented way to his small bachelor apartment. The most important thing in it was the computer. Apart from the unmade bed and a couple of chairs, there wasn't much else. The whole place was a mess except the computer table, where everything was as neat as a pin.

He said, "You look finished. Do you want to lie down?"

She lay on the bed just as she was, shoes and all, and he put a blanket over her. He sat down across the room.

"Please, Yoni, sit closer," she said between chattering teeth.

He moved the chair. She reached out from under the blanket, and he took her hand.

"Do you want to talk?"

"Does everybody know?"

"Know what? That you said it wasn't him when it was?"

She nodded with her eyes shut.

"Nobody knows that. I only knew it this minute."

"Nimrod knows. My parents will guess, and so will Uncle."

"I doubt it. Anyhow, they can't be sure. Listen, Nil. This is a very complicated business. I told Nimrod. If he opens his mouth to *anyone* with what he *thinks* he knows, I'll shove one of his date palms right down it."

Nili thought that image would once have made her smile.

"But what can I do?"

He rubbed his thumb thoughtfully against the side of her hand. She opened her eyes timidly and looked at him. He wasn't looking at her. He was thinking.

"If you admit to it now, you'll be in bad trouble," he said. "Valerie ... Dad ... your folks ... the grandparents ... No. You'll have to hold it now. At the same time we can't let that murderer get away with it."

"But they'll let him go!"

"They won't. Not at once. They'll question him. Try to get him to confess. If he doesn't, they'll release him, but they'll keep an eye on him. They'll hope he'll lead them to the other man."

"If they catch *him,* and ask me to identify *him,* I would!"

"Yes, of course. Which would be as good as admitting you lied before about the first one."

She half sat up and clutched his wrist. "Yoni, what'll I do? What's going to happen?"

"You're going to have to be very strong if you don't want the whole kibbutz, if not the whole country, down on you. Keep quiet. Go on with your life. I'll see what I can do."

"What do you mean? What can you do?"

"I've got a friend. I met him in the army. I heard he's in Shin Bet now. Maybe ... I don't know. I'll have to think it through."

She gazed at him. Shin Bet ... the secret service ... She had no clear idea what he was talking about, but she had a sense of relief, of having unloaded herself of a burden that Yoni was now picking up.

"Why are you helping me?" she whispered. "Why don't you hate me like Nimrod?"

"He doesn't."

"Yes, he does. So could you. I did something terrible."

Now he looked at her. "You made a wrong choice. But I've made some myself. One in particular."

"What?"

He let go her hand and stood up, turning away from her.

"Maybe I'll tell you someday," he said. "And when I do, I want you to remember that I didn't hate you about this."

SIXTEEN

The Trick

The big policeman who smoked a lot went down to Mustapha's cell and unlocked the door.

Mustapha was already on his feet. He had known all the time that this was coming. He had made a fatal error in not letting Feisal kill the girl. Of course she had identified him in the lineup, and now at last, after making him wait, letting him stew, they had come to take him for the first session of proper interrogation.

The fear was deep and hot, but he thought he had control of it. Enough not to show it to this man anyway. He just looked him in the eyes with no expression, but that no-expression said more clearly than words, "Do what you have to. I'm ready for you." These were the terms he fought on. Mistakes, especially stupid, sentimental mistakes, had to be paid for. That was a law of war. Everything else about the Jews he resented. For what was going to happen to him now, oddly enough, he had no resentment.

The man looked at him coldly and sourly. "Come!" he barked.

Mustapha went ahead of him along the corridor. What would the room be like? There would be no window. A desk, a chair for the interrogator, perhaps one for him, perhaps not. There would be two men in the room at least, one to ask the questions, the other to try to make him answer them. That was how it had been twenty-one years ago.

It was said they didn't use the same methods now. Well, that could only be because they'd found more effective ones. Mustapha didn't allow himself any illusions. His muscles tightened as they turned a corner.

Ahead were some stairs, leading up. That was unexpected. Interrogations usually took place in basements. There were good reasons for that. . . .

They entered a lobby in the back of the building. That was also surprising. It could give a man a faint possibility of escape. He glanced sideways at the double doors, through which he could see the sunlight flickering through the pine trees in the courtyard. The doors stood open. Nobody was holding him. What if he made a dash for it?

No. It might be a trick so they could shoot him trying to escape. The fear was bad, but he wasn't ready to die.

They stopped at a high desk.

The man behind it asked him if he was who he

was. He nodded. The man scribbled on a form. Then he turned it to face Mustapha. It was in Hebrew and Arabic. He read the Arabic.

At first he couldn't believe his eyes. It was a form saying he was released and asking him to sign that he had been well treated. The man behind the desk was holding out a ballpoint pen.

He looked up at the big man escorting him. "You're letting me go?"

"Looks like it, doesn't it?"

"I can walk out of here if I sign this?"

The man shrugged. "Why not sign it and find out?"

"I want to see my lawyer."

"You don't need her. We're not charging you."

This was not according to the blueprint. Mustapha had a struggle to hide the astonishment, the relief he felt. The man was watching him with narrowed, unreadable eyes. He turned back to the form and read it again. He didn't know what to do. He sensed a trap . . . but there was a chance of freedom. Just a chance . . .

He took the ballpoint pen and signed the form.

"This way."

The big man showed him to the door. He walked through it into the afternoon sunlight. There was a police car waiting outside. The big man went ahead, opened the back door, and said, "Get in."

"Where—?"

"Listen, you," said the man in a bitter undertone. "You're going free. You're just not going free in my city. Get in the bloody car before I kick you in."

He got in. There was nothing else he could do.

There was already another man in there besides the driver, and the big man got in after him. He slammed the door fiercely. The car drove away.

Mustapha was thinking feverishly. Maybe they were going to take him somewhere, kill him and dump his body. He'd never heard of their doing that, but he could feel their hostility. There was *some* trick to all this.

They'd kept him in his cell for days. They'd given him a lawyer who'd been allowed to talk to him alone. A woman . . . Not one of the ones he'd heard about, Jewish lawyers who genuinely tried to help Arabs who were in trouble. This one was young. One of theirs, probably—a police lawyer.

She'd asked him a lot of questions, quite politely but coldly. Of course, he had simply denied everything, said he had never been anywhere near Gilo. He provided an alibi of sorts—something he'd dreamed up before they'd arrested him. It wasn't much good, but it was just weak enough to sound genuine.

He explained why he had been hiding when they'd found him, said he'd been afraid they'd pick him up because of his record, afraid of interrogation after last time.

He got a shock when she mentioned Feisal. That nephew of his. Was he involved in politics? He couldn't say he didn't know, because he had been living in the same house with him. He said he might have been out in the streets a few times but had never taken part in any serious action. Which, till the day of the stabbing, had been true.

Did he know Feisal had left home and that his

mother ("your sister, right?") denied knowing where he was? No? Where could he be, this nephew?

Probably gone to Russia, he replied with a shrug.

Russia? Why Russia?

To study. Lots of Palestinians go to Eastern Europe to study.

Wouldn't his mother know about something like that?

Arab men aren't like the Jews; they don't bother telling their mothers everything they do.

She actually smiled at that.

He asked if his sister could visit him, bring him clean clothes and some cigarettes. She said no. He asked when the formal questioning would begin. She didn't answer. Her eyes were empty. She was certainly one of theirs.

She came every day with more quiet questions. Often the same ones. It made him very tense, but it was a far cry from the harsh sessions he had prepared himself for. There was a catch in it, for sure. They were so clever you never knew what they were up to.

And now this. Letting him go . . . driving him back to his village.

To his village! A shock went through him, and he jerked upright in his seat.

"You're not going to take me to my sister's door, are you?" he asked suddenly.

"Why not?"

He sat rigid. Was this it? Were they trying to get him killed by his own side? Arriving home in a Jewish police car was enough to mark him for death if the activists of Hamas got to hear about it and thought the Jews were doing him favors, maybe because he'd talked. . . .

The big man and the other man were exchanging smiles.

"Prefer a little walk, maybe?"

He nodded tightly. The car screeched to a halt by the roadside some miles from the village.

"Out you go, then, *arabush*."

The big man opened the door on his side, got out, dragged Mustapha after him by the scruff of his neck, and slung him onto the stony verge. Then he dusted off his hands, spat on the ground very near Mustapha's head, and got back in the car. It did a U-turn and roared away, leaving a cloud of dust to settle on Mustapha as he got to his feet.

He started to walk. His legs were shaking. He was out of condition after his imprisonment. And he was nervous.

Every now and then he glanced over his shoulder. It was stupid. As if anyone would actually be following him! He shook himself.

It was good to be out. The air was clear. No gas fumes or the prison reek of unaccustomed food, stale cigarettes, and the stink of toilets, just a pleasant country smell of dust, bruised scrub, and a vagrant whiff of goats. The road was empty, and the noon heat was too intense for birds. The silence was broken only by occasional faint insect noises and once by the roar of a jet. The sun was high and bounced off the heaps of rocks.

Away from the city, full of living proofs of the Jews' insatiable need to build and expand and make

179

their mark on the land, Mustapha could push his sullen admiration aside and think another way. The Jews tried to bring extra water everywhere, to green everything. It was unnatural. Everything they did, everything they built was unnatural, an interference, an intrusion on the land.

His own people knew how to live and build and grow food and leave the land looking much as it always had, as it was meant to.

He rounded a bend, and there was the village, far up ahead, straggling up two hillsides, looking not white and glaring like the Jewish settlements, regulated, hacked out of the rock, leaving it scarred and ugly, but like a natural jumble of stones. In certain lights you could hardly make it out. The vines and pomegranates, the olive and almond trees blended in because they were what belonged here.

Suddenly, for the first time in years, he thought of the orange orchards of his childhood, the village of his childhood, over the border in Jordan.

Jordan was Mustapha's birthplace. In Jordan lay his native village, from which, twenty-five years ago, at the beginning of the June War, what the Jews called the Six-Day War, his father had uprooted him and his sister, making them cross the river with him to the West Bank. The old man thought it would be safer there. What a joke! He had run straight into the enemy's mouth.

And he had left more than their home. His wife and four little daughters—Mustapha's mother and sisters—had been left behind, abandoned.

Mustapha had almost forgotten them. But he remembered the deep hatred he had felt for his father, who had callously taken the ones he needed—his only son, his eldest daughter—and run away from danger, leaving the weak and useless behind.

His father was dead now. Perhaps his mother was too. She had been sickly from all that childbearing and the hard life she led. But his sisters? All younger than he was. Where might they be now?

It was years since he had really thought of them, those little village girls with their submissive ways that hid naughtiness, their sweet, appealing eyes. . . . One in particular, the nearest to him in age. Nabila . . .

None of that. A fighter must have no close attachments. They tie a man, make him weak. He had had recent painful proof of that. *The girl* . . .

He stopped walking.

For the first time it occurred to him that he wouldn't be walking here if that girl he had stupidly allowed to live had picked him out in the lineup. Why hadn't she? Perhaps she had been too frightened, after the stabbing, to remember him. That must be it. What luck! Allah be thanked! His sense of shame at the stupidity of having saved her life relaxed its hold on him.

He walked on, gathering strength and speed. His legs were not trembling now. He was anxious to get back, have a good meal, a good night's sleep in his own bed. The village was in full sight now. It lay sleeping in the sun, as if deserted. . . .

Strange there was no one at all on the road. The West Bank side roads were not overburdened with traffic, but there was usually something.

This thought had hardly crossed his mind when he heard a sudden shout not far off to his right. He

181

turned his face toward it just as a gun fired. A bullet whistled over his head.

He dropped to the ground.

A curse burst from him. A trap. He'd run into a trap!

Curfew! There was a curfew on, and they hadn't told him! Now he'd be arrested for being out. That was their plan. How they must be laughing, back there in the compound!

He hitched himself in a series of knee and elbow jerks to the nearest roadside rock pile on the side the shot had come from. He lay in its scant shadow, in its scantier protection.

Another shot pinged off one of the rocks. Were they warning shots, or were they actually shooting at him? He'd never heard of anyone getting shot for being out during curfew, but if they were out to get him, they could always say he'd run, they could say anything. . . . He curled up, instinctively making himself smaller. But what was the use? They had seen him.

He heard booted feet scuffling and scraping as they ran and slipped down the hill. He thought, *I'm finished. Might as well die on my feet.* He rose slowly, his body resisting, his mind forcing it upright.

His hands went up of their own accord. A young soldier with a rifle pointed at him stood not five meters away, with another behind him. He shouted at him in badly accented Arabic: "Name!"

Mustapha gave his name slowly, waiting for the bullet that would end his life.

"Where you come from?"

"Jerusalem."

"Liar. On foot?"

"In a police car."

The soldier scowled. "Wait. Don't move."

He got onto a walkie-talkie he was carrying and muttered into it in Hebrew. Mustapha understood Hebrew, but he couldn't hear him. After a brief conversation the soldier switched off, lowered his gun, and jerked his head.

"Go on. Hurry. Get indoors. Curfew."

Mustapha, his heart beating thunderously, turned and walked on.

From behind him the soldier shouted: "Run, you—"

He broke into a run and into a sweat. He felt the soldiers' eyes boring into his back, the guns still there, the bullets still waiting. Now he knew. He knew what the trap was.

Pray to Allah Feisal had gone, and gone far. Because they hadn't really let Mustapha go. They were not finished with him—oh, no!

There would be a spy in his village. It might be anyone, a shopkeeper, a neighbor, even a child. A traitor they had turned and paid to inform on him. Hoping he would betray himself and lead them to Feisal.

SEVENTEEN

Ways to Help

Going back to school was hard for Nili, with what she had on her mind.

She thought everyone was looking at her, whispering about her, though nobody said much. One or two of the boys wanted to know the exact procedure of the lineup, how the suspects had acted and how they'd looked.

But most of the kids seemed to have their own concerns, and the whole tragic business inevitably dropped into the background, except when the newspapers brought it up again. There was still a campaign going on among some right-wingers to get the government to punish the Arabs wholesale and to increase security; the Jewish settlers on the West Bank, mostly religious American immigrants, were still "restless," and there were a number of incidents. These made Nili desperately uncomfortable. On days when people were buzzing with the latest settler outrage, such as when an Arab was attacked in the market at Hebron and badly hurt, she retreated into her shell and hardly talked to anyone.

It was hard for her, at these times, even to sit with the others in the high school dining hall. She would make a snack out of her meal and go outdoors to eat by herself. Even her best friends couldn't get through to her then, and among themselves they would murmur sympathetically that the whole business had made her a bit crazy.

One day, when she was sitting in the shade of one of the campus trees, brooding on her guilt, she saw Lev coming toward her across the grass. It wasn't possible just to get up and walk away from him, and anyway, in these moods she had no energy, so she just sat there.

He came under the tree and sat beside her.

"You are feel bad?" he asked.

The direct question got under her guard, and she nodded.

"I know what disturb you," he said.

She twisted her face around to him so fast she wrenched her neck. She'd suddenly remembered that Lev had been in her parents' room that night with Nimrod. Obviously he had discussed the business with Lev before she'd come home and there'd been that awful scene on the balcony.

Since then things had not changed between her and Nimrod. He wasn't speaking to her, but she knew he hadn't said anything to anyone else either. Yoni's word was law. But his command of silence had come too late to stop Nimrod from talking to Lev.

Now Lev was looking at her gently out of his pale, slanted eyes, so different from most people's. His hair was no longer slicked back but tousled and long on his neck. It made him look less odd, but he was still not accepted by most of the kids. Just because he was "one of the Russians."

But secretly Nili liked him. She couldn't help it. In his very difference there was a grown-up quality that made her like to be with him. She found herself looking into his unusual eyes, seeking something she couldn't find anywhere else. Lev *knew*—and didn't condemn her.

He settled his back against the tree.

"One time in Kiev," he said, "our neighbor, he go to police about us. He want favor of them. So he tell we make phone call to Israel and America. Not true. We not know someone in Israel or America. But my father in more trouble because this man tell he hear us."

"How did you know he did it?"

"I hate this man; he is in general a pig. Once he quarrel with my father, and he say he do something, so when police come, I guess who made the trouble."

"What did you do?"

"Plenty. I throw a stone and break his window. Hard to get things mend, so he cold a long time. I throw over his garbage. I steal his coal."

"Lev! You didn't!"

"Yes. Then he come to my parents, and he go mad. He say if my father don't punish me, he get me in prison. Then my father say, 'My son don't do this, and if he do it, I know why he do it, because

186

you go to police and tell to them lies.' You know what this man do?''

"What?''

"He run to his place and bring a bible. We don't have no more bible, is forbidden, but he have one he hide. He show my father this forbidden book, and he hold in his hand like this, and he say, 'I swear on God's name I not do like you say.' He say, 'Now you know I have this bible you can go to police and tell on me. Now you beat your son because he act without to know for sure.' ''

"Wow,'' said Nili, much subdued. "What happened?''

Lev shrugged. "My father beat me. Not hard. Say he do it not for neighbor but because is wrong to do against a man without to be sure.''

"But you were sure.''

"I think then, and I still. But maybe, for all that, I made mistake. Is better not to make trouble for someone if you not sure, one hundred percent.''

They sat quietly under the tree. Nili understood the story, and why Lev had told it to her now, and felt grateful to him, though her case was quite different. . . . When Lev suggested, after a bit, that they go back to the dining hall and see if there was any stewed fruit left, she nodded. He put out his knobbly hand to help her up, and they walked a few meters hand in hand before they let go, at the same moment, lest any of the kids should see.

Donna found herself worrying about Valerie.

She was aware of the irony. Valerie had taken her husband from her years ago. Donna hadn't known till just now that there was no anger left in her about this. Perhaps there had been, but the tragedy of Glen's murder had wiped it out.

Valerie was never seen around the kibbutz. She kept to her room. Dale, on the other hand, was about everywhere. She was seen going in and out of the various work branches, from the metal shop, where she collected dropped pieces to make patterns in the sand, to the sewing room, where she collected more dropped pieces to make patchwork pictures.

She hung around the children's farm a lot and got in the way, wanting to pet the animals and pestering the kids who were working there until they let her help feed them. Yoni mentioned to his mother that she nagged him to let her ride the tractor again, but he had to refuse. Rules were back to normal now.

People in the kibbutz were shaking their heads about this little "poor girl" whose parents seemed to have abandoned her to her own devices. It occurred to Donna that if Dale's parents were staying much longer, they'd have to get her organized somehow.

She mentioned it to Lesley, who mentioned it to Noah, but Noah was preoccupied and unable to make any decisions. His firm had given him indefinite leave, and he was just living from day to day, waiting for news. Meanwhile, what was happening to Valerie, holed up in that little room with her grief? The nurse in Donna, as well as the human being, worried. She wanted to go visit Valerie, but that didn't feel right.

One day Dale, who treated Donna as a sort of aunt, brought her tray to Donna's table in the *hader okhel* and sat with her to eat. Donna noticed she was sniffling into her salad.

She leaned toward her sympathetically. "What's wrong, Dale? Is it Glen?" She believed, with children, openness was the best way.

But Dale shook her head and poked her plate. "I hate this stuff. I'm so hungry."

"Are you dieting?" Donna asked in surprise. Dale sniffed and nodded. "Oh, forget it, kiddo. You need to eat when you're sad."

"I'm not sad," said Dale. "I don't want to be fat. They'll tease me when I get into a group here. Besides, Nimrod told me not to eat so much."

"Nimrod doesn't have to go hungry," said Donna, thinking: *Into a group? Is that on the schedule?* She looked at the rabbit food in the middle of Dale's plate and said: "How are you getting on? Have you lost any weight?"

"I don't know. I've been trying real hard."

"Come to the clinic after lunch. We'll weigh you."

They did this. Then Donna gave her a piece of graph paper and showed her how to make a weight chart that she could mark to show if her weight went down. While Dale was frowning over this, Donna took a piece of paper out of a drawer.

"Now here's something else to help. This is your official diet sheet."

Dale took it and looked at it. "I can eat all this?"

"Yes. There's no need to starve yourself. Only no snacks, okay? And here's a list of stuff you must never eat. Forbidden food. Like, imagine it's all blue and bubbling and bad-smelling and full of deadly poison that will make your hair fall out and your face turn purple and steam hiss out of your ears.''

Dale squirmed with glee. ''Eeeeuuckh! I'll never eat my forbidden foods! Never, ever!''

''Dale, how's your mother?''

The smile dropped off Dale's face. ''Awful.''

''What do you mean exactly?''

''She stays in bed most of the time.''

''Does *she* eat?''

''Dad brings her stuff, and Grandma, and Aunt Lesley. And they sit with her and coax her. But she like hardly eats at all.''

''And your dad? What does he do?''

Dale looked at her, a curiously canny look for an eight-year-old.

''Are you still buggy about him?''

''Dale! What a question! No, I'm not. But I'm worried about him. I've heard he leaves the kibbutz a lot.''

''Yeah. He drives to places.''

''What places?''

''I asked him. He just says 'here and there.' Like he's looking at the country.''

''Why doesn't he take you?''

'' 'Cause I don't want to go. I get sick in cars. Anyhow, I like it right here.''

''Do they ever . . . visit the cemetery?''

''Maybe. I don't know. Why should they?''

''To visit with Glen?''

''What for? He's gone.''

''Where, do you think?''

Dale frowned. ''I don't know. I think he's just— I don't know. What do you think?''

"I think he's in heaven," said Donna promptly and sincerely.

"You believe in heaven? Honest?"

"Oh, yes."

"Why?"

"I'm a Catholic, and that's what we believe, that after death our true selves, you know, our souls, will be near God and be happy forever."

Dale dropped her head and wrinkled up her nose.

"What?" Donna asked.

"But, like—Glen with wings and stuff—it's kind of silly." She looked up quickly. "Gee. I shouldn't say that. It's just—we're Jews, and Daddy says we don't know what happens after you die."

"But wouldn't you like to think of Glen still around somewhere? Don't you want to believe you'll see him again someday?"

Dale stared at her solemnly and then said, "I guess not. It's too weird. Thanks for helping me with my diet. I'll come Friday." And she took off.

Donna was left with a familiar feeling of unease. There was always this gap between her and all the people she lived with. The gap was not just between her religion and their lack of it, but between her religion and the religion that all the other kibbutzniks had tried to leave behind but that was still clinging around them like an invisible cloak they couldn't throw off: Judaism, with its emphasis on this life, its God, whom they called a God of love and mercy but who seemed to her a God of wrath and justice. A God without comforting promises and bargains and rewards, but only with commands. And punishments.

This God she could never come to terms with.

191

Fancy not being able to tell your child that her dead brother was not gone forever, that they would meet again someday. Gone forever! What terrible words of hopeless sadness! Somewhere she had read: "Who would believe that, if they could? Who could believe it, if they would?" Donna shivered.

Poor, poor Valerie! Lost in that neverness, without hope or comfort. Donna thought abruptly, *I don't care what she did to me when she was twenty-two. I must help her now.*

That night, when Yonatan came to visit her, as he often did, she said, "Listen, Yoni, I don't know what your father's plans are, but it can't be right for Valerie to lie in that room with her grief, not knowing when she can leave and get on with her life."

"Ima," said Yoni in a teasing, singsong voice, "it's not your business."

"Okay, okay. We'll see. What've you been up to today?"

It was a perfectly casual question, and she wondered why he averted his eyes.

"I went to Tel Aviv."

"Really? All that way! Whatever for?"

"I had someone to see."

"Anyone I know?"

"Maybe. Do you remember Danny?"

"Sure. You brought him home a couple of times when you were first in the army. Clever boy. Didn't he go into Intelligence?"

"Yeah, sort of."

"What suddenly put him in your head?"

"Just wanted to see him."

Donna narrowed her eyes. "Nothing to do with—"

He glanced at her and smiled a little. "You're quite a smart cookie yourself, Mom," he said in English.

"It's called intuition, fella. Something you poor old men don't have. So where does Danny fit into the picture?"

"He doesn't yet. But he might. I don't want to talk about it now. Listen, turn your intuition off and the set on, and let's watch *L.A. Law,* okay?"

EIGHTEEN

A Dilemma

A few days later, quite early in the morning, Shalom drove into the kibbutz. He parked his car and walked swiftly to Lesley and Ofer's home.

Lesley was at work, but Ofer was there, practicing his oboe. He looked up in surprise as Shalom came in. Shalom, while he was studying, was always short of money, and gas was expensive. He made the journey to the kibbutz rather rarely, and never on a working day.

"Hey, nephew! Good to see you. What can I get you—coffee?" Shalom shook his head and sat down. "How's your mother?"

"Nervous. She wants me to quit the restaurant. She hates my being out late, leaving her in the apartment alone."

"She should come here to live. You're never alone in the kibbutz!"

"Yeah, that's the worst thing about them! I

dream of living alone . . . but I can't leave Mother, she'd go crazy.''

"Aren't you ever going to get married?"

"How much does Mother pay you to ask me that question?"

They laughed a bit. Shalom lit a cigarette and then said, "Listen, I have to talk to you. Something extraordinary happened last night."

"What?"

"You know I work with some Arabs."

"*Nu?*"

"Of course, they've been off work for quite a while—curfews et cetera. But they're back now. Pretty fed up and bitter, but keeping a lid on it. They have to. If they show any resentment, old Nissim, our boss, will throw the book at them."

"Is he down on them?"

"Sure. He's from Morocco . . . one of the sort that says only Jews from Arab countries really know how to treat the Arabs."

"Maybe he's got a point."

"Not a point. What he's got is a big blunt instrument. He just hates them all, indiscriminately. But as long as he can hire them cheap and they remember that they're just work robots and not people, he'll put up with them."

"So?"

"Well. So Ali comes back. He's the nice teenager I told you about, the one who invited me home."

"Oh, yes, I remember."

"He's had a rough time, it seems. Our guys took him in, questioned him . . . just routine, but they

195

scared the hell out of him. Of course he had nothing to tell. Then.''

Ofer, who was leaning over, putting his oboe back in its case, paused and looked up.

"So. Last night he was serving in the restaurant because we were shorthanded—normally Nissim keeps him busy in the kitchen dishwashing—and he wasn't experienced as a waiter, so he got nervous and made some mistakes, and Nissim yelled at him, and Ali lost his temper and answered back. So naturally Nissim fired him on the spot, and not in a nice way, need I tell you. In fact, he made a really disgusting scene.''

"What kind of scene?''

"He actually said, 'It's a pity when our boys took you in, they didn't take your whole village in with you. I bet that child murderer's one of you. Nice and close to the spot, you lazy dogs wouldn't want to walk far to do the business. Pity the army doesn't just go in and flatten the whole place, root out that nest of scorpions!'

"I was standing there, and I saw poor Ali turn as pale as paper. He took his apron off and went out the back to get his jacket. I followed him. He was shaking all over. I said, 'Ali, I'm sorry. He doesn't mean it; he's just an ignorant slob.' He gave me a look. Like appealing to me without words. So I said, 'Get on with the dishes. I'll talk to him when he's cooled off.' Ali said Nissim had told him to get out at once. I said, 'Hang around. It'll blow over.' ''

"And did it?''

"We were very busy. Nissim needed every hand, so he acted like he didn't notice Ali was still around.

But when the place closed, I could see him getting ready to go for Ali again, and it wasn't right, Uncle. The boy works his tail off. The way Nissim treats the Arabs, compared with us, just makes me sick. So I went up to him and I said, 'Boss, let the boy off this time. He's the best worker you've got. We're all nervous just now. He didn't mean to get smart with you.' Nissim hemmed and hawed and finally said okay. He'd done a good night's business and was feeling mellow.''

''This was the strange thing that happened?''

''No. I was last to leave. After locking up, I was walking to the bus when Ali appeared from a doorway. Gave me a heart attack, to be honest! I never used to have the slightest fear walking the streets at night. Anyway, he walks along with me in the dark. He's in a funny state. If he wasn't a strict Muslim, I'd say he'd been drinking. Thanks me over and over, as if I'd saved his life. Tells me no Jew ever treated him so well. I was embarrassed because it's probably true: you treat an Arab worker the way you would anyone else, and they can't believe it. . . . He said he owed me.''

''Go on.''

''So listen. He's talking very quietly now, even though we're walking along the nearly empty road. The words are kind of stuttering out of him, like he's frightened of what he's doing. So here's the story.

''The people who live next door to Ali's family in the village have a visitor, a cousin, from another village on the West Bank. He suddenly appeared a couple of weeks ago after dark. Young fellow. Said he was in some trouble at home and asked if he could stay for a bit, lie low. Told the household to keep quiet about his being there. But of course, Ali's mother right next door noticed something odd—extra washing on the line or something—and asked her neighbor, who whispered the secret, swearing her to keep it quiet, and she did, except she sort of let it out to Ali.''

Ofer was listening intently. ''Don't tell me Ali thinks this young guy is—''

''Wait. At first Ali thought nothing of it. 'Trouble at home' doesn't have to mean trouble with the authorities. But after our people let Ali go, he talked to his mother, said what he thought: that killing kids isn't the way to fight. Maybe this had something to do with me; he knows Glen was in my family. He told his mother he doesn't blame the Jews for being really angry about it. But to his surprise, his mother acted strangely, like she didn't want to hear Ali talking like that. And yet when it first happened, she was also shocked about the murder, happening so close to their village, felt sorry for the parents and very worried that the army would come in and start destroying houses and so on. . . . Now she's behaving as if Ali were talking dangerously.''

''Which he was, of course. If any of the Hamas people heard him—''

''Well, they were alone at home, the two of them. But Ali picked up a couple of hints from his mother about this boy who was hiding next door. Just hints, you know, like 'We shouldn't be talking about patriotic actions being wrong when our neighbors are taking such risks.' She knows more than she's telling. And after a while Ali suddenly catches on. This fugitive from 'trouble at home' could be the man who murdered Glen.''

Ofer threw himself back in his chair with an intake of breath.

"Of course he's not sure," Shalom went on. "I think his point of view is, hiding this boy is very dangerous for the village, which, perhaps just because it's so close to the city, has always kept its nose clean. There's been such a lot of suspicion of them since the murder that it's been touch-and-go. The army's been there in force, doing their number—breaking into houses, smashing things at random, throwing their weight around, and frightening the wits out of people—but at least they haven't bulldozed any buildings, and now Ali thinks ... Listen, he didn't tell me this just out of gratitude."

"No," said Ofer. "Obviously not. If this young guy hiding out is the one, it would be better if the army just went in and got him. That would lift suspicion and fear off everyone else. But wouldn't Ali's mother get into trouble if she knew and didn't tell? And what about the neighbor?"

"Frankly I don't think Ali's thought about that. He's only a kid, and not very smart, and as I say, I think he'd had a drink or maybe he was high. . . . He's scared silly that this man, who could bring trouble to them all, is right next door. He wants me to do what's necessary without involving him at all. He seems to think I can."

Ofer muttered something under his breath. There was a long silence.

"So what are you going to do about it?" Ofer asked at last.

"Report it. I must."

"How can you know which house the suspect is in?"

"It's the one next door to Ali's. And I know which house is Ali's because I've been there."

Ofer jumped out of his chair in a spasm of movement and started pacing the floor.

"You'll be dropping this Ali in the *botz* with his own people, you know that. If they *ever* found out he'd blown the whistle, they'd kill him."

"You're not suggesting we don't do anything."

"Of course not. Of course not ... But what a dangerous stinking mess. Once the words are out of your mouth in the proper quarters, it's out of your hands. God knows what it'll lead to." He stopped pacing suddenly and said slowly, "Our people really could make your boss very happy."

Shalom said, "What are you saying? Collective punishment on the whole village?"

"A thing like this would give our right-wing policymakers a perfect excuse, and if you think there're enough peaceniks and liberals to stop them, with the country as angry and scared of terrorism as it is, you're kidding yourself. You don't know what we might be unleashing on those people if—"

Shalom stood up.

"Listen, Uncle, I'm a peacenik myself, but I'm not a 'vegetarian.' I want them to catch that butcher, and if they happen to shoot him in the process, I'm not going to cry. Provided it's the right man. I couldn't possibly keep this to myself."

Ofer looked at him.

"Do you know how many Arab villages were destroyed by us after the War of '48, and how many Jewish villages have been built on their ruins? Over three hundred.''

''But not since—not for years.''

''What we did once we might do again.''

Shalom faced his uncle with narrowed eyes. ''I think you are actually suggesting we keep this quiet,'' he said slowly.

Ofer turned away. ''Glen's dead,'' he said. ''We can't bring him back. Will damaging God knows how many other lives really achieve anything?''

''You're crazy, Uncle,'' said Shalom flatly. ''Think. Is it truly a secret you could keep? Because I couldn't. I'd never look my family in the face again.''

Ofer turned around. His usually calm and gentle face was suddenly red with agitation.

''I'm going to tell you something about keeping secrets,'' he said. ''Do you know what I believe? And this is very strictly between us. I believe my own daughter is keeping just such a secret, hiding it in her heart in a mass of guilt and misery. I think the other man they're looking for was in that lineup.''

Shalom gazed at him in horror and astonishment.

Ofer went on. ''Don't say it—I know. She should have identified the man if it was him, and she failed to, but she did it for a good, kind, innocent reason. If we, you and I, were to decide that the cost of revealing this secret of your friend Ali's was going to be too high, are we less strong than a fourteen-year-old girl who has held her tongue against all the pressure we could decently put on her?''

Shalom stood up. His mind had shot off at a tangent.

"If a connection could be made between this man Ali suspects and that other one—" he said slowly.

"We'd have both of them. Yes. And Nili might never be trusted again. And your friend Ali, who still trusts you, might find that in a moment of drunkenness or gratitude or whatever it was, he had brought destruction on his family—or more than his family. And probably signed his own death warrant."

Shalom turned away and made for the door.

"Where are you going?" asked Ofer sharply.

"I'm going home. I'm not going to listen to you. You're talking I don't know what."

"Treason? Say it."

He turned. His face too was darkened with emotion. "You said that. I didn't. And I'm not going to say what some people might think: that you're thinking first of protecting Nili. But have you thought what other deaths there could be, what other destruction? That man who killed Glen in cold blood—I see him as a tiger who's tasted human flesh and wants more. We let him get away with this for *any* reason at all, and who's next for his knife? I just can't believe you're serious. You're my uncle, and I respect you, but I reject your reasoning."

Ofer listened with his face turned away but said nothing. Shalom left, closing the door behind him quietly. Shalom never got angry enough to bang doors. But Ofer knew that in his nephew's heart were a deep sense of shock and a deeper determination.

Left alone, Ofer stood still in the middle of the

room. He was still standing there, lost in his thoughts, when Lesley came in.

"Ofer?"

He started and turned. His face was strained. She put her papers and books down on a table and went to him.

"Honey, what's wrong?"

"Lesley. I'm going to ask you now. Do you think Nili was lying at the lineup?"

She didn't move for about half a minute. Then she said under her breath, "Yes, I do."

"So do I. It's the only explanation for how she's been these last days. Listen. Shalom has been here."

"Shalom?"

"Sit down. I have to tell you what he told me. I think we have to prepare for Nili's secret to blow up in our faces."

NINETEEN

Nimrod Has a Headache

Lev tapped on the door of Nimrod's room in the high school dormitory. There was no answer, so he walked in.

As he did so, he half closed his eyes so as not to get irritated by the state of the room. He'd been brought up with very few possessions and very little living space and a mother who was fanatically tidy. The chronic disorder of this room, and the others in the building, tended to rattle Lev. His own small area of the room he shared with two other Russian boys was always tidy; it had gained him a reputation for eccentricity.

This room too was shared by three boys, and their belongings littered it from floor to ceiling. The floor was almost impassable because of snaking wires, cast-off clothes, sneakers, books, soda cans, sports equipment, an old stereo, and upturned crates used as extra tables. These in their turn were overflowing.

The walls were invisible behind shelves, posters, pictures, flags, charts, and anything that could be nailed, pinned, or stuck to a flat upright surface. From the ceiling hung mobiles, a kite, a model of a jet fighter, and a dangling notice saying NO WALKING ON THE CEILING EVEN WHEN HIGH. In one corner above the beds was nailed a Bedouin tent–like arrangement made of a sheet, with a huge watchful eye painted on it. The general appearance of the room was like some huge chaotic work of modern art.

The girls' rooms, Lev knew from peeping into them, were very little better.

Once a week, on eve of Sabbath, their house-mother forced them to tidy up, but since there was never enough storage space, it was simply a matter of pushing stuff under the beds. By Saturday the clutter had mysteriously reappeared and spread all over everything again like blown leaves.

Nimrod was sitting in a chair with his back to the door. If he heard Lev come in, he didn't give a sign.

"What is with you?" asked Lev, coming up behind him. "Why you aren't play football?"

"Got a headache," said Nimrod.

"Another one?"

Nimrod merely nodded.

Lev put his big hands on Nimrod's forehead. Hardly had his fingers made contact when Nimrod jerked his head and threw the hands off with an instinctive gesture.

"What are you touching me for?" asked Nimrod irritably.

Lev was startled, but then he laughed. "What you think, I am gay and make pass at you? It's not you I want to kiss, believe me! Sit and shut up and let me fix headache. No. Nimrod, let me do."

Nimrod sank back, but he was tensed as Lev gently and expertly massaged his temples.

"From what you have these headaches? You always have?"

Nimrod shook his head. Almost against his will, the warmth and movements of Lev's blunt fingers were easing the pain. There was silence in the room.

"You go to clinic," said Lev. "Get bullet. I mean ball."

Nimrod grinned. "You mean a pill. Or did you mean a bullet?"

"Why have pain if science can cure?"

"I think you've cured," said Nimrod, turning around. "It's much better now. Thanks. Where did you learn to do that?"

"My mother. She do in Kiev. Professional masseuse."

"She should do that here, instead of wasting her time in the laundry," said Nimrod. "There are enough headaches here to keep her plenty busy." He stood up. "Okay, I think I'll come back to class. What is it?"

"Math."

"Could you put my headache back till school's over?"

They laughed. Then Lev said more soberly, "What I said before. About not want to kiss you."

"Big relief to me. *Nu?*"

Blushing deeply, Lev confessed, "It's your sister I want to kiss."

Nimrod's face changed, closed. "Don't talk to me about *her*." Unconsciously his hand went to his forehead, and he frowned at the sudden stab of pain.

Lev, watching him, said: "Ah. From this maybe come your headaches."

"What?" asked Nimrod in a sharp, warning tone.

"My mother explain me that sometimes headache come from think bad thoughts."

"Well, my headache come from drink bad beer," said Nimrod.

"You drink beer?" asked Lev in surprise. "Is against rule."

"You don't say," said Nimrod sarcastically.

"From where you get beer?" Lev asked interestedly.

"You going to tell on me?"

"Me? To who, to KGB? You make a joke, I hope."

"You know there's beer and wine in the pub," said Nimrod.

"You go to pub? Is not for our age."

"Not officially. But the older guys don't say anything if we don't get outrageously drunk. I often drop in there for a drink," he said carelessly and not very truthfully. He had sneaked into the pub, in fact, three times in as many months. Two of the times had been this week.

Lev looked hurt. "Why you not ask me to come?" But he had more important things on his mind than drinking and quickly let the matter of the pub drop.

"Why you so angry at your sister it give you headache?" he demanded.

Nimrod raised a finger. "Watch it," he said.

"Watch your finger?"

"Watch what you're saying."

"How I can to watch what I say? I only can to hear what I say."

"*Don't be so smart.* Just keep off the subject of my sister, because I do not want to talk about her."

"Or to her?"

"Or to her—right."

"You make her very sad with your not talking."

Nimrod raised his voice now and said in English: "Lev, listen up. This is none of your goddamn business, do you understand what I'm saying?"

"Okay. Sorry."

Mollified, Nimrod turned away.

"Only I hate that she is so sad and she miss you and she cry—"

Nimrod whirled around. "She cries? She cries to *you*—about the way *I* treat her?"

"She have to cry to someone. She is very unhappy. She need you now."

"Why do you think she's unhappy, eh? Eh, Lev, old buddy, have you thought about that?"

Lev met his eyes steadily. "I think a lot about it."

"And I suppose you understand her better than I do."

"Yes. I think so."

"And treat her better too."

"Yes, that for sure. You treat her very bad just now."

Nimrod looked at him dangerously for a moment,

a moment during which Lev thought that the unbreakable rule about no fighting on the campus was about to be broken. But instead of hitting him, Nimrod just said, "Go to hell and leave me alone."

Lev shrugged sadly and left.

Nimrod went back to the kibbutz on the school bus that afternoon to go to the clinic. He preferred Donna to the ham-fisted nurse at school.

His headache had come back, and it was worrying him. He was never ill, and this stupid nagging pain was getting to him. Even more now that Lev had put the idiotic idea into his head that it was connected with his boycotting Nili.

The clinic was not as crowded as usual, and Nimrod had to wait only a short time before Donna put her head around the door and beckoned him in.

"What's your problem?" she asked him in English. "It's not often you pay me a visit."

"Headache," said Nimrod.

"Got it now?"

"Yes. Here. And across here."

"What kind of pain is it?"

"Like a regular stabbing."

They caught each other's eyes, grimaced, and looked away. Donna touched his head gently, tracing the pain.

"Worried about anything?"

He shook his head.

"What could be causing this, can you think?"

"Beer."

She took her hand away. "Ah. Aha. Oho."

"This is a private conversation, isn't it?"

"Oh, yes, don't worry—secrets of the consulting room. But if illicit visits to Ari the Godfather's den of vice are giving you headaches, what about not going?"

"Ari's okay."

"Ari is undiluted trouble. Like you, only worse. I wish you'd pick another hero, Nimmi-nimrodi," she said, teasing him with his baby name.

"*Shtuyot*—heroes!" muttered Nimrod. Ari wasn't his hero. Yoni was. But he wasn't going to say that to Yoni's mother, of all people.

"Oh, well, only two more years and the army will sort you out."

"And cut my hair and turn me into a nice regular killer like everyone else—I know," said Nimrod sourly. "Now can I have some aspirin?"

Donna turned away to the glass-fronted cabinet with the medicines in it. Just then the door burst open, and they both spun around.

It was Valerie.

Nimrod hadn't seen her for two weeks, and she had changed so much that for a second he didn't recognize her. She'd lost weight off her face. Her blond hair was pulled back and tied behind her neck instead of fluffed out around her face as before. She wore a cotton housedress that was crumpled and stained. Her blue eyes seemed to bulge almost crazily out of dark pits of shadow.

She ignored him and strode up to Donna, who looked alarmed, as well she might, because without warning Valerie shouted in her face: *"You leave my daughter alone!"*

"What—?" gasped Donna. "What's the matter? What do you mean?"

" 'Whaddaya mean?' " mimicked Valerie in a shrill, childish voice. "You know damn well what I mean! You are trying to take Dale away from me! Oh, I know *why*. Of course I do. You're paying me back. But it wasn't my doing. Noah chose me; he chased after me; he didn't want to stay here in this horrible hellish country with you. If you want to hate anything, hate Israel for driving him away. I just happened to be around. Oh, yes, that's how it was, all right!"

Donna glanced over Valerie's shoulder at Nimrod to signal him to leave. But Valerie grabbed her shoulder and shouted: "Don't you look away. I'm talking to you!" Nimrod heard a rattling sound and saw that Donna had let a bottle of pills fall on the floor. He knew he should leave, but the scene was mesmerizing, and he sat frozen.

Donna was trying to shake off Valerie's hand and reason with her, but Valerie wasn't listening.

"I know what you're doing. You're trying to get yourself a bit more of Noah by getting your hooks on his daughter!"

"Valerie! I swear—"

"This place!" Valerie ground out between her teeth. "This place! Already she's changed so I don't know her! She's never home! She's disappearing, vanishing into the kibbutz like—like some little animal in a forest!" Her voice rose hysterically. "Her clothes, her hair, her face, even her *name*—and now you've started on her *body*! Can't you leave me anything? She's all I have left, and you're swallowing her, all of you, and Noah doesn't even notice, he's not even *here*!''

Suddenly Valerie crumpled up and went down to the floor, her face in her hands. ''Oh, my God!'' she shouted in a raw voice, loud and terrible. ''I can't stand it. I can't bear it another day! I want my babies. I want to go home. . . . I want my mother!''

And while Donna stood above her, stiff with shock, Valerie began to bang her head on the tiles.

TWENTY

Yoni
Tells a Story

Nimrod seemed to wake from his trance. He was out of the room, out of the clinic, and halfway home at a run before he'd properly taken in the horrible climax of the scene.

He was swearing fiercely under his breath—every ugly word he knew in Hebrew, English, and Arabic. It seemed the only way of keeping away from him the unbearably pitiful sight of Valerie, broken, sobbing and banging her head on the floor. He wished with all his heart he had never seen it. He wished that it had never happened, that none of it, none of it had ever happened.

Suddenly the anger-monster surfaced, just shot out of his unconscious like a hungry shark. He found he had to suppress loud, primitive shouts of rage. *That bastard, that murdering bastard!* The cause of it all ... and still free, still on the loose, while so many people suffered in his wake!

On impulse he left the path and cut across the gardens, running as hard as he could until he came to Yoni's house. He burst in, just as Valerie had, without knocking, to find Yoni on the bed, with his arms around his girlfriend, Ilana.

Yoni lifted an outraged face and told him in no uncertain terms what he should do next. But Nimrod just stood there, white-faced and panting.

"Tell her to go. I have to talk to you."

"Tell *her* to go! I'm telling *you* to go!"

But Ilana looked at Nimrod, sighed, got off the bed, and pulled her blouse straight. "It's okay," she said. "See you later, Yoni." She strolled out past Nimrod, merely saying in English, in a not unfriendly way, "You owe me, butt-ache." At another time it would have sounded funny in her bad English.

Yoni didn't let him off so easily. He rolled off the bed and loomed over him.

"What the hell do you mean, walking into people's rooms without knocking? You're lucky we were just having a siesta or I might have had to cut your stupid ponytail off and throttle you with it!"

"Valerie's having hysterics in the clinic."

"What am I supposed to do about that?" asked Yoni angrily.

"You said after that day that you were going to do something about finding the ones who did it to Glen. Are you?"

Yoni seemed to lose his anger. After staring at Nimrod for a moment as if he had never seen him before, he turned away, lit a cigarette, and went to make himself a mug of coffee in the kitchenette on his porch. Nimrod sat down and switched on the computer and started messing around with the mouse in an effort to calm down.

Yoni returned with the coffee and stood in front of the screened window in a cloud of smoke.

"Your mother came to me with something interesting," he said at last.

Nimrod kept his eyes on the screen.

"Mom? What does she know?"

"Has it ever occurred to you to wonder why this guy saved Nili's life?"

"I don't believe he meant to. Do you?"

"Aunt Lesley thinks he meant to. She thinks—" He stopped. "Have you breathed a single word about Nili and the lineup?"

"No," Nimrod replied at once.

"Because what I'm going to tell you now is just as secret. It may not be true. But I've mentioned it to my friend Danny, who's with Shin Bet, and he's working on it with the cops in a very quiet way."

"Well? Go on!"

"I'm telling you because I want you to forgive Nil. If you understand better—not just why she did what she did but about *him*—you might get a better perspective on things."

Nimrod switched off the machine and turned around. "Tell me."

"Okay. Your mother thinks this guy recognized Nili."

"*Recognized her?* From where?"

"Not Nili exactly. But you know how she looks so much like your mother?"

"So what?"

"Aunt Lesley thinks she herself may have known

215

this man when they were both around your age. That this Arab, seeing Nili, thought for a split second it was . . . this girl he'd known long ago."

Nimrod scowled. What was he saying? That *his mother* had known the wanted man? The mere thought made him feel strange. "Ima? You're saying he thought Nili was Ima?"

"That's what she thinks may have happened."

"I don't get it!"

Yoni turned to face him and sat down, the cigarette burning between his fingers.

"Did she never tell you the story of how she crossed into Jordan on a sort of dare, when her class was initiating her into the youth movement?"

"She did *what*?"

"Yeah. It was in 1967, just before the Six-Day War started. And your mom had just gotten here about six months before, when Granddad and Grandma emigrated from Canada. She was having a rough time getting accepted—you know, like the Russians now, only there was only one of *her*. And she'd been a rich, spoiled teenager in Canada; I mean, it can't have been any fun at first. And one night the kids decided to give her a test, and they went down beside the river—"

"You can't get down there. It's all mines and barbed—"

"Well, you could then. Of course it was strictly forbidden, but the kids did it sometimes on a dare. And that night they gave your mother the choice of some things she could do that would make them . . . let her in, sort of. Be one of them. And she went for the most difficult and dangerous choice, which was

216

nothing less than to get to the old bridge, climb onto it, make a mark in the middle of it with chalk, and then come back to the others.''

"I don't believe this. She could've been shot.''

"Wait till you hear the rest. When she got to the middle of this rotten, shaky old bridge, she found she'd lost the chalk, so she decided to crawl over *to the other side* and find some sticks to place there instead, to complete the test. So she went over. And there she found a donkey she'd been watching for weeks from the culture house balcony.''

Nimrod was gazing at him as if he were talking about events on another planet.

"A donkey?'' he repeated dazedly.

"It belonged to an Arab worker in the orange groves over there. A man from that village you can see. He had a son, and your mother used to watch this boy working, and somehow she made some kind of contact with him. Waving, something, I don't know. And it seems this night the donkey had run away, and the boy had come after him, and so they met. And your mother, who had just begun to study Arabic, was able to talk to him a bit and—well, there was nothing to it. I mean, they exchanged a few words, and that was it; they went their separate ways.

"But then, after the War of '67, they happened to meet up again, because by that time the boy had left the village with his father and settled in Tubas on the West Bank.''

"What was Ima doing in Tubas?''

"Oh . . . just a class trip to see the new areas conquered in the fighting. And he was selling nuts or something in the market, and she saw him, and they talked again. She says she got the feeling then that he would never accept the Occupation, that he would grow up to be a fighter of some kind. She says it fits what she knew of him that he would get into trouble, though she also says she can't believe he'd become a murderer unless something bad happened to him.''

Nimrod was staring straight into Yoni's eyes. Now, unaccountably, Yoni narrowed his down to slits as if to stop Nimrod from looking into them. He even turned his head slightly aside.

''And bad things do happen to Arabs who rebel against us; you know that as well as I do. Especially bad things happened in the seventies. Young boys were taken in . . . not much process of law . . . very brutal interrogations—''

''Yeah, yeah, I know,'' said Nimrod hastily. ''Does that justify—''

''Nothing justifies, but some things explain. It doesn't take much to turn a man into . . . something different than he might have been. Injustice and pain, and especially fear, can change people very quickly. That's why you have to be so careful how you treat people.'' He stood up and turned back to the window. ''You can cause so much hate.''

''You're the one who's always saying you can't trust the Arabs.''

''Lately I've begun to reckon that if I were an Arab, I'd be saying the same about us.''

Nimrod was quiet. He just sat still, trying to think. Trying to imagine. Crawling over that broken bridge you could see from the top of the tel, meeting an Arab boy from the village—the thought of it shook

218

him. What a crazy and dangerous—and what an un-
believably daring—thing to do! A girl, a fourteen-
year-old girl!

That girl of twenty-five years ago was actually his
mother. Had her daring and recklessness been left
behind? Or had they become part of her life?

Nimrod asked abruptly, "Do you know exactly
what Mom does?"

"What do you mean? She teaches English and Arabic in the high school at Bet Alpha."

"But her other work. Her voluntary work for the
human rights group. She doesn't talk about it much."

"Some people around here, including Grandma,
are upset by it. Maybe that's why. She and her group
turn up some pretty ugly stuff and publish it, and
then they get it on their heads from the chauvinists
in the press. She doesn't want to make things tricky
for you at school."

Nimrod remembered a time when his mother's organization had published a report about how many
more kids were getting shot by soldiers in the territories than the army was admitting. Another time it was
interviews with Arabs who'd been tortured during
interrogations. Yes. The kids at school had been
angry, confused. He'd been glad his mother's name
had not appeared in the reports, even though he knew
a lot of the interviews had been done by her. He
hadn't told anyone that. He suddenly remembered
he'd had a spate of headaches around that time too.

"You should be pretty proud of what she does,"
said Yoni.

"Do you think her—her politics—her other

work—could that have anything to do with . . . what you just told me?"

"Who knows? But the point is this. If that man was the boy Aunt Lesley knew, grown-up and become a terrorist, then we know something about him. We know he was born in that village right across the river. We know that he lived in Tubas with his father and his uncle and sister, from May 1967. And we know his first name. If all those facts about him, or enough of them—he's probably changed his name—should happen to agree with the facts about the man in the lineup, then they have enough on him to arrest him again."

They sat for a while in silence. Yoni put his cigarette out and said, "Okay, that's it. Keep your mouth shut, and be nice to your sister."

"But why would she lie? Why didn't she identify him?"

"Maybe because . . . in that moment when he didn't let the other guy stick his knife into her, she had an insight into the man he might have been if we weren't all locked into this bloody situation. A situation in which soldiers like me can find themselves beating up prisoners and breaking their arms because they threw stones. Now get out of here, and if you see Ilana, tell her to come back and finish our siesta."

TWENTY-ONE

The Man on the Roof

Mustapha's nephew Feisal lay on the flat roof of his house of refuge, in the village near Gilo, smoking his twentieth cigarette of the day. He wished it were a proper cigarette, with something stronger in it than tobacco, but his cousin refused to try to get any of what he called "that rubbish" for him. So he had to be content to draw the smoke from the cheap, ordinary cigarette deep into his lungs and let it do the best it could to calm his nervous system.

Whenever he came up here, he had to be very careful. It was not just a matter of not letting people in the street see him. He had to be careful those in the house didn't see him come up here. They thought it recklessly dangerous for all of them. So he waited till the children were out and his cousin's wife went shopping and his cousin was at work, and then he crept up the stairs and crawled on hands and knees out through the doorway onto the roof, not raising his head above the low parapet that surrounded it.

There was a lot of stuff up here: pieces of unwanted furniture, swatches of tobacco leaves hanging on wires to dry, laundry. If he lay in a certain spot and didn't sit up, he couldn't be seen from neighboring rooftops, let alone the street. Didn't think he could. You could never be sure.

He was extra careful since the day, a week ago, when the woman next door had been up on her roof, hanging clothes, and had caught a glimpse of him. She'd looked away at once, but she had seen him.

But a man couldn't just stay locked indoors twenty-four hours a day, day in, day out. He had to get out sometimes. Otherwise he could go out of his mind.

Were they still looking for him? Did they know whom they were looking for? Not knowing anything definite was the worst.

He had known no peace since he had killed the boy. Not because he was in any way sorry—he was proud and satisfied that he had accomplished his mission—but because he was afraid all the time, awake and asleep. Afraid and alone. His cousin wouldn't listen, didn't want to know. He had no one to talk to.

And the girl's face, gaping, huge-eyed, haunted him.

Those eyes! Drinking him in, sucking his image into her brain, recording it so that she could describe him, betray him.

Why in the name of the Most Merciful had his

idiot uncle prevented him from shutting those eyes, and that gaping, telltale mouth, forever?

Nevertheless, he wished his uncle knew where he was. Word was out that they'd released him, that he'd gone back to Feisal's home village. Feisal was tempted to send him a message in the hope that he might try to visit him, but his cousin, a surly man made still more bad-tempered by Feisal's dangerous presence in his house, sharply warned him not to be stupider than he could help.

"They're watching him. They're not fools. If he came here, that'd be the end of all of us."

"When do you think it'll be safe for me to go home?"

"For my part I wish you'd go this hour."

"But you don't think the hunt's been called off."

His cousin looked at him with contempt. "Listen, you young imbecile. You did something. Don't tell me, I don't want your confessions. They're looking for who did it. They haven't caught him yet. So why should they call off the hunt?"

The implication—that they wouldn't stop looking till they caught him—sent a shiver down Feisal's back.

"But I can't stay holed up here forever!" he snarled, as if it were his cousin's fault.

"No," the older man agreed. "You're going to have to move on soon, because I've had enough. We're poor people, we can barely keep ourselves, and my wife has a weak heart. If they come bursting in here, it could be the death of her."

"But where can I go?"

"I've been thinking about it. You ought to keep

moving, not stay long in one place. I've got a plan: another village; another house; an activist, like you. Some people like trouble. He should be glad to help you.''

''But how will I move?''

''At night. Don't worry, I'll arrange that. Be worth it to get you off my neck.''

And tonight was the night.

Feisal lay on the roof on his back with the smoke drifting upward. The ordinary evening sounds of the village were all around him: children's voices, women's, the occasional buzz of an engine or crack of an ax, the cluck of chickens, footsteps. ... The sky above him was clear; the washing, with its clean smell, flapped in and out of his vision.

He wondered where he would be the next day. When it was dark, someone was coming in a car. It would drive into his cousin's backyard, which afforded some shelter from watching eyes; he would curl up in the trunk, and the car would take him to his new hiding place.

He drifted into an escapist sleep while the cigarette burned down between his relaxed fingers.

Suddenly there was a commotion that was no part of the mild, customary evening racket. Feisal jerked upright, and for a second his eyes roved the village below the parapet. Then, remembering where he was, he threw himself flat again.

The door to the roof was flung open, and his cousin, cursing, struggled through the flapping laundry, pulling half of it down in his hurry.

''You must get out!'' he hissed. ''Come quick.''

He half dragged Feisal down the stairs and threw

him out of the back door. It was twilight, but anyone watching must see him clearly. His cousin's harsh, unshaved face was set, his eyes glazed with fear.

"Where—?" began Feisal.

"Do I know? They're cruising the town, coming this way. Run. That way, into the hills. *Get away from my house!*"

Feisal's brain blanked out. Nothing functioned there. He stood helplessly in the doorway until his cousin abruptly raised both his fists in a gesture so threatening that he turned and fled, through the yard, out through a gap in the wall, and, bent double, along a narrow, littered alley.

Shalom was in the car with the soldiers. He hadn't wanted to do this, but Danny, Yonatan's friend, who was conducting the investigation now, had insisted.

Shalom was in a state of suppressed terror. He wasn't afraid for himself, of course, but for Ali, who, trusting him, had said too much. He must at all costs protect Ali.

He hadn't named him. He had been very careful not to, not to indicate in any way his source of information. He had told the authorities that an Arab he knew had told him there was a man hiding in a certain house in the village.

They had pressed him. Which Arab, how did he know him, how did this Arab know—? Shalom shut his mouth. He said only that he knew the house, had had it pinpointed by his source. He pointed it out, circled it, on an ordinance survey map that showed every building in the village. But they said it wasn't up-to-date; there'd been some illicit building lately;

things were not simple; there could easily be a mistake. He must come with them and show them.

They covered his head with a hood. Then they drove (surprisingly slowly, it seemed to Shalom) through the streets of the village.

Shalom indicated the twists and turns in the lanes that he thought led to Ali's house, but indeed, it wasn't simple. The village was built higgledy-piggledy according to no plan at all. From afar, in Gilo, he had been able to pick out the house, but now, in the tangle of streets and buildings, with no overview, he got muddled.

Danny and the two soldiers with him in the car were getting impatient.

"Is this the street? Well, you said turn left— *Nu!* I thought you said you could lead us straight to it!" They seemed to be almost taunting him.

The streets had emptied of people as soon as the car entered the village. But a couple of young boys were peering around the corner of a wall, watching them.

Danny said suddenly, "Those two!"

In seconds the car had jerked to a stop, the two soldiers had leaped out. The boys broke cover and ran. The soldiers gave chase.

"What's going on? Why are they trying to catch them?" Shalom asked agitatedly.

"Everyone knows everyone in these places," Danny said shortly.

One of the men came back empty-handed and panting. A few minutes later, the other one appeared, carrying a boy, who looked about twelve, kicking and struggling in his arms.

He brought him back to the car and bundled him into it. Shalom watched incredulously. What was this?

Danny seized the boy the moment the soldier shoved him into the back seat, pushed him onto his knees on the floor, held him there, and began to shout at him in Arabic. Shalom, who knew some of the language, understood that he was trying to get him to guide them.

Danny was shaking the boy and now began slapping his face with swift, practiced blows. They were not heavy, just efficient, and the boy's tears were chiefly of fright. "*Dai,* enough!" Shalom tried to interrupt.

"Keep out of this," said Danny sharply. And then he said to the boy: "The house of the man who works in a café in Jerusalem!"

Shalom's blood turned to ice in his veins.

He knew. Danny knew where he'd got the story. Ridiculous of him to imagine that Shin Bet wouldn't have put two and two together.

"It's not him!" Shalom shouted desperately. "Let the boy go. I'll find the house—I can show you—it's nothing to do with—"

Danny abruptly stopped slapping the boy and turned on Shalom with a quite different face. "Okay. Are you ready to stop messing us about?"

Shalom stared at him dumbly.

Danny opened the car door, lifted the boy out like a sack of grain, and dumped him as if he had no further use for him. Then he slammed the door. The boy stood dazed for a second and then ran like a rabbit for the nearest cover.

Danny had hardly looked away from Shalom.

"So let's stop pissing around," he said crisply. "Your co-worker Ali Husseini was the source. We're almost sure of it. We know he likes you; we know you've been to his house. We know where his house is, evidently better than you do."

"So why—?"

"We want the full story, my friend, nothing left out. The who, the where, the when, and the why. No protecting anyone, it's useless."

Shalom tried to moisten his mouth. "What do you mean—useless?"

"Information goes both ways and sometimes back again. We had to do some checking up. To find out who your friend Ali's neighbors are, we had to make some inquiries of our own. And I'm afraid *our* source is something of a two-way channel."

"What—what do you mean?"

"Well, let's just say he goes where the 'insurance' is. When he'd given us the info we wanted, he then almost certainly went to someone else about Ali. Your friend Ali's had it, man. He's history."

Shalom slumped in his seat. The hood was so hot it was making the sweat run down his neck and back. It was too terrible. He couldn't even address the harm he'd done, so he swerved from it.

"While we're talking and sitting here, the man could be escaping!"

"I hope so! Only he isn't, because we've got the village surrounded. Why do you think we're taking our time? We want him to bolt; it'll be as good as a confession. We don't actually enjoy taking houses apart looking for fugitives."

"I rather thought you did," said Shalom dully.

The other man suddenly lost his temper. "Oh, *sorry*. I didn't realize you were such a *feinshmecker!* This must all be very painful for your delicate liberal conscience. Aren't you damned lucky there are people like us to do the dirty work that keeps you safe?"

Something broke in Shalom. "If you mean you keep my family safe, I wouldn't boast too much about that! Whatever methods you're using didn't save my little cousin!"

"Yeah, we slipped up there all right. You can't win 'em all. Now do you want his killer punished, or perhaps you'd rather he was given some tender loving care?"

At that moment something started coming through on Danny's two-way radio. He listened for a moment and then said to the driver, "That's it. Go."

The car started off.

"Where are we going?" asked Shalom. Inside him was the beginning of an overwhelming feeling of guilt that was so big he dared not feel it yet. It was something he was going to have to deal with over many years.

"Back to town," said Danny laconically. "They've got him."

TWENTY-TWO

Shoot and Cry

Nimrod was not a stupid boy. He didn't think he was. Later, though, he was to wonder why it took him so long to grasp what Yoni had said to him, just before he told him to go look for Ilana.

Perhaps it was his having so much else to think about. His mother, the incredible story of the bridge and the Arab boy, the possible connection between that boy and the murderer—that kept his mind well occupied for quite a long time. After that he had to begin planning, reluctantly, how he would approach Nili, to make it up with her without having to abase himself completely, forfeit his pride.

He wanted to be sure he was not going to do this just because Yoni had told him to. And it was in order to be sure of that—to be sure he was doing it because he himself was convinced it was right—that he had to think quite a lot about Yoni first and about his own admiration for him, which had always been unquestioning, ever since he was a little boy.

Nimrod had been only eleven or so when Yoni first went into the army, after finishing high school. He vividly remembered his first sight of his big, handsome cousin in his uniform. He looked completely transformed in his khaki fatigues and lace-up boots, with the gun slung casually behind his shoulder. He, like Nimrod now, had worn his hair quite long at school (though his was dark and curly and didn't make a ponytail; it just hung around his face and neck). The army barber had cut it all off. In fact, Yoni had gone for broke and got a close crew cut. It made him look very tough and very male all of a sudden, as if a lot of young fat had been trimmed off him, as if this were Yonatan pared down to the bone. The man carved out of the boy.

But he wasn't changed inside. Not at first. He still knocked around at home, kidded with the girls, played computer games, threw baskets and kicked a football with Nimrod, laughed a lot, and teased their granddad about politics.

Yoni didn't really care about politics. Zionism, socialism, and all that—and his mother's Catholicism—he called all those isms "the Big Nothings." He said none of them amounted to anything important or permanent; "crazy" people lived and died for them, but sooner or later these Big Nothings all broke down and turned into their own opposites. Nimrod didn't understand, but he understood when Yoni said, "Enjoy life. That's my ism."

He even enjoyed the army. In the beginning.

He said it was good. The training was easy for

him. The other guys were great, and it was good to get out of the kibbutz—which he'd always said he couldn't wait to do—and feel yourself part of something bigger. They offered him officer training just because he was from a kibbutz—kibbutz boys were considered "the cream" in the forces—but he didn't want to be an officer. He said giving orders was just another ism. They made him a corporal anyway, but he was still one of the boys; it seemed his platoon did what they were supposed to, orders or no orders, just because they liked him. He was proud of that and said that in the army, comradeship and loyalty were what counted.

There was just one fly in the ointment.

Because Yoni's mother wasn't Jewish, he didn't "count" as Jewish either with the rabbis, despite his Jewish father. His grandfather had had a word with him before he joined up, telling him it might be better if he kept quiet about his mother's religion. Yoni wasn't one for keeping things quiet. But he saw early on that his grandfather was right. Some of the other guys were funny about Christians. Because of this "secret" part of his life, he'd once told Nimrod, he felt he had to outdo the others in training and other things. Be a better soldier so that even if they "found out," they could never accuse him of not being good enough.

Then, in 1988, he was sent with his unit to the West Bank and Gaza to contain the Arab uprising, the *intifada.*

After that he changed.

Nimrod didn't notice it at first. All he noticed was that Yoni didn't want to hang around with him anymore. He treated him as if they weren't related; he seemed to keep away from him. Yoni had his own room now, of course, like all the soldiers, and he kept to it a lot. At first the whole family grumbled that they scarcely saw him. It was Granddad who told them all to lay off him, that it wasn't all moonlight and roses in the army and that fighting the *intifada* was something you had to experience in order to know about it.

Nimrod didn't get it. He was hurt at each rebuff. He went on being hurt. He loved Yoni the way he always had, but he was so changed sometimes Nimrod felt he hardly knew him.

But now, after Yoni'd been so angry at Nimrod for bursting into his room, he'd talked to him in a completely new way. He'd treated him almost—not quite, but nearer than ever before—as an equal. He'd been open with him and confided in him. There was the beginning of a new, more grown-up relationship. Nimrod had felt very good about that as he came away from Yoni's room.

But something was bothering him. It was two days before he was ready to think about it—two days during which he still didn't speak to Nili but thought about everything else that Yoni had said to him.

Then, in the middle of one night, the words came back, words he had stored away and tried not to think about. Now he couldn't stop. He thought about them so hard he hardly slept for the awful question that kept recurring. Above him the big eye painted on the sheet nailed to the ceiling kept staring down at him, stern as the eye of God.

The next day at school he couldn't concentrate. He

fell fast asleep at his desk and was thrown out of class yet again by his teacher.

He didn't go to the principal as ordered. He went to a quiet spot behind a building and lay on the grass. He stared up at the blue, cloudless sky, and his face was one big frown. After half an hour he got up suddenly and walked out to the road and got a *tramp* back to Kfar Orde.

It was early afternoon. He went to his grandparents' house, but there was no one there. His grandmother was probably at her part-time job in the English-language library. But it was his grandfather he wanted. So he went out to the *refet*.

The smell inside the barns was good. He liked it better than the nonsmell in the toy factory. It was a strong, natural smell of dung, milk, and fodder and the rich smell of sweaty cowhide. He stood in the aisle between two lines of cows and watched them eating their feed and listened to them rattling the bars that held their glossy black-and-white necks captive. He reached to touch one, but it jerked back as far as the bars would let it and rolled its eyes. Cows weren't used to being petted.

His grandfather was in the milking shed where he occasionally filled in if someone was sick. He was hosing out the big jars for the milk but looked up with a pleased grin when he heard Nimrod's voice.

"Hi, Granddad."

"*Hi* there, son! Come to lend me a hand?"

"No, not really. When do you finish?"

"Now." He hung the last jar back on its hook and attached the pipes to it, wiped his hands on a clean rag, and together they emerged into the hot sun.

"What're you doing home so early? Is it a work day for you?"

"I have to go to the dates later. I wanted to talk to you."

"Are you playing hooky from school?" Nat asked suspiciously.

"It doesn't matter."

"Is that so?"

"This is much more important."

Nat sighed. "Well, at two generations' removed, I guess it's not my business.... So what's your problem?"

Now it was time to voice it. Nimrod said with more difficulty than he'd expected, "It's about Yoni."

His grandfather looked at him sharply. "*Nu?* What about him?"

They were walking through the heat. Even under the big shade trees that hung over the main paths, it was hellishly hot. Drops of sweat ran off Nat's face and arms, and his old legs trembled.

He'd done three hours' work in the sweltering heat of the milking shed, and he needed a long cold drink, a shower, and his bed, in that order. But Nimrod was his favorite grandchild, despite or even because of all his *meshuggassen.* He gave the boy's shoulder a little squeeze and said, "Out with it."

Nimrod said, "Did he do anything bad when he was in the army?"

Nat's mind, torpid with weariness a second before, leaped to the alert like a startled animal. He dropped his hand. *Quickly, quickly,* he thought, *I must think quickly. He's heard something or guessed something.*

The truth or a lie? Which? Oh, God, if only it weren't so hot!

"Why are you asking this now?"

"So there was something."

"Don't cross-examine me like that, son!" he said sharply. "I asked a simple question. Why are you asking?"

"He said something. It could—I mean, it could have been just a . . . general remark. But—"

"What did he say?" *Play for time. Think, man. He's so young. I don't understand it. I can't excuse it. How could a young, innocent kid who's seen nothing of life? It could damage him. Enough damage already! Enough! God, this country! I'm too old for all this!*

"He said," said Nimrod slowly and carefully, as if the words were hurting his mouth but would hurt more if he spoke them, "something about the bloody situation and soldiers like him . . . beating people up . . . and breaking—" He stopped. Then he made himself go on. "Breaking their arms."

They had reached the house. Instead of going inside into the blessed coolness he longed for, Nat led Nimrod under the sweltering shade of the grapevine he had trained above his patio. They sat down on garden chairs in silence. There was an overpowering smell of cut grass and flowers and the sound of insects among them, the sweet scents and sounds of the natural world going about its business. Nat needed that at this moment.

"Nimrod," he said shakily. "You know that in 1988, when the *intifada* really got under way, orders were given from very high up that Arabs who attacked the soldiers with stones were to be punished in that way.''

''By having their arms broken?''

Nat swallowed and said loudly, ''Yes.''

''I thought it meant—I didn't think they . . . really did it.''

''Well, some did. Some took it literally.''

''How did—how did they do it?''

Must I put the pictures in his head—those pictures on television that the world saw? Must I do that?

''I don't know,'' he lied for the first time.

''You must know, Granddad!'' Nimrod shouted suddenly.

''All right, I know! They caught them; they tied them up; they took rocks and clubs; they bashed their arms with them. It's very hard to break a man's arm that way. I'm quite sure that often they didn't, that it was just . . . heavy bruising. A beating. It was a punishment. A punishment that fitted the crime.''

''And Yoni did that?'' Nimrod's voice was shaking. ''Yoni tied men up and bashed them with rocks and clubs?''

Nat found to his dismay that he was crying, the way he had when Yoni had left that time, three years back, after he had come and told him. He couldn't help himself. His throat was aching, and the tears just came. But Nimrod didn't have the pity for him that Nat had tried, so hard, to have for Yonatan. Nimrod needed to drag it all out of him now, and he was ruthless.

''Granddad, did he? Answer me!''

''Once,'' Nat said. ''After he'd done it, he felt

237

sick and ordered his men to stop, but his platoon jeered at him.

"Later his officer got his unit together and asked who was having problems with the orders. Only Yoni put his hand up. His officer said if he didn't have the stomach to do his duty, he didn't deserve the benefits of security earned by others. He ordered him out on patrol with other men who—who were willing to do it, who did it without feelings. He told me he saw things he wouldn't have believed, beatings that went on and on. . . ." He took out a handkerchief and shakily wiped his eyes and blew his nose.

"It's what I'm always saying, Nimrodi. I've been saying it for twenty-five years. It's the cursed Occupation. You can't have a nice, kindly, humane occupation of one people by another. Never, not in history, not in this world. You can't liberate land, as the right-wingers called it when our forces won that miraculous victory in 1967. There were a million people on that 'liberated land.' The people weren't liberated. They were conquered."

"They started it. They tried to conquer us. They've never stopped trying. Someone has to lose."

Nat didn't seem to hear him.

"For a long while they kept pretty quiet, and we told ourselves what benign occupiers we were. We even kidded ourselves we were benefiting them— their standard of living improved; we kindly let them work for us, doing all the dirtiest jobs, of course— but the obvious fact is and was, we're on their backs and they hate us, so in the end, after twenty years, they got sick of it and started the *intifada,* the uprising.

"And for five years we've been fighting them in their streets, where, in my view, we've no business to be. Now, don't get me wrong. Don't think I don't know what would happen in any other country on earth if mobs of civilians ran at soldiers, cursing and hurling rocks; they'd be mowed down without mercy. But we haven't been so merciful. Hundreds of Palestinians are dead; hundreds more injured, young and old. But in all that time only a handful of our people have been seriously hurt or killed by all their stones. Because whatever they tell you, stones are *not* as lethal as bullets."

Nimrod sat with his hands squeezed between his knees, which were white as two stones themselves. He was not looking at his grandfather.

"But they'd kill all of us if it was the other way around," he muttered.

"I don't doubt it," said Nat. "We're right to be afraid of them. Their religion encourages them to die in battle, and they kill each other more than we kill them . . . they're murdering each other every day. For collaboration, for informing, for feuds, for nothing . . . Don't ask me to explain it. But the *intifada,* I understand that. There's always been only one way to win freedom: through fighting. It's the way we won ours."

"So why don't we give it to them? Why don't we just give it to them? The West Bank, Gaza, Golan—why don't we just let them have it?"

"It is fear, O little hunter. It is fear."

"What are you talking about?"

"It's a poem, Nimrodi," he said gently. "I mean, we don't give it back to them because we're afraid to. It's the hardest thing on earth to hand your enemy an advantage.''

They sat under the vine for a long time. Nat blew his nose one last time and put the handkerchief away. Then he put his arm around his grandson's shoulders. He felt Nimrod unyielding, as stiff as wood, holding himself tight. Old men can cry, soldiers can cry. But boys of sixteen don't cry.

''Do all the soldiers do it?'' Nimrod asked. ''Beating people, killing them?''

Nat shrugged. ''Most of our soldiers don't know what the hell they're doing in those streets,'' he said. ''They're confused, scared; anyone would be. They're trained for battle, not for street riots. They blunder about, pumped full of adrenaline, doing what they think they're supposed to. That's the worst of it. It makes no sense. We go there, they throw stones, we open fire or chase them and beat them—and for what? For what?'' He looked away at the green view of kibbutz gardens. ''For what great purpose was my sweet grandson turned into a brute even for five minutes?''

''Will I have to do it?'' asked Nimrod very quietly.

Nat turned to him fiercely.

''No,'' he said. ''You won't *have* to do it. And don't you do it. Don't you dare to do it and then come crying to me to make you feel better! I told Yoni I understood, but I didn't. I 'forgave' him, whatever that means, when he asked me to, but I've never been able to feel the same about him. I can't go through that again. Maybe I won't be alive to do it when it's your turn!''

Nimrod turned to look at him so suddenly he wrenched his neck, but Nat wasn't looking at him now.

"Shoot and cry, that's what they do—beat and cry. They do it, and then they're sorry, and it makes them feel good to be sorry. But it's not good enough. What's been done, the pain, the hatred, can't be canceled with tears, any more than Glen's death could be canceled if the killer came and begged his mother's pardon. So don't you do it, Nimrod. Don't you ever let anyone make you do it.

"Because, if they turn you into that kind of man, what it means to me—what it's already begun to mean to me—is that I should have stayed in Canada. That it's all been for nothing. That this wonderful country that began so bravely has a cancer eating it. *That's* what your generation has to fight and chase away, Nimrod. Not a bunch of hyped-up kids."

TWENTY-THREE

Lev at Work

Lev, who was doing his after-school work stint in the dates these days, worked partnerless that afternoon. Nimrod hadn't shown up.

Luckily the thorn cutting was nearly finished. The tall mobile ladders—the "elephants"—had to be trundled away to their summer storage. That was boring work—not as boring as the factory but three times as hot, of course. The trouble was, you didn't get paid for this; it was "kibbutz work," and his father was angry with him for opting for it when he could have been earning money.

More and more, though, Lev was feeling he didn't want to move into town with his family when the time came. He'd seen town. Didn't find it appealing, not after this . . .

When he listened, at the high school, to the kids who casually bad-mouthed the kibbutz, calling it boring and claiming they couldn't wait to get out, it hurt him. They talked about "parasites," lazy people who had to be "carried" by others; about the lack of opportunity; about wanting to travel; and, above all, about making money to have cars and clothes and be like Americans. It made Lev mad. All his life in Russia he'd regarded Americans as his enemy. The last thing he wanted to do now was be like one. Since the end of communism Americans thought they ran everything, and that made them dangerous, not enviable. Lev didn't like Coca-Cola, and sometimes he thought the world was drowning in it.

From what he could see, the kibbutz had a lot of problems, but it also had the cure for a lot of problems. There was no crime here. People didn't exploit one another or pollute the environment; they looked after one another. Kids were happy, you didn't have to worry about money or being ill or getting old, and most of the members were decent, honest, and hardworking. Lev felt at home here, even though the others didn't really accept him. So what? By the time he'd been through the army and come back here, he'd be accepted. The rate at which people who'd been born here were leaving, they'd be glad to have him!

Meanwhile, there was school, which Lev loved. He found it infuriating when kids fooled around and disrupted the classes.

Before what Lev thought of as the Nili business, Nimrod had been one of those kids. Once when he started fooling around in class, Lev suddenly lost his temper and shouted, "Shut up, sit down, stop it!" The whole class turned to stare at him, and he blushed a fiery red, but he held his ground. "He is disturb me!" he said.

"What a relief!" said the teacher ironically. "I thought it was only me." The class laughed, and Nimrod, also flushed with embarrassment, settled down. Afterward he tackled Lev, or was going to, but Lev tackled him first.

"Why you make stupidity in the lessons? Why you not want to study?" he asked his friend with quite unusual fierceness.

"Most of it's such boring garbage."

"You are *meshuggah*," Lev retorted. "Not one of it is boring. You are uncultured primitive."

Nimrod's mouth dropped open. "Who are you calling a primitive?"

"You. Only stupid moron don't want education. In Kiev we learn better than here, but here is more free. Now I see free is not so good if it lets to waste time and be insult to teacher."

"Oh, bullshit. I bet you raised hell in class there sometimes!"

"In Kiev we not dream, not *dream*, to behave like you."

Nimrod slouched off, muttering. But it took the Nili business to quiet him down. Since then he had sat in class in silence and done very little, either work or fooling. Lev almost wished he would fool around sometimes, be like his old self. . . .

But one thing he had done was put in a word for Lev with the boss of the dates. Now here he was, and here, today, Nimrod wasn't.

Lev finished his task on his own and walked home through the early June heat, dreaming of a cold

244

shower and a long iced drink. But thoughts of Nimrod intruded. Not like him not to turn up for work. Since the Nili business . . .

Lev promptly stopped dreaming of showers and drinks and began to dream of Nili.

He had not kissed her yet, but he longed to, and something told him she was coming around to him. She liked to be with him. Yesterday something wonderful had happened: she had come to sit with him at lunchtime quite openly, though her usual tablemates (all girls) were at another table, eyeing the pair of them and even whispering, knowingly and maddeningly. But Lev could easily put up with that for the intense pleasure of Nili's company.

He wanted to ask her why she had come to sit with him, but he was afraid to make too much of it, to seem too intense. (This was one of the things Israelis said about the Russians: they were too "intense.") She talked of small things and didn't look at him much. For his part, he couldn't take his eyes off her, especially her beautiful, rich dark hair, falling in the thick fringe on her forehead and in two glossy curtains past her cheeks. Once, when there seemed a danger of one of these locks trailing in her soup, he reached over and gently moved it behind her shoulder. She looked up at him, startled, and he smiled tenderly into her eyes—her indescribable eyes, blue-pollened daisies with thick black eyelash-petals, eyes he passionately wanted to put his lips to, so softly she would scarcely feel it. . . .

He heard the girls giggling at the next table and hastily attacked his pasta, nose well down over the plate, blushing hotly. Nili finished her lunch and picked up her tray.

"See ya," she said.

He looked up. "When?"

"*When?* Around. You know." But she was smiling at him. Did she know how he felt about her? Of course she did; girls did know. But did she know how he longed not just selfishly to kiss and hold her but to take away her sorrow, her guilt, to take it on himself and free her of it as if nothing bad had happened? Did she know that he would bear twice her pain if he only could?

He was reliving this moment and had entirely forgotten Nimrod when he suddenly saw him. He was running hard across a patch of open lawn in the direction of his parents' house.

Lev called him: "Hey! Nimrod!" He slowed for a second but didn't turn or stop. Lev swerved and went after him.

He didn't catch up until the door of the apartment had slammed behind his quarry. He knocked. There was no answer. He walked in.

Nimrod was alone, bent over a desk, rummaging, frantically it seemed, through the papers in the top drawer.

"What are you doing?" asked Lev.

Nimrod looked up at him. His face was very strange and alarming.

"Mind your own business!" he panted wildly.

Lev stood and watched him go through drawer after drawer. Some of the contents fell to the floor, and Lev moved forward and picked things up.

"What you look for?"

"Money!"

"Money of who? Your parents?"

"Yeah, why not? Who cares whose it is?"

"You steal?"

Nimrod stopped rummaging and stood up to face Lev. Now Lev grew seriously alarmed, Nimrod looked so wild and strange.

"What is wrong with you? Something happened?"

"I want to get out of here!" Nimrod shouted.

"But you can't," said Lev flatly. "It take more than money to leave your home."

Nimrod seemed to collapse inwardly. He kicked the lowest drawer shut violently and threw himself into an armchair. He was still breathing hard. Lev sat down near him and waited.

"My cousin Yonatan is an asshole," he said.

"I don't think so."

"You don't know. You don't know what he did."

More silence. Then Nimrod burst out, "And if he could do it, so could I! I know I could. If I had some shitty Arab at my mercy right this minute, I'd do something to him. I'd do something to him so he'd never hold a knife or a stone again. . . ."

His white face was suddenly suffused with bright color like raw meat, and his eyes grew glassy with tears. He dashed them away furiously and said, "I hate them! I hate them for making Yoni do that, for making me feel how I feel—"

Lev said softly, "Please forgive Nili now. Can't you?"

Nimrod threw him a look of astonishment.

"This is just *the* wrong time to ask, isn't it?"

"No. Is the right time."

"Yoni said it too. Only why should I do what he says anymore?"

After a moment to think, Lev said, "If he did bad, if he is asshole, he has to know how it's important to forgive. Himself first."

"He shouldn't ever forgive himself."

"You said you could do it too, what it ever was."

"But if I did it or anything like it, I wouldn't forgive myself. I'd be guilty forever."

"No. No one is guilty forever."

"Shtuyot! Shtuyot!" shouted Nimrod. "So we do something terrible and someone forgives us and then we forgive ourselves and then it's all over?"

"Yes, or we couldn't live, because we all do bad things."

"Some a lot worse than others! What about those bastards who killed Glen? You telling me they'll get over it?"

"Ah, them. They don't have nothing to get over. They think they done a great thing, kill the enemy."

"A little kid—"

"A little kid who will grow into a big kid who will be a soldier and come to sit on their backs."

Nimrod said nothing. He stood up and closed the desk drawers. Lev, sensing that the crisis was over, said, "Let's go shoot basketball."

They went out together. Nimrod said as they walked along, "Sorry I wasn't at work."

"Okay. The elephants went good into their houses."

They went to the basketball court. There were others before them, and they had to wait. They sat on a bench, and after a bit Nimrod said quietly, "Do you think that's what our soldiers figure when they shoot a Palestinian kid: that they're killing a future soldier?''

"Is not the same. They shoot because the kid throw stones and it make them mad. The kids is part of the fight now. Glen don't throw stones, don't do nothing, just walk in the street."

"So it's worse, what they did."

"Of course."

"A lot worse."

"Maybe. I tell you after I go in the army."

"I wish—" He stopped.

"What you wish?"

"I dunno. I wish . . . it was all over. I wish it would stop and be over. I wish the bloody Arabs would just let us live our lives."

That wasn't what he'd really wished. He'd wished he were sure that it was worse to kill Glen than to kill a Palestinian kid, that throwing stones made that much difference.

But at least Yoni had been sorry. At least he didn't think he'd done a great thing. At least he'd changed and become a different man.

Nimrod wondered if the murderers of Glen had cried and become different men.

TWENTY-FOUR

The Informer

Mustapha was on the run.

It wasn't because he knew the police and the army were closing in on him, which they were. He had not yet heard about Feisal's arrest. Nobody knew of this yet.

The Israelis had been clever in trapping the younger man. If they had gone straight to the house where he was hiding and ransacked it, as they sometimes ransacked such places, with all the village watching, and then marched their prisoner away, the whole country would have known about it within hours.

Instead, they had cunningly induced Feisal to leave the house and run to the edge of the village, where a carefully concealed ambush was waiting. They had captured him with minimum noise or fuss, simply throwing a blanket over him, handcuffing him, bundling him into a waiting car carefully hidden, and driving him away. The only person who saw this happen was a shepherd crouched behind some rocks, and he knew better than to mention it. In such situations, where there is danger from all sides, including one's own, a quiet tongue is gold.

No. Mustapha still had the hope that Feisal had got clean away. Even his mother had no idea where her son was. He had simply disappeared in the night about two days after the incident in Gilo, and she had heard nothing since. Heard nothing and wanted to hear nothing. Until the whole thing had calmed down, she was a pillar of silence, as if Feisal had never existed. But Mustapha could tell, from a certain look in her eyes, that she was proud of her son.

She said only one thing about the incident.

"Why didn't you kill the girl too?"

"Allah didn't will it" was all Mustapha said.

When Mustapha first got back after being released, his brother-in-law was far from pleased to see him. He had always disliked him, and not hidden his dislike, but now to his usual simmering hostility some new factor was added.

Mustapha supposed it was the disappearance of Feisal. Feisal was the only child of this marriage, a bitter enough blow for a man; but apart from any question of affection, he had worked in his father's fields and in his bakery, and now he was gone. With some justice, his father blamed the whole business on Mustapha. From the moment Mustapha reentered the house, his brother-in-law was like a cat on hot bricks.

At one point the first evening he tried to say something to Mustapha, but his wife gave him a look that silenced him before the first words were out. Mustapha guessed he wanted him to leave. But although Fatma was a pattern of Muslim obedience and service, Mustapha had lived in this family long enough to know who ruled. As long as Fatma wished her brother to remain, he would stay.

The trouble was, the Jews knew where he lived. They could pick him up here at any time. Yet if he left, they would take that as an indication of guilt. On balance, it was better to stay at home and act normally—unless anything happened.

He resumed his life. With Feisal gone, there was plenty to do in the family fields, where they grew eggplants, peppers, and other vegetables. But he kept very alert. He knew there was a watcher, probably a paid informer. He was suspicious of everyone around him, except his sister, whom he trusted.

One evening, after he came home from work, he had an unusually intimate conversation with her.

They were alone, and she was doing her cooking in her usual silent way. He sat at the table in the adjoining room (the kitchen was a tiny earth-floored annex) waiting to be served his dinner, reading a newspaper. Suddenly he said, without knowing he was going to say it, "Do you know if our mother is still living?"

Fatma, through the open doorway, answered at once. "Yes."

He looked up. "How do you know?"

"I get word sometimes."

"How?"

"People come and go across the bridge. Messages can be sent."

He digested this in silence. She meant the Allenby Bridge connecting Israel with Jordan.

"And our sisters?"

"Yes, why not? They are younger than we are."

"So you keep in touch and have never told me?"

"You never asked. I thought you'd forgotten."

He turned a page of the newspaper so as not to seem too interested.

"They still live in the old village near the river?"

"Why not?"

"Are they well?"

"They're hard up. How else, with no father to provide dowries? They had to marry where they could."

"They're all married?"

"Yes. Nabila is a grandmother."

He turned in his seat. She must be joking! He almost laughed at the preposterousness of it. Nabila! He remembered her, the next oldest after him, the one who had followed him around and pestered him, a little skinny thing ... Nabila!

"How could she be—a grandmother? It's nonsense!"

"Nonsense? Why? She's nearly forty. If my husband had given me a daughter at eighteen, I would have grandchildren."

He fell into an astounded silence. Nabila, a middle-aged woman! Little Nabila!

When the meal was set before him, he was surprised. It was rather lavish: meat-filled *kubeh* and four kinds of salad, including his favorite, cream cheese puddled with green olive oil and sprinkled with *za'atar*.

"What's this? So much?"

"Sayid made some extra on a deal. I found the money, and I made him give me most of it. I was surprised how much."

Mustapha tucked into the good food without more ado. He was too busy thinking about the strange unexpected news about his family to think about Sayid's sudden wealth. But when, the next day and the next, the food on the table was lavish, suddenly a warning rang in his head.

"More deals?" he asked his brother-in-law.

He nodded with a strange anxiousness in his manner and talked earnestly about how he had sold a big order of cakes to a stallholder in the Jerusalem Old City market for a wedding.

"Business is very good," he concluded, his fingers twitching.

"Not for many. You're lucky."

"It's about time," said Sayid. But his appetite was oddly small, and he was irritable and jumpy.

Now a dread suspicion that wouldn't be shaken off entered Mustapha's mind.

Would they have dared? His own brother-in-law? The thought was like explosives hidden in his head. He was afraid to look, to investigate, to find out, lest they blow up. For what must he do if it were true?

It was Fatma who confirmed it.

She came out to the field to find Mustapha a few days later. He saw her striding strongly in her long dress. She seldom moved fast. He stopped work and waited for her to reach him. He saw at once there was something wrong.

"You must leave," she said breathlessly. "Now.

Today. I have packed some things, very little, what you can easily carry.''

Fear thrilled through him. "Is Feisal taken?"

"Not that I've heard. But you must go just the same."

They looked at each other. Fatma, who had no fear, who had the inner strength belonging to a man, was now afraid. She, who never showed her feelings, grasped his arm and shook it, her eyes beseeching.

"Go."

"What's happened?"

"Just go."

Something in her face lit the fuse, and the fire began to race and sizzle toward the dynamite in his head.

"Sayid is the informer," he said slowly.

She turned away, clutching her hands to her chest. "I didn't say so. I didn't say so!"

"Deny it then."

She couldn't speak.

He brushed past her and ran back to the house.

It was empty. He found the bundle she had packed and picked it up. Then he looked around for what more he needed. He found it in the kitchen.

He left the house where he had lived for years without a backward glance and walked through the village to the bakery on its farther edge. He hid the bundle, so as not to arouse Sayid's suspicion. The very instant he had made the fatal discovery, he had cut himself off from any family feeling for the man, not thinking "brother-in-law" now but "betrayer."

With one arm stiffly held to his side, he walked in through the back of the shop, where the ovens were.

Sayid was alone there, pouring liquid syrup on a big round tray of baklava, exquisitely cut into a pattern like a magnified circular piece of woven cloth. He turned as Mustapha came in, and his nervous smile fell off his face.

He dropped the syrup jug on the floor and backed away, waving his hands, until he was backed against the long table where the leaf pastry was drawn out and rolled to the thinness of paper. He was a small, thin man, and Mustapha was able to put the knife in swiftly between two high ribs, but still the traitor's face burst into a hideous grimace of shock and agony. One hand, sticky with syrup, pushed against Mustapha's mouth so that he tasted sweetness. The other tried to tear out the blade. It was a long knife thrust in to the hilt, so the point came out of his back, and the snowy pastry on the table got spattered with blood.

Now Mustapha was running.

He had abandoned the bundle and walked out of the village, so as not to attract special attention. But once clear of it, he began to run as fast as he could.

He had a plan. He hadn't known he was making this plan, but it must have been for this that he had asked his questions about his mother and sisters.

He had to get out of Israel. He had to get back to his starting place, back to his birth village. There, with a mother and four married sisters, he might be safe—if he could evade the authorities on both sides, for the Jordanians would arrest him as fast as the Israelis if they saw him trying to cross the border, the border that was the river Jordan.

Instinctively he knew that his best hope was to try to work his way north up the line of the river. He must keep as near to it as possible (which was not very near, as its Israeli bank was mined, wired off, and guarded along most of its length) until he came to the point opposite to where his birth village lay on the far side. If he could cross *there,* he would have a good chance of slipping into the village without being seen by a Jordanian army or border patrol, because it was only about a mile from the river's edge.

Luck favored him. Quite soon he diverted around a village and, in a shed at the back of a barn, found a bicycle.

TWENTY-FIVE

Bruises

When Noah got back from his latest trip away
from the kibbutz and walked into his apartment, he noticed at once that something was
different. It wasn't Valerie herself, because she
was sitting with her back to him in an armchair, in front of the television, and didn't get
up to greet him. It was the room.

Noah looked around it with dismay. Onto
the plain furnishing had been imposed all
kinds of alien objects.

Prominently displayed on the whitewashed
wall was a big multicolored oil painting of
Jerusalem. There was a gaudy Persian rug
on the gray-tiled floor and a copper-based
lamp looking top-heavy on a tiny table. And
on every shelf and flat surface, standing uncomfortably on edge, were bright hand-
painted Armenian plates. The room, which
before had been utilitarian, nondescript, but

homely, now looked outlandish, overdecorated. Bizarre.

It wasn't as if he hadn't explained it all to her, as well as he could, when he had returned from Jerusalem that time. He'd told her he'd bought a whole lot of useless, stupid things that he didn't want and had no use for. He couldn't cancel them because he couldn't remember where he'd bought them. As to why, he said it was a compulsion. "Therapy?" she had asked, seeming to understand, and he had said gratefully, "That's it, therapy."

But now, while he'd been away in his rented car, these awful tokens of his fit of craziness had been delivered, and instead of just dumping them somewhere or sending them back, Valerie had accepted them and set them all out.

"Well?" said her voice over the back of the chair. "What do you think?"

"Why did you do it?" he asked.

"A surprise for you."

A surprise. A punishment more like.

"I told you—"

"Yes, I know. But you see I knew you were lying."

Dismay turned to alarm. "Lying? Why on earth should I lie?"

"Naturally, you wouldn't want me to realize at once that you want to go on living here. That your buying these ... objects ... was like a woman buying things for her new home."

Having dropped this bombshell, she switched off the TV and got up and came around the chair to face

him. He gasped. She had an ugly lump on her forehead and two black eyes in a face as livid as cheese.

"Val! My God, what's—"

"Oh, this?" She touched the lump. "I got that
banging my head on the floor. And nobody hit me;
my eyes went black by themselves from the banging,
Donna said. Your Donna is a neat gal when the cards
are down, isn't she? She's a good nurse too. She
knew exactly what to do."

Noah had nothing to say. He averted his eyes from
her. He didn't know he'd gone as pale as she was.

"A tranquilizing jab. Just the thing. Then she
brought me home. 'Rest and I'll be in to see you
later,' she said. 'Tell Noah you walked into a door.'
But I figured, the truth shall make you free. Well,
me, anyway."

He ignored this. "Does it hurt?"

"No. Nothing hurts just now. Must be the jab.
Well, look around. Do you like your little gray home
in the Middle East?"

He needed to sit down. She watched him while he
did, and there was quite a long silence. Then he said,
"Well, I went a bit crazy. It was your turn. Who can
blame you?"

He felt suddenly weak with emotion. He subdued
it and stood up again.

"What about a drink?"

"What about a cuddle, pal?" she said quietly.
"Wouldn't that be more like it? Tender loving kisses
on my self-inflicted bruises?"

He came and put his arms around her and held
her, but he felt empty, and she knew it.

After a moment she moved away and said flatly, "I guess a drink would be better after all."

She poured them both a drink from a bottle of local brandy that Nat had quietly left for them. Neither of them liked brandy or usually drank much at all, but they both drank this rather fast. Noah, glancing at her, felt afraid without knowing why. Something shattering was coming. What was it?

"Where have you been?" she asked conversationally.

"Nablus. Jericho. East Jerusalem."

"Ah. Arab watching again?"

"Yes."

"Tell me, what are you hoping to get out of all this? You're not hoping to spot . . . him, are you? The one out of all of them who killed Glen? I mean, we're both a little nuts, but are you that far gone?"

"Val, it's important to me."

"So I gathered. Only, if you must leave me alone for hours and days on end, while you go Arab watching, I'd like to know more."

"I suppose . . . No, of course, not him. But in my eyes a lot of them look alike. They've got a—a look. Especially when they're looking at me. I look into their eyes and try to understand where we are with them."

"Do you show yourself to them or just drive on by?"

"No. I don't drive by. I park the car, usually in the middle of a town, and I get out and walk around, and . . . look at them. And look at them looking back at me."

"In Nablus and East Jerusalem."

261

"Yes."

"In a rented car with Israeli plates."

"Yes."

"You do know that's not safe."

He said nothing.

"If anything were to happen to you," she said in the same brightly conversational tone, "how do you suppose I'd feel about that? No, I'm only asking. My son killed. Then my husband. I mean, have you thought anything about that? About me?"

He hung his head. At last he said, in a tone of desperation, "If only—if they'd only find . . . the right Arab, if I could see him face-to-face, I wouldn't feel compelled to do this."

He saw her jaw stiffen. "You know what?" she said. "You're acting like a lunatic. An irresponsible lunatic. First you go out and buy up half of Jerusalem. Then you put yourself in the way of getting yourself hurt, or worse. Perhaps you want to leave your bones in this killer country with Glen's, add your blood to all the blood this piece of earth has soaked up?"

She put her hand over her face very sharply, almost slapping herself. Then she swiftly pulled it down and sat very deliberately facing him.

"Noah, look at me, please."

He looked up.

"I made a complete, total spectacle of myself today. I accused your first wife of trying to get you back, of trying to steal Dale away from me. Then I fell down and started banging my head on the floor. I think I may have done this in front of Nimrod."

Noah dragged air into his lungs. It was deeper than a sigh.

"I told you once before, Noah. Or was it more than once? I want to leave here. I want to go home. *I am going* home."

"What do you mean?" he asked quickly.

"Well, I don't seem to have much of a family anymore. I don't have my son because he's dead. My daughter is changing from my cute little caterpillar into a kibbutz butterfly. As for you, I don't think I have much of you anymore either."

"Valerie, that's not—"

"But you're not my only family. I've got another one. A mom and a dad, and a sister and a brother. They're all still around. . . . I phoned Mom today, when I got back from my head banging. She said I was to come home, that they'd pay, that I could stay with them. I asked her to book me on to the first flight available after tomorrow."

"You? Just—you?"

"Yes," she said, watching him steadily.

"What about Dale?"

"Who?" she asked politely. "Oh! Do you mean *Dahlia?*" She drew the name out, *Daaaaahlia.* "Well, no. I'm not taking Dahlia because she wouldn't want to come. She wants to stay here. In the kibbutz. With her Nimrod and her Nili and her Yo-na-tan. And her wonderful diet that is shrinking her before my eyes."

Noah thought if she didn't drop this casual bright tone of voice, he might start yelling at her. He knew he would never forgive himself if he did. So he said as quietly as he could, "What makes you think I'll agree to your going without me?"

"What makes you think I'll wait for your agreement? Our marriage is over, Noah."

The words hit him like ice water straight in the face. It wasn't even the words so much. It was the awful truth of them that he hadn't known.

He was winded, speechless. She took his glass from him and carried it to the sink to wash it. While her back was turned to him, he muttered, "And what, in your opinion, is going to happen to me?"

"Oh, that's easy," she said, drying the glasses. "You have to make up for having run away before. You'll stay here in Israel. You'll try to win back the respect of your parents and your sister. And maybe even the love of the only son you've got left. And you'll probably do it, just by not being a *yored* anymore—isn't that the word? An emigrant, a deserter, which you've been all these years? The worst mistake I ever made in my life was to encourage you to be a *yored*. It's something you've never forgiven me for."

Noah stood very still. She didn't love him. Had Glen's death—and the part Noah had played in it, by insisting he come here—broken her love, or had it started breaking before? Still, he marveled at how well she knew him. She knew and understood him better than anyone living.

He thought, *This is the ultimate irony of my messed-up life.* Donna, the Roman Catholic, still here, roots down, an Israeli. Valerie, the Jewish wife, hating Israel with all her heart, taking him away from it once, and fleeing from it again because she sensed, before he knew it himself, that now—probably far too late—he wanted to stay.

TWENTY-SIX

The Shoplifter

Dale was in the kibbutz store, the *col-bo*. She was shoplifting.

She walked slowly around the shelves, looking at the displays with her hands innocently behind her back. When she thought she was out of sight of the old kibbutz lady who was sitting knitting at the checkout counter by the door, she snatched some chocolate bars and stuffed them quickly into her jeans pockets. There was plenty of room in them since she had lost two and a half pounds in two weeks.

When she had as many as she dared take—three in one pocket, four in the other—she strolled toward the exit. Her hands were shaking, and her heart was beating so hard she thought the woman must see it knocking bumps in her chest. On the way she picked up the first thing that came to hand—a package of balloons—and toyed with it for a while as if trying to decide whether to buy it.

"You have a birthday, Dahlia?" asked the lady kindly.

This seemed a good reason to be looking at balloons. "Yes."

"*Mazal tov!* You are what age?"

"Eight. Nine." The lady blinked. "I mean, I will be nine next birthday."

"Good. Good," said the lady blandly, and added, "How you are thinner now!" and gestured admiringly.

Dale hesitated. She half wanted the lady to stop her, take the chocolate bars away. If she did that, perhaps she could take away the terrible feelings that were eating Dale up inside. But she just smiled, and Dale walked out.

Two minutes after she'd left, the checkout lady left too, locking the store behind her, and hurried to the clinic, where Donna was doing her morning stint.

"It looks as if your little protégée is about to break her diet," she said, and told her what Dale had been doing.

Donna wasted no time. She asked two waiting patients to come back later and she too shut up shop and took to her bicycle.

She went first to Noah and Valerie's apartment. She didn't want to go there, but she went anyway. She knocked. Valerie came to the door. When she saw Donna, something like a smile crossed her bruised face.

"Hi," she said.

"Hi. How are you today?"

"Okay. Better. I'm packing."

"Oh?"

"Yep. I'm flying back to Canada tomorrow."

"All of you?"

"No. Just me."

Donna didn't show her intense curiosity and puzzlement. She just said, "Is Dale here?"

"Is she ever? No. I haven't seen her since early morning."

Donna excused herself. After that she had to think, to put herself in Dale's place. Where would she go to be private for an illegal binge of stolen chocolate bars?

She found her eventually. In the cemetery—almost the last place she thought to look. It seemed very strange, very pitiful to see the little girl sitting by her brother's grave, still without a marker, just a heap of raw earth covered with dead flowers, stuffing herself grimly with one chocolate bar after another. Her face was smeared with chocolate and tears and the product of a runny nose. She was still heaving with aftersobs. Almost the most poignant thing was that she had smoothed the wrappers out one by one and spread them on the mound. An offering.

Donna, after watching the scene for a few minutes from a distance, almost overpowered with sadness, laid her bike on the ground and went to sit beside Dale. Dale didn't seem to notice her and stuffed the last bit of chocolate into her mouth. There was a moment's pause, and then her stomach rebelled. She managed to twist herself away from the grave just in time.

Donna held her forehead. When it was over, Dale

just crouched there on hands and knees, panting, worn-out.

"What is all this, kiddo?" Donna asked, stroking her hair.

"Mom's going!" Dale gasped furiously. "She's going to leave me here!"

Donna said nothing for a moment, looking past her at the chocolate wrappers on the side of the grave.

"Did you tell Glen?"

"Yeah," said Dale bitterly. "But what's the use? He can't hear. He's dead. What'd he have to go and get killed for and make everyone crazy?"

"Who's crazy?"

"Mom and Daddy, that's who! Daddy keeps going off, and Mom's going home to live with Granny and Gramps, and I'm staying here because *she doesn't want me!*"

Donna let a renewed bout of sobbing play itself out. Then she sat Dale up with firm hands. The temptation to wipe all that gunk off her face was almost overpowering, but she held back. It would be good for Valerie to see this, to see how vitally important she was to the one child she had left.

"I think you've got it wrong, babe. Come on."

She stood up and pulled Dale to her feet.

"Where're we going?"

"To straighten a few things out with your folks."

Later—quite a lot later, when a few home truths had been aired and Dale's immediate future, as Dale and not Dahlia, had been settled—there was a knock on Yonatan's door. It was his father.

"*Ahalan,* Aba," said Yonatan, his heart jolting in

his chest. Here it came, perhaps—the heart-to-heart he had dreaded. It had to happen before his father left for home.

"What's this *ahalan* business?" Noah asked curiously. "Whatever happened to *shalom?*"

"Old-fashioned. It's trendy to say *ahalan* now."

"But that's Arabic, isn't it? The Arab greeting."

"Sure, why not?"

"Seems odd to me."

"Aunt Lesley told me the Arabs say to her, 'You've taken our land, you live in our houses, you eat our food, and now you're stealing our language.'" He gave a wry shrug. "That's how it is with conquerors, I guess. Sit down, Aba. Want something—coffee?"

"No, thanks. I came to tell you what's happening, so you won't get it from gossip. So here's the story. Your stepmother's leaving for home tomorrow and taking Dale with her. But I'm staying."

Yonatan turned away to hide his confused feelings. Good news—bad news? He just didn't know.

"You're staying. Why's that?"

"I have unfinished business here."

There was a brief pause, and then he said, "Actually, some more important news came just now. They've caught Glen's killer."

Yonatan jumped up in a spasm of excitement and then sank down again, ashamed that he was so much more moved by *this* piece of information.

"Both of them?"

"No. The younger one. The one who—"

"And the other?"

"They'll get him. They know who he is. The boy talked right away. It's his uncle."

"And is he—"

"The one Nili . . . couldn't identify? Yes, as it happens, it is. But, Yoni, I hope we can all agree to regard that as—as a natural . . . mistake. He probably looked different when she saw him in the lineup."

Yoni looked down. "Sure," he said. "Sure."

"Could easily happen. And nobody around here needs to know it was the same one."

"If only the police and the press don't cause unnecessary trouble."

"We can still pass it off as a mistake. I don't blame Nili, and if I don't, nobody else has the right to."

Father and son sat silent for a while. Then Yoni looked up. "When you say you're staying, you don't mean here? In Kfar Orde?"

"You got something against it?"

Yoni flushed. "It's not that. It's just—I mean, what would you do in kibbutz? It'd never work."

"I've quit my job, of course," Noah said casually, as if throwing away some empty piece of packaging.

"Seriously? Why? It's your life."

"It has been. Far too much so. Now I'm going to try for a new one."

"But not here!"

"Tell me why not. One reason."

Yoni drew a deep breath.

"You're a successful man; you're a *macher;* you're used to a rich, luxurious Western lifestyle. How can you turn around and give it all up at your age?"

"My father did."

"Things were very different then."

"I don't see much difference. The outside world we both operated in is still the same, or worse. Israel's still here. The kibbutz is still here."

"Barely."

"What do you mean?"

"Dad, I hate to break it to you; you've been completely turned another way since you got here or you'd have noticed. The kibbutz movement is played out. Finished. On its last legs anyway."

Noah looked astounded. "Rubbish."

"Oh, no. It's not rubbish. Why do you think practically all of my generation—post-army youth—is leaving? They're sick of it. Don't see the point of it anymore. The pioneering, the ideology—finished. Isms that have served their turn. We want something better."

"Better. How better?"

"Our parents and grandparents built all this, set it up for us. Where's the challenge? Anyway, a lot of us want to travel and get ahead. It's too small for us, kibbutz. Besides, we're all kind of demoralized because it's just not what it used to be."

"If you feel that, why are you still here?"

Yoni said, "Because of Ilana. It'll take time to shift her!" But he said it as if that weren't the whole answer. Noah waited. "Well, things are changing fast. Of course, you know most kibbutzim are up to their hair roots in debt because of all their dud investments in the eighties. To hell with ideologies, they've got to start being practical. There's talk of incentives, permanent management jobs, more industry, less farming. And even differential salaries—"

"*What?* Paying people different rates for different jobs? But what would make it a kibbutz if—"

"Dad, that's the point. If the kibbutz is going to survive, it's got to get rid of all that baggage about equality and move with the times. Capitalism's won more than the Cold War. The kibbutz will be nothing but a history village or a museum if we don't make some pretty drastic changes."

Noah frowned at him. "What on earth does your granddad make of all this?"

"He thinks it stinks. Complete betrayal of principle. But nobody listens to the old people."

"More's the pity," said Noah. But he looked very thoughtful. "Kibbutz capitalism! A commune for the nineties . . . needing management skills and financial advice . . . You know what, son? Maybe I'm not going to be so out of place after all."

Yoni gazed at him. All the pain and resentment of his fatherless upbringing swept over him. "Mom always said you go the way the wind blows."

If this thrust hurt Noah, he didn't show it. "Well, this might just be a wind that would suit me. Speaking of your mother . . . has she lived alone all these years?"

"I think that's something you should ask her. But if you have any ideas about getting back together with her, Dad, forget it."

Noah met his eyes. "And you? Have I hope of getting back together with you?"

Yoni, embarrassed, stood up and moved away. "You don't know me, Aba," he said in Hebrew.

"I'm the son of your body, but you don't know me at all."

"I'd like to get to."

Yoni was silent. His father had spent his life out in a cutthroat world, he'd seen enough of how people acted in that world to have lost his illusions, up to a point. But if his son were to turn around now and say, "I've shot at unarmed people in the streets. I've beaten up helpless prisoners. Do you still want to get to know me better?" he knew he would see in his father's eyes all the shock and horror of a man who knew nothing, actually, about the realities of survival. To take away a man's last illusions is a terrible thing—even if he is the father who ran out on you.

If he stays, thought Yoni, *if he really lives here, becomes Israeli, he'll find out gradually; he may be able to understand. Meanwhile, it's not his forgiveness I need. What does he know?*

"Aba, don't you think we'd better . . . just see how it goes?"

Noah, who, from the profound hunger and pain of his heart, desperately longed to embrace his son, withstood the longing because he knew he had no right. He stood up too and moved with dragging reluctance to the door.

"Is the computer okay?" he asked as casually as he could.

"Sure. Thanks. It's the best."

"Good. Good." Noah's feet seemed to be rooted to the tiles. "Will you come and say good-bye to your sister?"

"Of course."

"She loves you like mad," he said with a tremor

273

in his voice. "You've been great with her. She'll miss you."

"She'll miss the kibbutz."

Noah, in the doorway, gave a rueful smile. "She'll be back. One day. We'll have to make sure it's still around for her."

Nili was once again sitting on one of the little kids' swings when she saw her uncle coming toward her.

He had waved at her half an hour before, signaled "Stay there, wait for me!" So she'd stayed and swung and waited, though as the minutes passed, she grew restless and uneasy. What did he want with her? Could it be anything to do with . . . her secret?

By the time he came back she was all jittery. She'd stopped pushing herself back and forth with that soothing motion, and her hands were sweating on the chains.

He smiled at her—his sweet, sad smile that she could hardly bear, it churned her insides up so badly—and sat on the next swing. It was evening; all the little kids had gone. Their playground was empty, and she and her uncle, giants on the little swings, were alone in the sunset.

"Thanks for waiting," Noah said. "I wanted to talk to you."

Nili said nothing. She looked at the scuffed ground under her feet. Her guilt was growing again inside her, her double guilt, and with Glen's father next to her, *Out out out!* wasn't working.

"Nil," he said slowly, "I think I know a little of what you're going through."

She became absolutely still. She didn't raise her eyes.

"Would you like to tell me?"

She shook her head fiercely. Tears were coming— telltale tears. Oh, what was he doing? What did he want from her? A confession that would damn her forever in his eyes? She'd held it in so tight, so long. If she let it out now, it would burst like hot lava and burn them all up—herself first!

Noah said gently, "Okay, darling, don't say anything. Let me say it. I *know*. About the lineup. I've known a long time, and I don't blame you. I did at first, you know, that awful day in Jerusalem when I was so angry and when I scared you and your mom, but then I began to understand . . . what a basically kind, brave, generous thing it was for you to do."

She looked at him now, through a prism of tears. He was like a fantasy person in a rainbow—a magic rescuer.

He reached between the swings and hugged her to him, chains and all.

"Oh, you poor little scrap!" he muttered in her ear. "Don't you realize the whole thing was down to me?"

"You?" she faltered.

"Of course. I should have traveled with you. I should have taken proper care of you both. Everything that happened, everything you've suffered, could have been avoided if—"

She pulled back. "You mean, you forgive me?"

"No. Because there's nothing to forgive. I want you to forgive me for putting you through all this misery."

Nili stood up. It was so strange. She did it without the slightest physical effort, as if her sheer, sudden lightness had lifted her to her feet. A little more of it, and she would rise in the air like a helium balloon.

Noah stood up too, more slowly, and took her hand. "I'm not going back to Canada," he said.

Nili gasped with happiness. "Uncle! You will stay with us? And Dale too?"

"Not Dale," he said heavily. "She's going home with her mother."

She stared at him, questions forming in her mouth. But she had learned how not to say things that might do damage. She squeezed her uncle's hand, and he smiled and offered her his handkerchief to blow her nose.

TWENTY-SEVEN

The Big Bang

On the night in June when the Israeli general election results were announced, there were two loud bangs to disturb the rejoicings in Kibbutz Kfar Orde. One was, in reality, nothing that mattered, but it gave everyone a terrible fright. The second was something more serious, but nobody took any particular notice of it.

The election campaign had been fiercely fought in the cities. In the kibbutz the politically active members went in buses to Jerusalem to demonstrate. Nearly all of them would vote for the peace parties anyway, so there wasn't much campaigning within the kibbutz.

But Nat campaigned energetically, although the tragedy in his family had interrupted his efforts. He hated the sitting government with a deadly hatred. He feared that the young people, those in the top high school class, who

277

were old enough to vote for the first time, didn't realize how important this election was, might not bother, or might cast their votes flippantly. They seemed, many of them, totally bored with politics. To Nat this was an outrage against democracy.

He called a meeting in the high school dining hall and lots of kids came, not only the top class, because they knew Nat believed in reconciliation and peace with the Palestinians, and they didn't see how he still could.

"If we don't get this bunch out, we can kiss all possibility of a peace settlement good-bye!" he cried in his imperfect Hebrew. "They're stalling! They can't face the problems of peace! It's so much easier to keep the hatred and mistrust going, to demonize the other side, to refuse to understand that the Palestinians have a case and need a state of their own! The only thing that will ever make it change is if we put ourselves in their shoes and try to recognize their humanity!"

"You can still say that? After what happened?"

"Yes! Yes! Yes!" cried Nat, banging the table.

"Explain to us. We don't see it."

He straightened up, summoned his strength, and spoke from his heart.

"If you stand on the tel of Kfar Orde and look south, you can see the broken remains of a bridge that once linked us with the other side of the Jordan. It was just a little footbridge. My dream is to build it again, to have our people and theirs crossing it, both ways. It's the only way we can be secure, the only way we can survive!"

278

*"I'd feel more secure building a nuclear bomb!" called a voice from the back.

It was a kind of black joke, and although nobody laughed, there was a faint murmur of agreement from a few. Then they saw the look on Nat's face, and there was a moment of absolute silence.

Then he exploded.

"Be ashamed, you young fool! What are you saying? Do you want to destroy everything we've built? To make this beautiful, historic, precious land uninhabitable and littered with burned-up children? Think, think! Use your imaginations! In destroying them, we destroy ourselves! They are like us! No worse, no better!"

"They are worse than us! We don't go stabbing their children in the streets!"

"We shoot them instead! Does that make us morally superior?"

"We shoot them when they attack us! We're fighters! They're killers!"

"What would you do, you, you, each of you, if they'd been on our backs for twenty-five years? Would you be sitting quiet or would you be out there throwing rocks? You, who talk about nuclear bombs, you call yourself superior?"

The meeting ended in uproar.

Later Nat added more, in his head: *When I hear such things, I know that to kill one child is not the worst. You may be killing children too a year from now if we can't settle things!* But he didn't say that. Not to these students on the brink of their army service, many of them deeply afraid in their hearts, though afterward he thought, *I should have. But they were already angry with me. You can't convince the young by making them angry. Perhaps you can't convince them at all. They have to find their own way. They are unreachable.*

Yet Nat and others like him had their effect, because on election day, Nat's side—a coalition of left-wing parties—won. Not by much—a narrow margin—but the leader who was not interested in making peace was ousted, and another, who claimed he was, was elected. And those who believed in compromise and coexistence, and who still had faith in good sense and reconciliation, rejoiced and allowed themselves to entertain a new hope after the long years of stalemate and frustration and, for many like Nat, shame.

Lev burst into Nili's room in the high school without knocking.

He'd never done such a thing before, but now he was too excited to let a mere door stand in his way. He was already shouting with triumph before he threw it open.

"We did it! *We* did it, we Russkis, it was our vote that made the difference, what do you say to us n—"

He stopped dead on the threshold.

Nili was standing there in nothing but her little white panties, looking so beautiful, so beautiful that the breath was knocked out of him.

He should have retreated, she should have snatched something up to cover herself, but neither of them moved. He gazed at her spellbound for a few timeless seconds, paralyzed by her sweet loveliness exposed to him and not hidden, no, she was not hiding, she was letting him see her, look his fill . . .

But he must stop looking, he must behave properly, and so must she, and as if by common consent, she slowly turned her back, and he slowly turned his. And they stood there, with their backs to each other, he with the image of her beauty still stirring him, and she, without conscious thought knowing that what had been in his eyes was exactly what she had been lacking until now, not sorry that he had seen her and that she had let him look at her—not a bit sorry.

But what now?

In both of them was the longing to turn, to move toward each other, to embrace. But he didn't, and she didn't. For him it was not right to take advantage of this moment, which in any case was enough and more than enough for now, enough to fill his dreams to the brim for the next little space of time, days or weeks, before moving closer to her, step by slow, loving step, closer and closer, as now he surely would. . . .

For her, there was a shadow of disappointment. She was used to another kind of boy, the kind who saw his opportunity and seized it, who didn't see any reason to hold back from what was apparently offered or even just available.

Nili had been kissed by several boys in the dark after parties, just because it was time—she was nearly fifteen—it was time, and the boys did what boys do: They grabbed and they kissed. . . . It wasn't right for her, but it was the expected thing, what other girls did, part of the local behavior. Now she knew what had been wrong, and she knew she would kiss no one till Lev and, the way she felt now, no one after him either. The disappointment vanished, and she drew in a deep, happy breath.

Briskly she put on her Sabbath shirt and pulled on her best jeans. "Lev, you can turn around now," she said lightly.

He turned. She was smiling. He smiled back with the whole of his face. Though part of him longed to see her again as she had been before, he was glad she had got dressed. It was right for them.

"I can to take you to the party?" he asked.

"Sure. I'll be proud to go with one of the Russians who won us the election," she said, and offered him her hand.

As they walked together to the bus that would take them back to the kibbutz, to the celebrations, he said, "Where's Nimrod?"

"He got a lift back with some other boys, earlier," she said. "A 'good' lift, not a *tramp.*"

"Did he—has he said anything to you?"

"No. But he kind of—things are better anyway." She gave him a shy look. "Since they caught him, the one who did it, everyone's—nobody's—people feel better."

Lev squeezed her hand and let it go as they came into sight of the others. That was one good thing anyhow.

But they hadn't caught the other man yet. They were still looking for him. When they did catch him, what then? Would her deed be revealed? Would her misery be renewed tenfold?

Suddenly, halfway to the bus stop, Nili came to a

halt. She didn't look at Lev but clutched his hand again and stared away across the fields, unseeingly.

"What?" he asked anxiously.

"I want to tell you something," she said.

"So, tell me."

She stood perfectly still, as if entirely alone, frozen in her thought. When she spoke, her voice seemed to come from a distant place.

"In the morning," she said, "before we got the plane to come home, me and ... Glen ... we had a fight."

There was a long pause. The bus had come, and some kids getting aboard were waving at them to hurry, but Nili didn't see them, and Lev took no notice. He was listening with the deepest part of himself to what she was trying to tell him.

"He didn't want to come to Israel. And I ... didn't ... want him to come," she said in a faraway, floating voice that was full of tears. "We quarreled. We—"

He put his arm around her. "That is okay," he said. "Even if you didn't like all things in him, that doesn't make it your fault he died."

She turned to him swiftly and put her face against his chest for one moment. Then the shouts from the bus driver penetrated their privacy, and they turned around and ran.

Nimrod was busy. He didn't care about the election and had decided to add some real fun and excitement to the celebrations.

Actually the plan was not his idea. It had originated with Ari, Ari the Godfather. He was wilder than Nimrod had ever been, but just now Nimrod had decided he was a better hero than Yoni.

Ari, insofar as he liked anything at school, liked science. He'd devised a foolproof scheme for giving the whole kibbutz something to talk about other than the election results. His eighteenth birthday having occurred on election day, he'd celebrated by voting for the farthest-out right-wing party there was, the one that advocated transferring every Arab in Israel and the occupied territories across the border by force. He didn't think twice about what this would involve; he just voted for this bunch of lunatics because he was feeling crazy himself at the thought of soon going into the army and having to face the furious stone throwers in the stinking alleys of Gaza and Nablus.

Now, while most other people were putting on their best clothes and preparing the *hader okhel* for the party, he was in the old culture house with a small group of his followers, who included Nimrod.

The weather-warped door, normally kept locked, had been prized open and pulled shut again behind them. The electricity was still working, but there were no bulbs in the sockets, so someone had brought a powerful flashlight. Now they were bent over a rickety table, on which was a big tin can that had once held corn. It had different contents now: magnesium stolen from a building site in the local town, alkali from the school science lab, and gunpowder carefully extracted from bullets filched from the magazine of a father's gun.

When this had been ritually mixed by each of them, they packed it down and sealed the tin. Ari attached one end of an electric cord to it, and the other to a broken light bulb. This was fitted into a socket after making sure the switch was off by testing it with a good bulb. The group of boys, all quite a bit younger than Ari, was high on excitement. They were giggling and pushing one another.

Nimrod, on Ari's instructions, ran to the outside door and looked down at the kibbutz below. The sky was nearly dark, but he could see that the lighted paths leading into the center, toward the lit-up dining hall, were all but empty; one or two latecomers were hurrying away from him, toward the festivities. Faintly Nimrod could hear the music and even the voices. The party had started. It was safe; no one would be hurt; it would just be a tremendous laugh. Off with the old government, on with the new—not with a whimper but a bang!

He ran back along the corridor and into the big hollow hall. He stood for a brief instant, looking at it in the spooky light of the single flashlight. This was where they'd all used to come, all the members, for the concerts, the plays, the lectures ... BT. Before Television! Pity in a way. Well, but they'd abandoned it, as they'd abandoned so much that his grandfather had told him had made the kibbutz special. It didn't matter what happened to this old place now!

He hurried to the group around the ramshackle table.

"All clear," he said in a conspiratorial whisper.

The boys turned their bright, excited eyes on their leader. He looked around at them and nodded.

They moved swiftly down the corridor to the outer

door. There was the switch—another switch, on the same circuit, that would trigger the fuse they'd made. Ari stood with his finger on it, took a breath, and said, "Go!"

They pushed past one another through the doorway and ran like mad down the hill as Ari flicked the switch and hurled himself after them.

The explosion rocked the kibbutz.

Lesley and Ofer, sitting at one of the long trestle tables with Nili, Donna, Yoni, Ilana, Noah, and Nat and Miriam, leaped to their feet in shock. Miriam clutched her heart and screamed. Nat grabbed Nili, who was on the other side of him, pushed her under the table, and then turned and clasped Miriam in his arms, leaning over her as if to protect her from falling masonry.

Donna, after an initial jump, sat in frozen calm, only clutching Yoni's knee under the table. Noah turned white, half rose, and stared around him wildly, having no idea what it was or what to do.

All around them people were jumping up. Someone grabbed a microphone and called for parents to get their children into the shelters. Soldiers home on leave grabbed their guns and rushed outside, and the women soldiers began helping with the children and old people. Yoni was not in uniform and stayed with his mother, waiting for orders.

Within minutes the first shock was over. The children, many of them crying with fright, were hustled out; people who were on the defense committee hurried off to their posts.

Throughout all this, people were turning to one

another, ashen-faced, asking in shrill voices: "What was it? A shell? No, didn't sound like one—more like a mine! That could mean someone's trying to get across. Or maybe our armory's gone up! Don't say it—couldn't be—it would be more than one bang—no, it was just the one—some fireworks, maybe!"

Yoel, the general secretary, was at the mike, saying, "Okay, everyone! Please be seated. A patrol's on its way. Everything's under control!" The small orchestra, mostly made up of elderly people playing mandolins, regrouped and began to play a ludicrously jolly tune. A lot of people burst into nervous laughter.

A girl in uniform came to Miriam. "Do you want to go home? I'll take you."

Miriam just shook her head. Her face was white, her eyes closed. She leaned against Nat's shoulder.

"Leave her," he said.

Miriam murmured faintly, "What was it? What was it? Is it another war?"

"No, sweetheart, no," said Nat. "It's just some accident; it's nothing. Please, honey, relax, it's okay, it's okay." He soothed and stroked her, his mind afire with fear, not for himself but for her. She looked terrible. There was a blueness around her mouth.

Donna bent over her. "Don't move her," she said. "I'll get her an injection of heart stimulant. Keep her still." She hurried away.

Lesley saw Nili's eyes peering up at her from under the tablecloth and smiled. "Come on out, hon. I think it's all over." She helped her out. "Hiya, brother!" she called to Noah at the end of the table.

"You look a bit spooked! Thought better of staying with us?"

He shook his head and sat down slowly. Not this time. This time he wasn't leaving. . . . Images, memories were flashing through his mind, seemingly at random. The most vivid was the face of Glen's murderer.

Noah had been allowed to go to Jerusalem to see him, had psyched himself up for it, and when it had happened—when his long, fraught imaginings of this moment had come true and he had found himself looking at the man who had actually taken his son's life—nothing changed. Nothing was solved. Here was no demon stabber, just a closed, sullen young face, a face like a hundred others he had looked into during his obsessive ramblings.

He had asked him *why?* rhetorically, knowing in advance that there would be no satisfactory answer. There was no answer at all. The boy just stared at him as if across aeons of time and space, an alien who couldn't understand his language. And yet . . . he understood the question. There was an Arabic-speaking prison officer there to make sure he did. And still the boy had sat there, sullen-faced and silent, refusing even to look at Noah.

Again Noah's frustrated anger had risen, like poison in his mouth. He felt later that if the guard had lashed out at the young killer, beaten an answer out of him, Noah might have stood by. God forbid, he might even have helped. . . .

From this fearful look into himself, Noah had known with certainty that, as Shalom had said, "It's in all of us." Violence, hatred, the willingness to inflict pain to gain one's ends ... Was this—his own bewildering, destructive rage, his desire to punish—part of his answer?

Kill a child ... No. No. Noah could never do that! But beat, furiously, mindlessly, a boy scarcely out of childhood, to get an answer to his question "Why did you kill my son?" Could he be sure, now, that he was above that? Could he go on hating others who were not above it? All this flashed, once again, through Noah's brain as he sat in the echoes of the explosion.

Suddenly Ofer said, "Where's Nimrod?"

But before they could start to worry, he was there, sliding into his seat next to his father. He looked flushed and tousled; the elastic band that held his *kuku* had broken, and his hair hung over his shoulder, making him look girlish and innocent. But his eyes were full of half-suppressed gleams.

"Where have you been?" asked Ofer. "Thought you were sitting with friends."

"I was just coming," Nimrod said.

"So what's going on out there?"

"Dunno. Came from somewhere near the tel, I think," said Nimrod. "You should see everyone running around. Someone really stirred the ant heap...." He was on the verge of laughing when he saw his grandmother's face.

His own face changed so completely that Yoni, who happened to be looking straight at it across the table, caught his breath with a sudden instinctive suspicion.

"What's wrong with Savta?"

"It was the explosion. It gave her a bad scare,"

said Yoni. "Not just her. Some old people have weak hearts, you know."

Donna came half running back and gave Miriam an injection. Nimrod watched in dawning horror.

"She'll be all right, though!" he almost shouted. "She'll be okay! She will, won't she?" He looked around at them all with an air of baffled desperation.

Yoni was watching him. "Let's hope so," he said grimly.

Nimrod, who had never in a million years thought of anything like this, felt all the blood drain out of his face into his fingers, which hung down on either side of him like lead weights so that he couldn't move.

TWENTY-EIGHT

The River—
The Border

Mustapha, if he had planned it, could not
have chosen a better time than election night
to arrive at the sector he had been aiming at.
There were no stray kibbutzniks wandering
about the perimeter of the kibbutz, other
than the regular few guards who were supposed to patrol the fences and gates. And
they were few and far between that night.
Who expected anything? It was a quiet border. The trouble was in Jerusalem, in the occupied territories, or on the fringes of
Lebanon in the north. Not here.

When the "big bang" went off, even these
few rushed away from their normal posts to
find out what had happened, and in the general
hubbub they didn't return for hours.

Mustapha was not very tired. The bicycle
had borne him safely and with minimal effort
along even quite main roads, and no one had

stopped or challenged him. He was just another Arab on a shabby, lightless bike.

He took care not to ride fast. He knew that the murder of Sayid would not be discovered for some hours, and that when it was the Israeli police would not be particularly interested—even if they were notified at once—in the death of an Arab at the hands of another Arab. They'd write it off as some family feud and not hurry to investigate.

Of course, as soon as Shin Bet, the secret service, realized the connection between the dead man and itself (he was its paid informer, after all), it would put two and two together quite quickly. But by then Mustapha had every hope of being safe across the river.

He got off the bike and hid it in some brush about half a kilometer south of the kibbutz. He left the road and made his way down to the track, rutted by army vehicles, that ran alongside an area that had been raked smooth. This raked area was several meters wide—just bare, harrowed earth—and beyond it was a wire fence, to stop anyone from getting any nearer to the river, which was the border. Along the fence at regular intervals were signs. They read DANGER. MINES. Beyond that was a second wire fence. Beyond that again was rough sloping ground, stony and covered with thistles and dry scrub growth. Below somewhere, invisible from here, was the river, winding its way in loops and curves between Israel and Jordan.

Mustapha knew his danger. His knowledge tingled in every nerve of his body. The raked ground was there to show footprints. Evidently there could be no mines laid here or the mechanical rake would touch them off, so this part was safe to cross. Where, then, were the mines?

Between the two fences? Or beyond them?

He walked along the track for some distance, keeping his eyes and ears open, nerving himself. He had no option but to sprint across that open space. He must reach the fences and pass them and then get down to the riverbank and across the river. Crossing the river would be the easiest part. He had crossed it before, years ago. The river was like a friend compared with the deadly dangers on either bank.

In the distance he could see the high perimeter fence of the kibbutz.

He knew this place. It was here that the girl had lived, the other girl, the one he had allowed to fill his mind when he was still a child. It was here that he had come, one night of reckless daring when he was fifteen, and stolen, to show his courage to his superiors, some tokens, among them a small faded photograph of a pretty, smiling girl in a bathing suit. . . .

He had watched this place and thought about it when he was a boy. When he was a man, he had thought about it again, differently. It had become the place that symbolized his sentimental weakness for the girl, the place-to-be-destroyed. He had often dreamed of destroying it. Now if he was not careful, and lucky, it might destroy him.

He rounded a bend, and suddenly, across the river, on the hillside, he saw his native village. Its lights were coming on, twinkling through the deepening twilight, friendly lights, calling him to come where he had been born, where he would be safe.

He turned at right angles, and in a series of leaps so he touched the ground as few times as possible, he bounded across the raked earth.

He had reached the fence. He lay down swiftly at its foot.

He was breathing hard. Fences were nothing. You lay down and slid under them, holding the lowest wire up with your thumbs. But this was razor wire, no room for thumbs. He had to take off one of his shoes, and press it upward to raise the bottom strand.

He couldn't do it. He couldn't squeeze under! He slid back and used a stone to make a scrape on the hard earth where the thickest part of him—his chest—had to pass. He was panting, and his eyes were everywhere, behind toward the kibbutz fence, along the track each way. . . . No lights. No sounds. He scraped frantically, then tried again. Not with the shoe, the shoe added thickness. He put his arms to his sides and pushed himself sideways.

The razor-sharp pieces on the wire tore his shirt, scored his chest. He gritted his teeth and pushed through the pain—through the pain—through! The first fence was behind him.

But now came the really bad part: the space between the two fences. The distance was not much, but every step across it might touch off a mine that could blow up under him as soon as his foot fell on it. He examined the ground with his eyes. It was dry and rough and looked as if no one had ever been there. Presumably the mines had been laid quite a long time ago, and weather and weeds and tufts of grass now disguised their hiding places.

It was getting dark. He could hardly see. He would

have to take a chance. The mines could not be every-where. With luck he would miss them. *"Inshallah . . ."* he muttered, took a breath, and stepped forward with a big stride.

The ground took his weight. For a split second it yielded a little, and his whole body was washed with terror. But nothing happened. Gasping rawly with the fear he could not suppress, he took another giant step.

Nothing!

His last step was a leap that brought him sharply up against the second fence. He nearly bounced off it and fell backward, saving himself only by grasping one strand, which tore the flesh of his hands. But he held on until he had regained his balance.

Now he must lie down, exposing the length of his body to the possibility of mines. He couldn't do it. He couldn't force himself. Instead, he struggled out of his shirt and tore it in two, wrapping each half around his bloody hands to use as gloves, and began to swing himself upward.

As soon as his feet left that fatal ground, he felt as if he had wings. Ignoring the new cuts inflicted by the wire on his legs, he surmounted the fence and flung himself down onto the ground beyond. Safe! He'd done it!

He didn't stand up. He rolled and pulled himself through the brush, down the slope. Soon he was out of sight of the track, but he didn't stand up yet. He thought he should crawl and slide all the way down to the river, but blood was oozing from the shallow cuts on his chest and hands, and soon he was pricked and grazed all over from the stones and thorns.

It was nearly dark. He thought he could chance it.

He stood up cautiously, and, bent over, he scrambled down toward the river. If he looked up, he could still see his village, in front and to the left of him. Every now and then he let himself look at it, to keep his bearings, but most of the time he had to watch the darkening, rough, treacherous ground. Twice stones rolled under his feet and he fell, but he was up again at once, scrambling forward and downward. . . . It seemed he would never see it.

Until at last, there it lay, there it was: the river!

It came into sight quite suddenly, as he humped his body over a little rise in the ground. It glittered close below him, and he could hear its soft chuckling sound, which seemed to speak to him: *You're going to make it, ha-ha-ha, you're going to make it!* Mustapha began to chuckle himself, and think of Nabila, his sister, and how she would be astonished when she saw him, how she would feed him full and wash his hurts and burn with pride at his cleverness at getting through. . . .

He stopped. There was something man-made here, on the bank. A few broken struts. . . . He knew this place. This was it! He'd forgotten till this moment! This was the bridge that the girl had crossed, that he had watched her cross as he had crouched in the grass on the far bank . . . the night his father beat him, the night she had stolen his donkey, the night he had told her his name and she had given him the chocolate. . . . The night that had changed him. But not forever. He had reversed the change so that he could be a man and throw himself into the struggle.

He stood for a moment, his eyes wide with memory.

A shiver passed over him and recalled him.

The bridge was gone. Just a few rotten sticks. What was he waiting for? The river was at his feet. Its cool water called to him like a command. "Cross! Cross! I will wash your hurts and make you safe!"

He stepped forward eagerly.

Miriam was in bed and asleep, and once more Nat was sitting beside her with his cat, Tuli, on his lap, keeping vigil. Donna had said Miriam would be all right. The doctor was due in the morning.

Noah sat not far away. Nat's son, Noah, so long estranged. He had said he was staying. But he had said that once before.

Nat was full of disturbed feelings. Did he want Noah to stay? Another marriage broken. Another child—little Dale—"left behind." Could this be good? Could this be a source of pride?

Miriam had said, "Don't be hard on him. He's staying. That's what counts. He'll stay with us. Maybe he and Donna . . ." But Nat didn't deceive himself. It was far too late for that.

Yet it was good—no denying it—to have his boy sitting there near him, so quiet and unobtrusive, yet so supportive.

But there was nothing quiet and unobtrusive about Nimrod, who kept bursting in, creating currents of agitation in the room.

"Is she okay? She'll be okay, won't she?"

At last, after one of these burst-ins, Nat phoned Lesley and said, "Les, take Nimrodi off my back, will you? I appreciate his concern, but what she needs is quiet."

But he felt a great tenderness for Nimrod. Even after Nat had told him those terrible things, upsetting him so much that he had run away from him, he still loved his grandparents. He was a good boy.

Nat sat by his wife and stroked Tuli's bony old back, sensed his grown-up son near him, and felt an unaccustomed, and temporary, peace steal over him.

They'd won the election, anyway. What a blessed relief! Things were going to get better.

Lesley put the phone down and said to Ofer, "Where's Nimrod? Dad says he's being a pain, popping in and out."

Ofer said nothing but went out into the darkness. He saw Nimrod in the distance, walking slowly away from his grandparents' house, head down.

"Nimrod! Come here!" his father called.

Nimrod hesitated, then came.

"Savta will be okay. Leave them in peace now. Come and sit with us."

Nimrod shook his head. "Where's Nil?"

"She and Lev are at Yonatan's. Where's your crowd?"

Nimrod said, "Dunno." He looked totally downcast.

Ofer peered into his face in the lamplit darkness. "What's up, son?"

"Nothing. I think I'll go to Yoni's."

He sloped off. Ofer watched him go and then went back into his house. Lesley was writing on her old word processor.

"Working? I thought this was a night off."

"Doing an article."

Ofer went and leaned over her shoulder. In green letters on the screen, he read:

A mysterious blast spoiled our celebrations for the election of a new government. Perhaps it was an omen. . . . We mustn't assume everything will now automatically get better because we have a new prime minister. We must remember that this was the same man who ordered the breaking of stone throwers' bones. Once we thought that because our leaders were from among us, we could trust them as we trust our own family. Now we know the demands of "the street" can make an extremist of any politician. . . . The peaceniks have not won yet, and if they relax, they never will.

Ofer gave a little grunt. He straightened up and went to where his oboe was lying on the table.

"What do you think?" asked Lesley, typing busily.

"You're your father's daughter. What a pessimist!"

"So cheer me up."

Ofer lifted the instrument and began to play a nursery tune called "Our Big Green Kibbutz Truck." He played it very slowly, like a learner, frowning and puffing laboriously on every note. Lesley looked up at him and burst into song. *"Ha'auto—shelanu—gadol ve yarok . . .* Weren't those the days of innocence! I do love you, you funny old musician!"

* * *

At Yoni's, a party was in progress. The kibbutz one having broken up, some of Yoni's friends, plus Nili and Lev, were having a small one of their own. They'd taken some food from the dining hall, and Yoni had some beer. They'd put music on the stereo, pushed back the few pieces of furniture, and begun to dance.

Nili and Lev were in each other's arms. They were dancing slowly, softly, to music that was meant to encourage a quite different kind of dancing. While others jumped and gyrated around them, they formed a little island of intensely tender, almost private movement. Lev's chin rested on Nili's head. Her arms were around his neck, his around her waist. The eyes of both were closed. They were lost.

Yoni was not dancing. He was sitting on the bed with a glass of beer, holding Ilana's hand and thinking.

When Nimrod slid in, looking pea green, Yoni stood up, faced him, and turned him, and before Nimrod knew what was happening, he was outside again.

Yoni spoke English, keeping his voice low. "Listen, I can see the appeal of it. And the way you carried it out was brilliant. So when they catch on to you—which will be tomorrow—and the whole kibbutz jumps on you with both feet, you can take refuge with me. Don't tell anyone I said so."

Nimrod gazed at him like a hypnotized rabbit.

"I—"

"Just one thing," Yoni drawled. "No looking down your nose at Nili after tonight. Okay? Because you could have killed Savta with your brilliant trick." He opened the door with a bow. "Meanwhile, come in and have fun. The condemned man ate a hearty dinner."

He was just shoving Nimrod none too gently back into his room when the second explosion happened.

Epilogue on Two Hills

This second bang was not as noisy as the first. It seemed to come from much farther off. People returning to their homes clutched each other and then broke away, half laughing. Not knowing yet what had caused the first bang, but having the assurance of the army that it wasn't due to enemy action, they thought this second one was something similar. Perhaps it was some army exercise, or some quarry dynamite set off by mistake. . . .

Nobody was very worried this time, although Nimrod, for one, was extremely surprised.

The next morning the remains of the first explosion were traced to the culture house (which had absorbed the blast remarkably and showed little on the outside except broken windows). The appalling rumor started to circulate that it had been an "inside job"—some kind of prank.

This caused such a sensation that when more rumors started that the second bang had been a mine at the river's edge, nobody had much energy left over to react. The general belief at first was that some animal, a gazelle perhaps, or a dog, had set it off.

Having come up with this explanation, everyone went back to shock and horror about the awful probability that some of their own kids had deliberately set off the blast that had ruined the celebrations and nearly given Miriam Shelby a heart attack.

To many, especially the old-timers, this seemed like nothing less than the betrayal of every principle of mutual responsibility and trust, marking the total failure of their educational system.

There was no question this time of not bringing the police into it. The army had already called them, and by eight A.M. an investigation was in full swing. Loyalty didn't come into it. Everyone was furious and determined to find the guilty ones. There was no one to hide behind, nowhere to hide, and by eleven o'clock Ari and Nimrod, after a brief, tense conference, had turned themselves in. The other four soon followed suit.

To tell the truth, all of them, including Ari, had been so shocked by the outcome of their "bit of fun" that they were almost eager to face the music. Nimrod, for his part, hadn't slept all night, despite having tried to drink himself into oblivion at the party. At first he blamed Ari in his thoughts for leading him astray, but that didn't last. He couldn't honestly put the blame on anyone else. He kept torturing himself with the thought of what his grandfather would think of him, whether, as with Yoni, it would seem to him a crime for which there was no real forgiveness.

He knew this was a turning point. The sight of his grandmother's pale face and blue lips, and his grandfather's frantic anxiety, had shocked him into a completely new state of mind.

And it turned his lingering sense of righteous outrage against Nili onto its head. How—*how* could he have abused her like that when he himself was capable of something so mad, so dangerous?

Late in the party, swimming in remorse and apprehension about what was coming to him, he'd sidled up to his sister. She was sitting on Yoni's sofa, with Lev asleep with his head on her lap.

"Nil."

"Hmm?"

"Sorry."

"Okay."

"Brother and sister?" he'd asked in beery but heartfelt tones.

She gave him a very grown-up look, as if she were the older—his older sister.

"You're drunk," she said tolerantly. "Stop talking *shtuyot* and go to bed."

He went, meekly. To bed, but not to sleep.

The kibbutz grapevine was working overtime. Long before anyone could inform Nimrod's parents officially that Nimrod was the culprit, Nat's "spies" got wind of it.

So the first Lesley heard was a phone call from

her father, distracted and raging. He said he would *never* get over it, never in his life, and that if he were a younger man, he would take great pleasure in beating Nimrod black and blue. Lesley flew into a fury.

She turned to Ofer, who was sitting alertly behind her as she put down the phone. "It was Nimrod," she said between clenched teeth. "Just wait. Just wait till I lay my hands on him!"

She started to rush out of the house, but he jumped up and stopped her.

"Slowly, slowly!" he said. "Take it easy. Don't take it so personally."

"*Personally!* He's our son and he's done this!"

"He's also a son of the kibbutz. They'll deal with it."

"Will they! Will they! And what will they do, pray tell? Do you know what would have happened when we were at school if anyone had done anything half as awful as this? A trial by the other kids, probably expulsion, or at least a whole term's suspension, hard work at home, and ostracism."

"They may do that now."

"They will not! They won't do anything like that. There'll be endless talk, endless waffle, and in the end they may send him home to work for two weeks. And when he gets back to school, he'll probably be greeted as a hero. That's what the kibbutz ethic, and peer pressure, have sunk to! *God,* I'm sick of this place!"

Ofer let her go and turned away. Lesley raged on.

"If the kibbutz doesn't deal with Nimrod in a—an appropriate way, a kibbutz way, if they leave it to us to punish him, then to hell with communal education. Ofer, I'm very serious!''

''I see you are,'' he said.

''We've been told the kibbutz takes responsibility for them, that parents are there to give them love and support, that that way they grow up to respect the commune and to be good, caring citizens. Rubbish! Rubbish! It's all gone, it's all changed! More and more freedom, more and more individualism and materialism, more and more live-and-let-live. And less and less idealism, less and less socialism, less and less the way of life that made us unique in the world, that gave us our pride and made all the sacrifices worthwhile!''

''Sacrifices . . . ?''

''Yes, dammit, Ofer, sacrifices! Don't tell me you've never thought of how much better we could be living outside! We could both have been earning good salaries all these years. I could have done far more work for—for the causes that I care about if we'd moved to town. But we thought the kibbutz was important enough to stay and work for. And look what it's got us!''

''You're blaming the kibbutz for Nimrod's . . . behavior?''

''Yes! No. Partly. What I'm blaming the kibbutz for is not being the kibbutz anymore. We've stayed in this—this hot little hellhole, and the only point of it all is if it's *still a kibbutz* with kibbutzic ideology and communal life and kids coming back after the army to carry it forward instead of scattering all over the damned *world,* anywhere but here! We're forty, Ofer, forty, we're giving this place our best years, and for what? So that they can take our kids and raise them as selfish hooligans? So that they can turn it into a place where the manager of the *refet* earns more than a teacher because cows make more money than children? That's what's on the program! Payment for meals, payment for health, payment for schooling, it'll all come, and if it does, I tell you, I'd rather be comfortable and cool and independent in a nice high-rise in Ramat Gan!''

She was shouting, but now the look on Ofer's face stopped her.

''Personally I would rather be dead than in a nice high-rise in Ramat Gan,'' he said quietly.

Lesley closed her eyes and breathed deeply. They stood silently until she opened them. She went up to him and put her arms around him.

''So would I,'' she said. ''Forgive me. I'm so angry. He could've killed Mom.''

He kissed her.

''He's not a selfish hooligan,'' he said gently. ''Only sometimes. And it's our fault too. We've evidently been too busy with our own lives.''

''I deny it. To my last breath! Some kids' villainy has actually got to be *their fault!*''

''Which also lets the kibbutz off the hook. Right?''

She sighed. ''Oh, what the hell. Give me time. I'll get over it.''

''And so will your father, don't worry.''

''Yes,'' she said, with the hint of a grim smile. ''Or I might have to remind him of the time he told me about, when *he* was sixteen, and he and his gang let all the air out of those car tires and nearly caused *several* fatal accidents.''

She left the house by herself and walked up to the top of the tel. As she had once retreated to the culture house, and before that to her river in Saskatoon when she was a child, now she came up here in troubled moments. The heat was fierce. The herons stood as still as decoys on the little islands in the fish ponds, and the lush, tousled tops of the date palms were motionless.

Drenched in heat, she stood and surveyed her small world, the world she had bad-mouthed to Ofer in her fury. It was incredibly beautiful and profoundly important to her. She knew they would not leave. They were rooted here. There were advantages to city life, village life, suburban life. She might tell herself that in a different environment, a different, stricter school, Nimrod might not have been such a rebel. (Nice word! "My son's a rebel; yours is a *meshuggeneh;* hers is a delinquent!") But the fact was, she didn't believe, not in her heart, that there was a more honest, *striving* life than the one they had made in Kfar Orde.

Besides, Lesley loved it.

Her eyes moved over the familiar landscape and came to rest on a blotch on the dried-out slope of the opposite bank.

It looked like a man's figure, as still as everything else on the scene. Just lying there.

Was it a fold in the hill that she had never noticed? Or some shadow, or a piece of wood? She screwed up her eyes. No. It was definitely a sprawled body. It lay there in the sun without moving.

She wished she'd brought Ofer's field glasses, the

ones he watched birds with. Should she go and get them, and perhaps tell someone else?

Yes.

She turned swiftly and ran down the wooden steps.

Mustapha had opened his eyes just before she turned.

He had long since lost track of the hours he had been lying here in the sun since he had stopped being able to drag himself along. He had kept going for a long time. All night, from the time he regained consciousness . . . he didn't have any idea of how much or how little ground he had covered. He thought it must be many miles, but one part of his brain, which was still functioning, more acutely, it seemed, as his body grew weaker, knew it could not be so far.

Because all night he could see the lights of his village. They were not getting noticeably nearer, for all his struggles. They were still away in the distance, taunting him now: "Get here and you'll be safe. . . ." Mocking him as the river had with its false promises, the treacherous river . . .

Which side of it had betrayed him? Had he splashed through it and then trodden on the mine, or had the mine blown up under him and then he had dragged himself to the other bank? He remembered being wet through, so wet he couldn't feel the blood for hours, not until morning when the sun dried his clothes and his sweat and he could still feel the wetness of the blood, the blood of his life, running from his shattered leg.

The awful thought had tormented him all night: Was his leg still there?

He had not looked. He couldn't feel it. He couldn't feel much below his waist. . . . He dreaded the pain. But much more, he dreaded death, and fought against it.

Now he dragged himself back out of its very throat. The heavy weights that were pressing him down into it had to be fought against, no matter what broken horror lay behind him on the ground. He struggled up through the layers to wakefulness.

He felt the sun burning his face. He saw its brightness through his eyelids. He forced them open.

He couldn't focus on anything near. But what he could see was a hill, a hump against the sky beyond the river. He saw a figure standing on it, and he remembered, with a great and sudden clarity, the girl. He remembered looking at her from this side to that, years ago. Now, as then, she turned and was gone.

He closed his eyes and made another effort to move forward. A desperate effort. He felt the blood begin to flow again, and he fainted.

When he opened his eyes again, the hill was still there, and there were people on it. A number of people . . . they were moving and pointing, pointing at him. He wondered if they could see him.

If those people could tell his people, they would come down from the village and fetch him.

Could they do that? Could those gesturing figures dancing before his eyes against the sky, could they cross the river, somehow—even by a signal—could they tell Nabila her brother was bleeding?

If there were no war, no struggle, then they could tell her. Or they could come themselves, across the bridge . . .

He kept his eyes wide open, looking at the hill, and now the sun showed him a word. A white word on the hill's flank.

He thought, *I am dying; that word is not there.*

But he could see it. It was in his own language, written for him to read.

It said *salaam*.

He closed his eyes, but he could still see it.

Peace.

Glossary of Hebrew, Yiddish, and Arabic

Aba—Dad

adoni—sir

agora—a tenth of a shekel (Israeli currency)

ahalan—Arabic greeting

arabushim—derogatory term for Arabs

ben-kibbutz (literally, son of kibbutz)—a boy born in the kibbutz

beseder—right, okay

bo-i—come (to a girl)

boker tov—good morning

botz—mud, or a kind of thick coffee (in the botz: in trouble)

col-bo—kibbutz store

dai—enough

dod—uncle

dodi—my uncle

ephronim—special ladders on wheels for use in fruit plantations

feinshmecker (Yiddish)—gourmet, one who won't eat coarse food

gadol—big

gesheft (Yiddish)—business

go'al nefesh (literally, sickening to the soul)—something horrible

graise (Yiddish)—big

hader okhel—dining hall

Ima—Mom

inshallah (Arabic)—a common Muslim prayer meaning "As Allah wills it"

ivrit—the Hebrew language

keff—a treat, a good time

kinder (Yiddish)—children

klaine (Yiddish)—little

kubeh—Middle East savory

kuku—ponytail (slang)

l'hit' (short for *lahitra'ot*)—so long, good-bye

l'khol harookhot (literally, to all the winds)—for heaven's sake

lo hashuv—never mind

macher (Yiddish)—one who makes things happen, a big businessman

mahair—go fast

ma shlom'ekh?—how are you?

mazal tov—congratulations

meshuggah—crazy

meshuggassen—crazy acts or behavior

meshuggeneh—crazy person

miscainah—poor or unfortunate girl (or woman)

motek—sweet child

muglev—coward

nu? (Yiddish)—well?

refet—cow shed, dairy

Saba, Savta—Granddad, Grandma

salaam—peace

sbeng—slap

Seder—the Passover service

shalom—peace

Shin Bet—secret service

shtock—shut up

shtuyot—rubbish, nonsense

tramp—a lift

tsoros (Yiddish)—problems, troubles

yarok—green

yored—emigrant

za'atar (Arabic)—a seasoning

The Enchanting Story
Loved By Millions
Is Now A Major Motion Picture

LYNNE REID BANKS'
THE
INDIAN
IN THE
CUPBOARD

It all started with a birthday present Omri didn't want—
a small, plastic Indian that was no use to him at all. But
an old wooden cupboard and a special key brought his
unusual toy to life.

Read all of the fantastic adventures
of Omri and *The Indian in the Cupboard*

THE INDIAN IN THE CUPBOARD
72558-4/$4.50 US/$5.99 Can

THE RETURN OF THE INDIAN
72593-2/$4.50 US

THE SECRET OF THE INDIAN
72594-0/$4.50 US

THE MYSTERY OF THE CUPBOARD
72595-9/$4.50 US/$5.99 Can